PARIAH'S MOON

Book One of *The Pariah of Verigo*

Ian Thomas Healy

Local Hero Press Edition

Pariah's Moon
A *Pariah of Verigo* Novel
Published by Local Hero Press, LLC

1st Printing
Local Hero Press: trade paperback, February 1, 2017
Printed in the United States of America

ISBN-13: 978-1971445380

Cover art by Karyn Lewis Bonfiglio
Book design by Local Hero Press, LLC

Books by Local Hero Press

The *Just Cause Universe*

Just Cause
The Archmage
Day of the Destroyer
Deep Six
Jackrabbit
Champion
Castles
The Lion and the Five Deadly Serpents
Tusks
The Neighborhood Watch
Jackrabbit: Big In Japan
Arena
Hero Academy
The Path
Cinco de Mayo
Search and Rescue
Rooftops
Plague
Soldiers of Fortune
Just Cause Universe Compendium
Destroyer of Earth
Flint and Steel
The Club
Jackrabbit: Rinse and Repeat
Posse
Extinction Event
Rain Must Fall

Pariah of Verigo

Pariah's Moon
Pariah's War

Three Flavors of Tacos

The Guitarist
Making the Cut
The Scene Stealers

Collections

Airship Lies
High Contrast
The Good Fight
The Good Fight 3: Sidekicks
The Good Fight 4: Homefront
The Good Fight 5: The Golden Age
Muddy Creek Tales
Caped

Other Novels

Assassin
Blood on the Ice
Funeral Games
Hope and Undead Elvis
Horde
The Murder Squad (2026)
Roast Wyvern (and Other Recipes)
Starf*cker
Strings
The Oilman's Daughter
Troubleshooters

Nonfiction

Action! Writing Better Action Using Cinematic Techniques

CHAPTER ONE

It was such a small thing, but great nations were brought down by such acts of audacity. Its perpetrator, Giele Stillwater, considered nothing of the ramifications as he held himself above his love.

Terika, Princess of Aelfland, smiled at him as she lay amid the soft pillows of her boudoir, showing the adorable dimple in her cheek. The imported Verigan silk wrapping the goose-feather pillows was cool and slick against the back of his head. The sheets were ivory white muslin and scented with a rose perfume that mingled with the spicy scents of their lovemaking. Wax candles burned on tables and dressers, their comforting flicker pushing the evening's shadows off into corners. Incense burned in a small brazier on the princess' headboard, filling his head with the smoke of cinnamon-wood and cloves. The soft glow of candlelight highlighted the sheen of sweat covering her skin, made flawless through expensive oils and lotions, and the steaming baths with the finest soaps and shampoos from the royal chemists. He loved the soft curves of her aristocratic body, much more pleasant to touch than the thin, hard bodies of camp whores who serviced the men of his unit.

How fortunate was he, a common soldier in the King's Army, to have found the love of a princess? She'd warned him to be cautious and discreet, for the King required that she should remain chaste. The reality was far different and much more sensual.

Her almond-shaped eyes, flecked with green and gold, shimmered as he sprawled beside her, wearied from his exertions. "You have such a gift for making me happy."

"It was my pleasure, my lady." He leaned down and kissed her full, soft lips.

"If only we could make this moment last forever." Her delicate fingers toyed with a tassel hanging down from her canopy.

"I wish that as well," he said. "What must I do to remain yours forever?"

She laughed, like musical notes from an orchestral reed pipe. "Giele, I'm royalty. I do as I please, or have company as I please." She rolled over to straddle him. Fresh desire stirred his loins once more. "And right now, I'm pleased to have you here . . . and *here*." She repositioned herself.

He caressed her smooth, pale thigh with his tan, callused hand. Before he'd ever lain with Terika, he'd feared some kind of reprisal would be exacted against him for daring to touch royalty. The princess assured him that such experiences were normal among royalty. Her father's own exploits were the stuff of legend. In his youth he'd selected commoner women of beauty for his concubines, and had even married one and fathered Terika with her. Terika told Giele she wished to keep him as her own concubine, regardless of whatever lord she might find herself married to for political purposes. She was his princess, and he believed her, even when she'd first allowed him to take her. The gift of her virginity had convinced him more than anything of her sincerity. "Even though I'm a common soldier?"

She kissed him. "You are a most uncommon soldier, dear Giele."

Outside the palace, a cold autumn rain battered the windows and walls. Lightning flickered and answering peals of thunder rattled against the palace walls. The crackling fire, luxurious curtains, and a thick bearskin rug warmed Terika's chambers. Before their loving, he'd thrown a couple logs into the fireplace, and the Dwarven steam radiator emitted a quiet hiss in the corner. Woven tapestries, some hundreds of years old, lined the stonework walls, showing scenes of peaceful mountain heights, forests, and the seaside. Terika loved to look at them on days such as this, when the storms kept sensible folks sequestered indoors. From a more practical viewpoint like Giele's, they trapped heat within the chambers and kept the room comfortable and warm in spite of Autumn's damp chill. In this boudoir in her high tower, he felt safe in a way he never had in the field.

"Not tonight. Tonight, I'm not a soldier. Tonight, I'm yours." Right then, he was prepared to give away everything to spend the rest of his life with Terika.

"Oh, Giele." She kissed him and they cuddled against one another, lovers hiding from the rain.

Lightning flared and thunder gave its immediate answer as the storm's fury centered over the thousand-year-old palace. Giele tensed, for in that brief flash he'd seen the silhouette of a man where none should be—behind the window's silk curtains. His reflexes kicked in, honed by twenty years in the military. Terika shrieked as he rolled the two of them off the bed to the floor, where she might be safer from a potential assassin. He grabbed the nearest weapon within reach—a letter opener from Terika's bedside table—and flung himself across the room. Fighting naked would put him at a disadvantage against a clothed opponent, but Giele didn't have time to seek out his uniform from the pile of discarded clothing. He heard the unmistakable sound of steel sliding from scabbard and knew with grim certainty he had but one chance to kill the would-be assassin.

Terika gasped as the killer thrust a dagger through the curtain toward Giele's belly. Twisting away from the attack, Giele plunged the letter opener downward into the assassin's throat. Bright blood sprayed the diaphanous silk of the curtains, making a sticky black blot against a sudden burst of lightning beyond the window. The invader clawed at the bubbling gash in his neck. Giele knew the wound he'd inflicted wouldn't be fatal—the letter opener made a poor weapon. He kicked the assassin's feet out from beneath him. Leather shin guards caused painful shocks against Giele's bare foot. The shadowy killer yanked the curtain from its hooks as he fell. A spray of blood stained the silk as it tumbled around him. As he squirmed, sluggish and dazed on the floor, Giele grabbed hold of the man's head through the curtain and smashed it twice against the corner of the stone hearth. A great quantity of blood spilled out, this time from the man's ruined head. His struggles ceased.

Terika squeaked in terror, her fists jammed against her mouth, as the dead man's blood spread across her chamber floor to soak her rug. Giele realized he must have looked equally terrifying, with the would-be assassin's gore streaked up his arms and chest. Nevertheless, there was a time for blubbering and this wasn't it. There could be more attackers on the way. "Call for the Guard!" Giele flung aside the curtain to look upon the attacker.

The Elf's hair was cut military-short, the same as Giele's, and his armor bore the rose insignia of the Royal Palace Guard.

"What in the hell? A traitor?" Giele muttered.

Someone's heavy mailed fist pounded against the bedchamber door.

"I'm sorry, Giele. I have enjoyed you." Terika crawled back into her bed. Confused, he turned to look at her. She drew a deep breath and then screamed, "Help me! He's going to kill me! He killed my guard!"

Giele stood in shock. What game was she playing?

Terika pulled her blankets up to her neck as Palace Guards crashed through the door, pistols and crossbows at the ready.

Giele looked to Terika in confusion. Instead of fear or terror, he saw naught but a conniving, sly smile on her face, and realized something had gone wrong in the worst way. He'd been duped. His hopes for a future with her shattered like his heart, and without a moment's hesitation, he turned and dove through the window.

Glass crashed all around him and the sharp edges raked new furrows amid the scars from three wars. The shock of pain and cold rain against his naked flesh took his breath away as he tumbled down some ten feet from the Princess' tower to hit the steep slope of the roof below. His momentum carried him down the rain-slick slate tiles and he cast about, desperate to stop his tumble before he went sailing off the roof to break himself upon the cobblestone courtyard four floors beneath. Lightning struck a nearby minaret and the resultant explosion of thunder seemed to shake his very bones loose from their sockets. The silver plating on the palace towers, which made the castle shine like a star in the daytime sun, reflected the sudden flashes and almost blinded him.

Bullets and bolts shattered tiles, but not one struck Giele's naked flesh. In the Army, he had always scoffed at the substandard training of the Palace Guard, but now he was grateful for their poor aim. What they lacked in accuracy, though, they made up for in organization, and whistles shrieked above him as they raised the alarm.

He reached the edge of the rooftop and his questing fingers caught the drainpipe as his body swung out into space. Desperation lent him strength as he dangled in the rain, above the yawning open air. He managed to grab the pipe with his other hand and shimmied along it. A palace wing jutted out twenty feet away and if he reached it, he might yet avoid a lengthy questioning session with the Royal Torturer.

Beyond the palace walls lay the rest of Morningstar City, wreathed in a mist of steam and smoke from flues, trapped by the cold autumn storm overhead. Its peaked roofs looked like tiny mountains poking through the fog. Gaslights on the cobblestone streets made diffuse yellow glows amid the gray tile roofs. Copses of trees poked up between the chimneys like dark giants. If Giele could escape the palace, he could disappear into the streets and alleys of the city. Then he could figure out what had happened and why Terika had betrayed him. Beyond that, he'd need time to plan his future, for it could no longer be as a member of the King's Army.

Before he'd covered half the distance toward the next wing, the drainpipe separated from the roof and bent. Cold rainwater sluiced across him and stung his fresh wounds. He realized the pipe would not hold for long. He saw a window a few feet away, and pumped his legs like a child on a swing. The slippery pipe swung out even further from the roof, and he hung over a long drop for a moment. He heaved another kick and as the pipe swayed back toward the wall, released his grip and crashed through the window into a hallway lined with tapestries. More shards of glass dug into his vulnerable flesh, and only by the grace of God's Blood did he avoid making himself a eunuch.

Giele picked his cut and shivering body up from the glass-littered floor and tried to ignore the pain as more splinters poked into the soles of his feet. He had never been in this part of the palace before and had no idea which way to go. The guards made the decision for him as a gaggle of them erupted into the hall from the stairwell at the end. He dashed in the other direction as they shouted orders to halt.

As he sprinted, cold and bleeding, through the labyrinthine palace, he cursed himself for his ultimate foolishness. His were not the actions of a twenty-year veteran, a Grove Colonel in the King's Army. He'd be fortunate if the Guard only killed him for his transgressions.

The Palace Guards were far more loath to shoot their pistols within the confines of the palace. The King wouldn't appreciate damaged masonry, even in the pursuit of a criminal. They had no such fears about crossbows though, and bolts shattered against the walls or stuck in tapestries as Giele raced down the corridor. He rounded a corner and startled two maids pushing a laundry cart. They shrieked at his sudden appearance— wild-eyed, bloodied, and naked. He would have apologized had he any breath at all to spare. Instead, he overturned the cart in his wake in the hope of delaying the pursuers.

He found a familiar corridor as he rounded a corner. A quick left turn led to a staircase. He scurried down the stairs into the kitchens and shocked the early-morning cooks as they prepared the breakfast banquet for the King and his guests. The Palace Guards' whistles and shouts continued to sound behind him, as well as the whistle of one saucy bakery maid who must have found his nude form pleasing enough.

A guardsman appeared in front of Giele. He grabbed a heavy iron pot from a counter top and hurled it at the guard. The pot struck the guard full in the face with the crunch of his nose shattering. It seemed Giele's presence had alerted the entire Palace, but he was close to escape. He put his head down and rushed for the door where street vendors sold their produce and meats to the chef.

Palace Guards moved in to block that route, so Giele shoved a startled scullery boy out of the way and dove down the garbage chute.

He was not a large Elf; the hard life in the military had kept him trim and fit. Even so, he could have become wedged in that narrow stone pipe. Had he been wearing a single stitch of clothing, he would have died, stuck in that ludicrous, stinking tube. Instead, his blood and sweat provided sufficient lubrication, and he wriggled downward through slime and black rot to drop from the chute's mouth into the icy river below.

The Silver River had been sculpted and diverted by dams over hundreds of years until it no longer lived up to its name. Instead, the sluggish muck flowed along a stinking culvert filled with Morningstar's garbage and sewage. With the heavy rain, the Silver crested high along its banks as it often did in the autumn. Giele hoped for some flooding in the low-lying areas to better aid his escape. He struggled to stay afloat in the frigid, reeking water, fearful of the diseases and poisons that might enter through his wounds, but he was determined to stay in the river until he reached the middle of town. A sodden rat perched on a floating piece of wood scrap hissed at him, and Giele recoiled, striking his head on one of the massive stone buttresses that supported the palace overhead and making himself see stars. Cold gray light diffused in from the outside to give the underside of the palace a surreal look. Slime mold and algae coated the stone walls and ceiling, stinking of sulfur and decay.

He saw the portcullis a bare moment before his body slammed into it. He clung to the rusted metal, dizzy from the impact and the knowledge that his plan to swim to safety had evaporated. The iron was pitted and slick with algae and age, but unlike the garbage chute, Giele couldn't fit in between the bars. Diving down, he found the grate embedded deep into the river bottom. He would have to find his way off the Palace grounds on foot after all. He climbed from the filthy water and ran along the narrow ledge beside the river, feeling the entire Palace hulking over him like he was an insect and it was a foot ready to stomp. Somewhere ahead he would find a way to get back inside the building and, with luck, another way to escape. He was so cold, he struggled to draw each breath. Frigid water, blood loss, and exhaustion had all taken their toll, and he was running on his last reserves of strength.

Then a guard stepped out from behind a fortification tower and pummeled his mailed fist into Giele's face. His consciousness fled with his hopes of survival. His last thought was of Terika, and why she had betrayed him.

Chapter Two

Sharp fumes assailed Giele's nostrils and he jerked awake, head throbbing and body aching from his recent flight and failed escape attempt.

A Palace Guard stepped away from him and closed a bottle of smelling salts. Giele shook his head to try to clear it. Despite the powerful inhalants, he still felt groggy. Dried blood caked the inside of his nose, making it difficult to breathe. He tasted more blood in his mouth, although his tongue was swollen and dry. He sat in a high-backed wooden chair with his wrists bound tight behind him. His hands were numb from the cut circulation and his shoulders ached from his arms being stretched around the chair back. Stone walls rose around him, and beneath his bare feet lay a hard-packed dirt floor littered with old straw. No brilliant gaslight there; the light came from a pair of flickering torches against one wall. The smoke curled upward to disappear against the shadowed ceiling.

A beardless Dwarf with long black braided mustaches ending in tiny silver beads stood atop a crate so he was at eye level with Giele. He had a simple leather skullcap over his shaved scalp, and a badge of office pinned to his chest; he was Melanus, the Chief of Palace Security. He stared at Giele from beneath beetled brows and picked at his teeth with a silver pick.

"You're in a lot of trouble, Army. What's your name? And don't lie to me because we'll find out the truth."

As Giele was still naked, Melanus could see the tattoo on his chest that identified him as part of the King's Army. All recruits got them upon graduation from Basic. It was their rite of passage from untrained civilians to the commissioned elite. He'd begun with a single oak leaf, done up in great detail by a skilled artist who lived among the teahouses and bordellos of Lower Morningstar. He'd added to it with each promotion from Leaf Archer to Branch Lieutenant, Bole Major to Grove Colonel. The tattoo spread across his chest like a copse of proud, ancient trees. It had taken an entire week of leave to complete the intricate forest decorating his skin following his last promotion. Now, with it gleaming dull platinum under the flickering torchlight in the windowless stone chamber, Giele had never been so ashamed to bear that mark.

Despite feeling dizzy from blood loss and the blow to his face, Giele raised his head with what pride still remained within him. "Giele Stillwater, Grove Colonel, 136th Regiment of the King's Army."

Pain exploded in his face from another heavy blow from the Dwarf's gnarled fist. "You're nothing now, Army. You understand that? You're only alive at the King's request."

Giele tasted coppery blood and spat to one side, careful to avoid striking Melanus with his spittle, despite an overwhelming desire to mar that badge of office with a crimson stain. Jigan forces in the First War had captured him once. Splinters under the fingernails, knotted ropes, even going so far as to paint him with honey and dump ants on him—nothing had been out of bounds for his captors. Even under circumstances as dire as those, he'd resisted giving up any more information beyond his name and rank. They tortured him like professionals; this Dwarf was but a dabbler, surrounded by amateurs. Even so, Giele knew that any moment, Melanus could summon the Royal Torturer, and then he'd be in for it. "I presume," he muttered around swollen lips, "that the King said nothing about me being damaged."

Melanus struck him again, straight on. Giele turned his head at the last moment to avoid having his nose shattered, and instead took the blow on his cheek. Perhaps he deserved the punishment for his actions of late, but no officer of the Army could accept such treatment without a spark of resistance. At that moment, he realized his feet weren't bound to the chair.

Amateurs, he thought.

He lashed out with one foot and caught the Dwarf in the side. The impact sent Melanus flying one way and tipped Giele over the other. Palace Guards leaped forward with guns leveled, their fingers quivering on the triggers, eager to unleash death.

"Hold!" Melanus got to his feet and nodded at Giele once, as if acknowledging he'd gotten a good, fair shot in. Then he stalked over to the guards. "Which of you horse's asses secured the prisoner?"

"I did, sir," said a tall, rangy Elf whose pointed ears stuck out like wings from the sides of his head. He gulped and stiffened to full, nervous attention.

Melanus drove a hard uppercut into the guard's crotch. The man groaned and collapsed with a stream of vomit leaking from the corner of his mouth. "Next time you'll remember to secure all of his limbs, won't you?"

The guard gurgled and blubbered and the Chief took it as acquiescence. He turned back to Giele, twirling his finger in one side of his mustaches. "You got that shot for free, Army. Don't think the next one won't cost you a finger, toe, or testicle."

Giele didn't respond. He'd given his name and rank, and displayed his resolve to remain uncooperative. Nothing more was required of a prisoner.

"Get him up," said Melanus "Hobble him. We're to bring him to the King."

The guards kept close watch over Giele as they untied him from the chair. His hands prickled as blood flooded back into them. Less for his own modesty than for decorum, they pulled a robe over his head and tied it at the waist. They bound his hands behind him once more and stuck his legs into cuffs separated by an inflexible length of iron. He'd be able to walk in an awkward, stumbling gait, but would be unable to run. Thus accoutered, they marched him through the Palace. Staffers stood aside and whispered to each other as he was paraded past them. He kept his head down; this was no time for haughty pride. The guards moved around him in a close phalanx, keeping him well-covered from all angles. He thought at first they would bring him to the King's Hall or Office, but soon he realized they were escorting him up a familiar tower.

They brought him back to Terika's chambers.

Terika herself laid on her bed, dressed in a gown and clutching a stuffed bear to her chest, a relic of childhood. Tears of humiliation streaked down her cheeks. The Royal Physician knelt between her legs, various brass scopes attached to articulated arms on the leather harness over his shoulders. With all the devices attached to his head, he looked less like an Elf and more like a giant spider. He swung one away from his face and turned to the King. "I'm sorry, my Lord. She has been thoroughly . . . despoiled."

Distant thunder rumbled in counterpoint to his mood as King Teirol Morningstar of Aelfland drew up to his full height. Giele had never before seen him up close. Normally he stood behind a balcony during troop reviews. He was tall, with the shoulders of a warrior, not yet hunched by his age. Giele would have given him even odds in a battle against a man half his age. He'd ruled Aelfland longer than Giele had been alive. His image graven on the coins of the realm didn't do justice to his stately jawline and nose sharp and slender as a bird's beak. His features remained youthful thanks to the efforts of the Court Physician. His hair flowed in great silvery curls to fall past his pointed ears and around his shoulders—the sign of nobility. Only commoners and the military kept their hair shorn to keep lice away. The wealthy bathed regularly and the soap shops and perfumeries in Upper Morningstar always did a brisk business. He had been roused from sleep, and wore a heavy dressing gown against the chill of the evening.

The King's philosophy of benevolence through strength had made Aelfland an expansionist nation. Hence, Giele had fought three wars, quelled one uprising, and done so all with great pride. He'd been willing to die for this man, the leader of Aelfland, and stood before the King expecting that would be his fate. A son confronted by a disappointed father could not have been more ashamed than Giele.

"Is this him?" demanded the King. "Is this the man who dared spoil my daughter's purity?" His fair skin turned an ugly shade of crimson as he turned to a skeletally-thin Elf who was wrapped in layers of dark blue silks. The Elf's countenance was darkened by a hood which sloped down over his forehead. Only his predatory eyes gleamed from within that shadow. Giele knew him by reputation and description: Iago, the Court mage.

Terika had lied to Giele. Her intention to make him her paramour had been a sham; she'd known full well that revealing him as her lover would land him in chains. What court game was she playing with him as the pawn? Anger flooded through him, but he was too exhausted to nurture it. He'd been a fool, and knew it now, far too late to do anything to change his fate.

Iago raised a bony hand and verdant energy crackled between his fingers. His measured motions betrayed not the least bit of fear or concern at the King's wrath. No mere ruler of Elves could stir him after he had commanded demons and entreated with spirits. Giele flinched as the energy leaped out to surround him. His hair stood on end and queasiness wracked his gut, as if the energy sapped his very life force.

An answering green glow arose from beneath the sheet covering Terika's legs.

Iago turned to King Teirol. "Yes, my Lord. It was he." His smooth, oily voice seemed to seep right past the King's fury. "But . . . he did not take her flower this eve."

"What?" The King's eyes widened.

"They have lain together several times. At least a dozen, I should think, my Lord. I sense no trace of another man's energy. Only he has placed his mark upon her."

"Can you repair the damage he's done?"

Iago lowered his head with an unfriendly smile under his hood. "Not now, my Lord. Perhaps if tonight had been the first time. Now I fear she has been permanently . . . spoiled."

A vein pulsed in the King's temple. He held out a hand to one of the guards. "Sword."

One of the guards drew his rapier, bowed, and handed it hilt-first to the King. Teirol yanked the weapon from the man's grasp and shoved him backward.

Giele prepared to die at the hands of his liege. He bowed his head. He had wronged the throne, and deserved to die for it. He hoped at least the King would be merciful and make his death quick

"Father, wait." Terika had set aside her stuffed bear and sat with her head held high despite the embarrassing invasion into her chambers. At that moment, she looked every bit the princess with whom Giele had fallen in love: beautiful and innocent.

Hers was the solitary voice that could have stayed the King's vengeful hand. "What, Terika?"

"I have never asked you for anything before today," she said. "But I ask you now to grant my request and spare this man's life."

"You dare to petition me after this?" Teirol slashed the sword down in fury, cutting into the mattress. A cloud of goose feathers burst out and floated in the his wake as he stalked back and forth. "Breath and Bones, you have a lot of nerve to make demands after this. You must have known this would make you impossible to marry."

She bowed her head, but did not lower her eyes in deference. Instead she glared at her father. "Yes I did, father, and I am prepared to accept the consequences. But what will it serve to slay this . . . pawn?"

Giele winced to hear the word come from her lips. He knew she'd used him for her own nefarious purpose, and it stung like a stiletto.

"It will settle my mind somewhat to take the life of the man who dared rut with my daughter. For shame, Terika. A commoner."

A spark of prideful anger lit in Terika, and she raised her head again. "My mother was a commoner, Father, lest you forget. And Giele isn't a commoner. He's a decorated officer in your Army."

The King turned away from her. "Your common blood shows with your behavior, Terika. You should be ashamed to be so thick-headed. I care not what you do after you are wed, but your whoring with this . . . this *peasant*." He spat the word like it had been poison in his mouth. "You've ruined any chance for me to forge an alliance through your marriage. He shall pay for his offense against you and against the throne."

"Father, please! I am the one who has defied your wishes, not he. If nothing else, spare his life"

In that moment, Giele realized how he'd been used. When Terika told him she could make love to whomever she wanted, she neglected to add the most pertinent detail: not until *after* she wed.

For months rumors had floated about Terika's possible union with some powerful Jigan warlord. Giele had done his best to ignore such talk, for it made him sick with jealousy. Terika told him she wouldn't allow herself to be used for political gain, and the proposed marriage arrangement would never occur. She had her eyes on a larger prize: the throne of Aelfland itself.

The many times she and Giele met and made love ensured that she couldn't be made whole by magic, and thus made herself undesirable as marriage material. Her betrayal made him dizzy. He was nothing more than a tool to her, a cockerel with legs, as they would have said in the military.

Except . . . she had fought to keep the King from slaying Giele where he stood. Maybe somewhere in those eyes into which he'd spent so many hours gazing, a spark of affection still burned for him.

Teirol glanced back at his daughter's earnest expression. His fury wavered. Nobody in the room dared to even draw breath. "God's Blood!" he roared. "You devious little whelp!" He hurled the sword to one side where it stuck quivering in the masonry, and raised his hand to strike Terika.

The Princess lifted her chin, ready to take his blow. The corners of her mouth twitched into an almost-imperceptible smile. She knew she'd won, and so did Teirol. If her common blood had made her choose so far beneath her station for a lover, her royal blood showed now in her political savvy. Someday, she would be a powerful and terrifying ruler in her own right.

Giele would never live to see it. Of that much he was certain.

The King lowered his fist. His teeth were clenched so his jaw muscles stood out in sharp relief. "Very well. Conduct the prisoner back to the dungeon while I decide upon a suitable punishment." He pointed at

Terika. "I give you my word that he shall not be killed, but nothing more."

Terika nodded, keeping her triumph well-hidden. Only a slight twitching at the corners of her mouth indicated her pleasure. She'd bested the King with her court game, and both knew that in doing so, he lost power and she gained it. "Your rule is benevolent as always, Father."

He frowned. "You may not think so in a moment." He turned and grabbed his Physician, hauling the man to his feet by his collar. "You will perform whatever medical procedures required to restore my daughter's maidenhead. Surgery. Black magic. I do. Not. Care."

Terika's carefully-composed expression of studious victory began to crack and her eyes widened in horror.

"M-my Lord," stammered the Physician. "Even with surgery, such a correction would be detected instantly."

"Perhaps an accident, my Lord," said Iago. "Unusual calisthenics or even horseback riding have been known to prematurely split a maidenhead."

The King stamped his foot. "Do what you must. I so command you. My daughter will be married as a virgin. I will not see my treaty dissolved because of her foolish and juvenile indiscretions."

The Physician bowed and swallowed hard in fear.

"It shall be done, my Lord. We will bend our heads to research immediately." Iago turned to Terika. "My Lady, please lie back, raise your gown, and spread your legs apart." He smiled in a smarmy way that made Giele shudder despite his temporary reprieve.

The King whirled and stalked from the room, leaving Giele kneeling helpless and wondering what Teirol meant by promising nothing more than not to kill him.

CHAPTER THREE

Giele lay sick in the stone cell in the dungeon, his head spinning from injuries and fevered from his recent dip in the Silver river. It might have been the same one where Melanus had awakened him, or it could have been someplace different. All dungeons were cold, damp, and stank of urine, vomit, and death. Hours passed while he sprawled on the cool stone. A passing spider paused on its sojourn across the floor near Giele's face, as if regarding him in pity or contempt. He watch its progress until it disappeared into a dark corner, in search of one of the thousands of flies which ranged through the dungeon. They buzzed around his head and touched down to taste his wounds. He didn't have the energy to wave them away, so he suffered their distractions. Teirol had promised not to kill him, but was that the same as letting Giele die from sickness or starvation? His thoughts whirled helpless like a leaf tossed about in a gale, until he snagged on the memory of Terika's face.

He'd met the Princess by pure accident.

The 136th had spent six months patrolling and securing the Jigan border. The Jigans, Elves from the frozen southern half of the continent, coveted the great trade routes of the Aeresic Ocean, and the shining star of Aelfland was all that lay between them and their goal. Three times in Giele's tenure as a soldier the

Jigans had come marauding north, marching upon the free Elves of Aelfland. Three times, the King's Army had fought off the invaders and sent them running for their ice caves and windswept steppes where the forests would no longer grow.

In the Third Jigan War, Giele's company had seen a lot of action amid the giant, ageless pine trees with boles thicker than the length of a wagon which made up the southern Aelfland forest. The behemoths were of such dense, sturdy wood that it required concentrated magic to knock one down. A few fallen trees were as effective a delay to a marching army as a fortified wall. Sometimes the battles raged on for days across clearings of tundra scrub while the impassive, titanic trees waited around the edges. Arrows hummed like cicadas along with the thunder of cannons and the screams of Giele's dying men. Snipers hid amid the forest, sometimes suspending themselves in rope slings in the shadows under the high branches with pine needles glued to their armor.

Giele lost a third of his men to the Jigans, either in open battle or from the hidden snipers overhead, and another third to a nasty fever which swept through the ranks. His unit had been one of the lucky ones. The 109th Forest Regiment and 24th Engineering Corps had been decimated and he'd absorbed those pitiful few survivors into the 136th, just to have a few more hands to draw bowstrings or pull rifle triggers. Just when it seemed all hope was lost, a dispatch arrived from Morningstar City. King Teirol's diplomats had hammered out an uneasy truce with the Jigans. The war, it seemed, was over for the moment, and fresh troops arrived to give some relief at last. The 136th was rotated away from active duty and recalled home.

Despite their heavy combat losses and exhaustion, the 136th made the most of the six hundred mile journey from the border to the northern coast where

Morningstar City sat at the mouth of the Silver River like a jewel on the face of a maiden. They grieved the fallen, cursed those who'd slain them, and found their way back from the darkness of front-line combat to the bright hope of returning to their home garrison.

As the troops marched north, the giant evergreens gave way to smaller trees which bore leaves instead of needles. The air carried upon it a hint of the sea from the Aeresic far to the north. No longer did Giele awaken in the mornings to find frost decorating the metallic parts of his gear in delicate patterns. It was spring in Aelfland, and the forests were bursting with life. Birds called to one another or raced about, seeking food for their new hatchlings. Flowers colored the clearings with scarlet and gold. Angry squirrels chattered at the racket of the soldiers as they marched with lighter hearts. Once Giele saw a tigress shepherding her kittens up a hill and away from the approaching soldiers. He could have ordered a squad to pursue her and chase them down, but had no desire to slay such a noble beast who had enough sense to stay away from the arrows and bullets of a traveling army.

When they reached the Silver River, the troops gave a great shout of joy, for that meant home was less than a hundred miles north. They bathed in the gentle currents and dined on fresh fish every night. Many Aelflanders lived along the Silver, and stopped their work or came out of their homes to watch the column march by. Children waved and gave flowers to the soldiers, and more than one child would return home with a goofy grin, an overlarge helmet perched over his ears, and a desire to someday travel north to Morningstar to join the King's Army.

Forests gave way to orchards and cultivated fields, and Giele was careful to keep the column from traipsing across freshly-sown fields. The farmers were happy to provide provender to the troops who kept them safe from the rampaging Jigans. Although it was spring and many crops hadn't yet borne fruit, farmers had early vegetables and plenty of herbs, and the additional variety in the soldiers' diet was a welcome change from the dried fruit, biscuits, and jerky upon which they'd subsisted for months.

After the fields, the countryside returned to forests once more. This was the King's Forest, kept uncut by royal decree except for the Highway. It was a national treasure of Aelfland. It was a reminder to all Elves that as a race they'd come of age among the trees. Giele had grown up deep in the Forest, hunting rabbits and pheasants under the cool canopy of leaves, reading tracks amid the sun-dappled forest floor. He grew restless, for he'd always felt more at home among the trees than in the smoky, cobblestoned metropolis of Morningstar City.

The arrival of two welcome wagons some twenty miles out from the city further strengthened the soldiers' spirits. The first contained a boisterous driver and his two assistants, hearty Dwarves all, who laughed loud with the soldiers of the 136th as they unloaded fresh fruit, bread, and six casks of cinnamon ale. When they uncovered the cleaned and spitted fat pig, ready to cook over an open flame, some men openly wept at the prospect of fresh meat instead of dried. Giele set his Majors to distribute the goods among the men after detailing a crew to dig and prepare a fire pit, and promised them all they'd dine on the coast the following afternoon, to great cheers.

The second wagon was decorated with garish pink and red silk, and held a selection of women all too eager to separate Giele's men from their coins for a few minutes in a tent. The rolling bordello was managed by a severely-dressed Elven madam whose no-nonsense attitude scared away more than one green Leaf Archer eager to dip his wick for the first time. Giele had spent his share of time among camp whores and wasn't opposed to the practice, but companionship wasn't what he needed at that time.

He closed his eyes and massaged his temples. The sounds of revelry and merriment were far too similar to those of death and destruction for his tastes.

"Sir?" asked Bole Major Kiler. "Do you need anything?"

"God's Blood, I need quiet, Kiler!" Giele snapped.

He stiffened, and Giele felt ashamed for his outburst. Kiler was a good soldier and a better man, and he deserved better than anger. "I'm sorry, Kiler. The noise of these laughing jackdaws is making my ears ring. What I need is some quiet space to feel a bowstring between my fingers without others shooting back at me, and a fat rabbit or pigeon in range."

"I understand, sir. Enjoy yourself."

Giele strung his favorite bow, slung a quiver of broadheads, and climbed into the saddle. "I will, believe me, Kiler. You have command until I return, probably not until morning. Try to keep the men from drinking themselves stupid or fighting over the women."

Kiler saluted before taking a deep draft of ale himself.

Giele rode off through the trees and wandered without purpose or destination in mind. He let his mare choose her own path and kept his hands clear of the reins. An hour later, he happened upon a game trail and dismounted. He tied his horse to an oak tree, strapped on her feedbag, and set out on foot.

At last, he began to relax and unwind from the journey with the troops as he followed the game trail. Before night fell, some animal would feel his arrow and fill his belly. He'd hunted in these ancient deciduous woods many times over his lifetime. The smell of rich loam was like the aroma of fresh baked bread, spiced with wildflowers and spread with sap. Brooks burbled in the language of the world, and birds and insects answered in tongues of their own. He found a *stinkfern* by its acrid, tangy odor, and rubbed its leaves across his exposed neck, arms, and scalp. The sharp-smelling juice would repel the clouds of biting gnats and mosquitoes for many hours.

The gentle breeze blowing through the forest carried with it the breath of the distant ocean, and Giele tasted the hint of salt on his lips. He reached out to caress strands of moss which dangled from the lowest branches of a heavyset elm. Although inedible by itself, tiny yellow mushrooms grew amid the moss. Giele picked a handful and slipped them into a pouch; they would add a delicious buttery flavor to whatever animal found itself spitted upon his arrow. Inspired by the mushroom discovery, he foraged for more to add to a meal. Underneath an innocuous broad-leafed plant with five-pointed white flowers he found a tuber which could be roasted amid the coals of a fire to reveal a sweet yellow pulp within its blackened crust. A handful of sour berries and some spicy basil leaves would transform his meal into one fit for the King himself.

All he needed was the main course to make itself conveniently available.

He selected a waiting spot and climbed up to perch on the lowest branch of an elm tree that might have been as ancient as the world. The light grew gray as clouds obscured the afternoon sun, bringing with them a stronger, cooling breeze. He sat there for a long time, breathing the musty odor of moss and tree bark and listening to the drips on the leaves as moisture condensed upon them until it fell. A stag passed beneath him and paused to sharpen his antlers against Giele's tree. He could have shot the stag between the eyes, but he wasn't in the mood to kill something so large. With the patience of an experienced hunter, he waited for another opportunity.

Then a fat rabbit indeed loped across the trail. His eyes gleamed like polished hematite, and his tail was as brilliant as a freshly-laundered pillow. Giele could taste it already: wild hare with roasted tuber and spicy basil. Barely daring to breathe, he drew the arrow's fletching to his cheek.

A stick snapped and someone else's arrow struck the forest loam beside the rabbit. It leaped away as Giele's arrow stuck into the very spot where his dinner had stood a heartbeat ago.

He heard a feminine voice utter a frustrated "Breath and Bones," and turned to see Princess Terika Morningstar, the sole heir to the throne of Aelfland, sitting on a dappled horse. He'd been so intent upon seeking his prey that he'd never even heard her approach. She wore beige cotton riding pants, tall leather boots, and a ruffled white silk blouse under a rough twill jacket, the sort of fashionable utilitarian clothing the wealthy enjoy when they choose to act like commoners. Her fawn-colored hair was caught up in a felt cap which strapped under her chin and framed her face like a portrait in a locket. She didn't ride sidesaddle like most ladies of the day, but straddled her horse like a proper rider should.

Giele froze. Time slowed to a standstill as he drank in the sight of her. Indeed, his breath stopped and his heart must have as well, for Terika was by far the most beautiful woman he had ever seen. In her, he saw the serenity he needed, the purity he craved after months of blood and stink and rot. At that moment, she was like some goddess of old, given flesh and life and laughter, and he wanted to tear her hat aside and plunge his rough hands into her hair, to taste her skin, to feel her breath against him.

One of her ladies-in-waiting sat astride a gelding nearby and studied her fingernails as if she'd rather be anywhere but in the forest. Her impatient sigh broke the trance Terika's appearance had laid upon Giele. Time started to pass at its normal breakneck speed once more, and he knew he had none to waste. He would risk anything for the chance to brush his lips against her slender wrist.

He dropped from his perch to the ground and bowed. "My Lady." He retrieved her arrow. God's Blood, he sounded like a stripling recruit. Would his voice break next?

"Bandits!" shrieked the lady-in-waiting.

"Nonsense, Fallah," said Terika. "He's a Grove Colonel. Of the 136th, I presume?"

Giele straightened up and stood at attention. Breath and Bones, he was a rutting *officer*, and he would comport himself as such. "You have an excellent eye for detail, my Lady." She must have recognized both the rank and unit emblem stenciled upon his cloak.

She smiled at him with a dimple in one cheek. Her eyes sparkled like the star of her namesake. "Thank, you Grove Colonel. My father has entrusted me to the care of wonderful tutors. I see we both sought the same rabbit."

Giele handed her arrow back to her. "You shot first, my Lady. The kill would have been yours."

Her lip curled in a well-practiced pout. "I'd have hit him too, the little devil, if I were a better archer." She held a bow which was too long for her height and looked to have an unbalanced pull to Giele's practiced eyes.

"If I may observe, your bow is too long and curls awkwardly along the top arm, my Lady. You'd have spitted that rabbit neatly with a properly-sized bow."

"What's your name, Grove Colonel?"

"Giele Stillwater, my Lady."

"Then Giele, I command you to show me." She slipped off her horse, despite her lady-in-waiting's protestations of mud, insects, snakes, and for good measure, bears and tigers.

He took out his kit and made some quick modifications to her bow, restringing it three inches shorter, and trimming the top arm as best he could to correct the flawed construction. He clucked his tongue in irritation at whatever pathetic civilian bowyer had let such an inferior weapon out of his shop. The 136th's bowyers would have used it for kindling. Having made his repairs, he asked her to try it. She took it back and drew it with awkward grace.

"No no no." Without thinking, he moved in behind her to correct her grip and stance. As he did, he caught the hinted scent of flowers and perfume on her skin and hair. No woman had ever smelled so good to him before. His hand brushed hers and it was like he'd touched a match to a fuse. She turned her head to look back at him and something in her eyes called to him. Had she felt the same spark? Breath and Bones, it made his heart race. He'd fought wars at the King's command, but this young woman and all she represented was the reason why. Now he had her in his arms, like a reward for a job well done. She was the opposite of the bawdy camp whores he'd left behind; in his eyes, she was perfect. But she had commanded him to teach her, and he would do whatever she asked. "You're standing all wrong. You're still carrying it like you're on horseback. You've got to learn to shoot like an infantryman before you can be in the cavalry."

The lady-in-waiting gasped at Giele's scandalous behavior. "My Lady, I must protest at this boorish man's familiarity."

He bowed his head. "I apologize, my Lady. I forgot whom I addressed."

The Princess sniffed at her companion. "Next time, Fallah, I'll leave you behind since you don't see fit to hold your tongue." She then smiled at him. "Never fear, Giele. You may call me Terika. Now please, I am but a raw recruit now—not even qualified to be a Leaf Archer. Will you show me the correct way to shoot?"

And that was how it began. He gave her a shooting lesson there in the forest under the watchful eyes of her chaperone. She thanked him and they went their separate ways.

The following morning, the 136th approached Morningstar City along the Highway. The palace's silver-sheathed minarets gleamed in the sun over the gray-tiled roofs of the city. The King's Forest grew to within a hundred yards of the city walls, giving way to a broad grassy pitch where children played and women walked together. A bazaar was spread along one side of the Highway, where merchants hawked wares from far-off lands like Dewar, home of the Dwarves, or even the Verigan Colonies across the ocean. They called to the soldiers from their colorful tents, waving bolts of silk, mosaic steel blades, or ornate wood and brass constructs. The children cheered as the 136th passed them by, and many marched alongside the troops.

Morningstar's gates were open wide, and would remain so unless the city itself was threatened. The palace sat near the city center, straddling the Silver River, surrounded by the mansions of the wealthy, in turn ringed by Lower Morningstar, where the common and less-than-common people lived and worked. Plumes of smoke and steam rose from the factories along the harbor, and the rich, sour smell of urban garbage and woodsmoke shocked Giele after being in the clean, pristine King's Forest.

A commotion near the rear of the company made Giele look back. His men moved aside to let the Princess overtake the command ranks. When she drew alongside Giele, she smiled and asked if he might return to the palace with her and make sure she got a proper bow. He left the 136th once more in Kiler's hands. Kiler would report in at the city gate, and then bring the troops to the garrison on the south side of town where they would be integrated back into low duty.

Giele rode with the Princess to visit the best bowyer he knew of in the King's Army. They spent a full afternoon checking measurements, pull strength, and curvature until he was satisfied he had found her the perfect weapon.

For the first time in his life, the Army wasn't the sole reason for Giele's existence. He awoke each morning with thoughts of Terika. He rushed through his duties in the garrison, delegating many of them to Kiler. His own work was of such slipshod quality that had he been a lesser officer, he'd have been busted back to Leaf Archer. He didn't care. He had his time with Terika to look forward to.

Under his tutelage, she became a skilled archer. Their early shooting lessons took place under the watchful eyes of her ladies in waiting in the palace courtyard. They were never alone, and Giele hated it. Although he never again saw Fallah in the Princess' company, she always had some other servant attending her nearby. Giele longed to take her away, just the two of them, where he might dare to speak the feelings that were growing in his heart. He knew she felt the same in the way her gaze lingered upon him far longer than it should have, or how she stood a little closer to him than necessary, or found reasons to brush against him.

In all the time his daughter spent learning to shoot, the King never once looked in upon her.

"Doesn't he have interest in your progress?" Giele asked her one afternoon as they walked the courtyard.

She twirled her parasol in disdain. "My father's interest in me is how soon he can negotiate a treaty through marriage. I'm a tool of state to him, nothing more."

"It's a shame he doesn't see more than that in you. He doesn't see the beauty or the grace that I do."

She smiled like the sun coming out from behind a cloud. "You're such a romantic, Giele, the last of a dying breed in these modern times. At least you sound sincere, unlike those empty-headed toadies and courtiers who always try to endear themselves to my father through me. Sappy nonsense. God's Blood. Is it any wonder I hate this place? It's the most beautiful prison in all of Aelfland." She made a rude gesture toward the stonework walls of the palace, beyond the manicured lawns and gardens. A Dwarf's mouth fell open in surprise at her vulgarity and dropped his plumb line upon his assistant. They cursed and argued for a minute before returning to their ongoing restoration work. The palace was a thousand years old; it took great effort by many skilled Dwarven stone artisans to keep it from collapsing under its own weight.

Giele unfolded Terika's hand from the rude position it held, and dared to kiss the back of it, lingering longer than he should have against her soft skin with its floral perfume. Had they been alone then, he would have bared his soul to her. She seemed to know what he meant to say, for she reached out and touched a delicate finger to his lips, and smiled.

Soon, their spring shooting lessons transformed into summer excursions into the King's Forest beyond the city, where Terika could aim at natural targets in the rough and wild woods instead of the carefully-sculpted courtyard. She changed her hoop skirts for proper riding attire, her parasol for a bow and quiver.

One day, she ordered her ladies-in-waiting to stay behind. They were dismayed and raised a great fuss, but Terika so reminded them that she would be in the company of a great soldier in the King's Army. "I swear I will guard the Princess with my life," Giele told them, and meant every word.

They left the palace grounds and rode along the cobblestone streets of the city. The bazaar remained along the Highway, and had been joined by both a traveling theater troupe and wrestling ring. Unburdened by the expectations of the ladies-in-waiting, Giele and Terika delayed their journey to the Forest long enough to watch a pair of Dwarves box each other bloody and to hear a minstrel sing a bawdy tune about lusty women and strong wine.

In spite of his brave words to Terika's servants, Giele was as awkward as a schoolboy with Terika as they left the Highway to travel into the wilder part of the King's Forest. He made clumsy, adolescent mistakes like following a game trail the wrong way and blundering into a patch of stinging nettles. Instead of speaking with authority, he stammered and tugged often at his collar to relieve the burning of embarrassment upon his neck.

On that hunting trip, Terika bagged her own fat rabbit. When she brought it down, she laughed and threw her arms around Giele's neck and kissed him. He twisted his fingers into her hair like he'd dreamed of the first day they'd met. She tasted sweet, like wild mountain honey and blueberries straight off the vine. She moaned as his lips went down the side of her neck and his hands clasped the small of her back beneath her blouse, his skin on hers. "Oh," she gasped.

Like a bolt of lightning, Giele realized he was seducing the princess of the realm, and leaped back as if scalded.

"What's the matter?" she cried.

"I cannot do this. I must not. It's wrong. You're royalty, and I'm . . ."

She wrapped her arms around him again and put her head against his chest. "I'm terribly lonely, Giele. I feel so safe with you."

He returned her embrace, breathing in the scent of her hair. "If only I could be more to you."

"Perhaps you can. But not today. We've been gone too long already. They may have roused search parties and set dogs after us."

A week passed where Giele had no contact with her. His duties as Grove Corporal filled his days and dreams of Terika filled his nights. He grew nervous, haggard, even short-tempered with his men to the point that Kiler took him aside and asked him was everything quite all right.

"I'm fine, Kiler. I'm just not sleeping well."

"Perhaps the garrison's physician should prescribe you a mixture." Kiler tapped ashes out of his pipe.

"Perhaps you should mind your own business, Bole Major." Giele clenched a fist where Kiler wouldn't see it.

"Sir, if I may say so, you should take more care." Kiler lowered his voice. "You're speaking her name in your sleep."

For a moment, Giele felt the first glimmerings of panic. But Kiler was loyal, and honorable, and he would never betray his commanding officer and friend. Giele knew he could count on Kiler no matter what. His warning was meant without hidden meaning. Giele smiled at him. "Thank you, Kiler. I'll do my best to control my nighttime mutterings. You'll make a fine Grove Corporal someday."

He shrugged and lit a fresh bowl. "I suppose so, sir."

Then Terika sent for Giele, requesting another hunting excursion.

When he joined her, she told him she hoped to bring down more than just a rabbit, and cautioned her staff she'd be gone the entire day. Once they'd ridden well out of sight of Morningstar City, Terika led him to a secluded grove by the Silver River.

"Come." She slipped off her horse and led him by hand deeper into the grove.

"My lady?"

She spun around and in a decisive motion, untied the sash of her riding cloak. Underneath was naught but bare flesh. "Love me, Giele," she said. "I want to feel your skin against mine, to feel you within me."

Giele's common sense left him and he took her there in the grove beside the river. It had been a long time since he'd been with a woman, but the skills returned to him in minutes. His lips and fingers caressed her soft skin, lingering in her most intimate places. She opened herself, inviting him to love her. She cried out with his first thrust and he realized he'd taken her flower, a gift which she could bestow upon but one man.

She'd chosen to give it to Giele.

"Don't stop," she gasped. "Be my paramour, Giele." They passed the entire afternoon there in each others' arms. He reveled in her body, and she embraced his. When the time came that they had to return to the palace, she whispered to him that they must be cautious. Certain people in the court would try to use their relationship as leverage against the King should they discover it. Giele agreed that discretion would be paramount.

From then on, their relationship became much more careful. Stolen kisses behind the stables. Embraces in the darkness of the courtyard. Were it not for the great difference in their stations, he'd have taken her and married her. He had fallen for her head over heels, like a moonstruck youngster. As it was, he had to be satisfied with their trysts when and where they could schedule them. They met in the grove thrice more over the summer. She grew bolder as the days began to shorten. In a laundry room under the castle he made frantic love to her. The fear of being caught added to their excitement. While the orchestra played at a masquerade ball for summer's end, he pressed her up against a pillar behind a curtain and they made their own quiet music.

The one place he was never permitted to visit was her chambers. Giele longed to share a real bed with her, not just a pile of leaves and green branches in the grove or damp sheets in a steaming underground grotto. "A man should be able to lie with the woman he loves," he said. "I want to sleep beside you, and wake up with you in my arms."

She kissed him. "Perhaps I can arrange something."

He'd been so intoxicated with her, he never realized she hadn't returned the sentiment to him. At least now he knew why.

On that cool Autumn morning Giele received an envelope which bore her seal and sigil. Inside it, he found a card scented with her perfume and written in her familiar, flowing script. She'd instructed her most trusted servant to let him into the Palace after dark, and to bring him to her where they could lie together as man and woman.

The cautious part of his mind warned him against such a risky plan, but his heart overruled it. He had chosen instead to seek out his Princess, and never mind the consequences.

Those consequences would come soon enough, he feared. Giele's reverie vanished like smoke into the wind as the door to his cell flung open and two Palace Guards hurried in and hoisted him up by his arms, followed by the Dwarven Chief of the Guard. "On your feet," Melanus said in his gruff voice. "The King commands your presence."

Giele's fate, for better or worse, had been decided.

CHAPTER FOUR

The guards hauled Giele in his sickened state up to the Throne Room. King Teirol conducted official business in his offices behind the Throne Room, but affairs of state and things he wished to do in public took place before his courtiers. It was a grand room, one of the first built in the palace. Great buttresses held up a high arched ceiling, from which hung huge tapestries depicting pivotal events in the reign of the Morningstar family. The polished marble stone floor reflected dozens of brilliant gaslights, which illuminated the room in a fiery amber glow. A ribbon of carpet led from the tall double doors like a river of blood, and ended at the three marble steps before the dais. The King's throne sat upon it, an ornate monolith carved from the trunk of a single thousand-year-old tree. It gave off an unnatural gleam from the countless layers of lacquer and devoted polishing hands it had seen throughout generations of Aelfland's rulers.

Teirol sat upon his throne like some great bird of prey, garbed in his high-collared vermilion robes of office. A golden crown with a device of emerald and silver leaves perched upon his head and his scepter rested beside him. His face betrayed no emotion as the guards half-carried, half-dragged Giele along the carpet. His jaw was set firm like a statue's, and a cold rage burned in his eyes that muted whispered conversations among the courtiers, who looked twisted and monstrous in Giele's fever-distorted perceptions. The King's subtle anger filled the air of the throne room with tension, like the air before a lightning storm or a battle line before the first arrow is fired.

Giele couldn't focus upon the King for more than a moment at a time. His eyes rolled in his head like they'd been disconnected. He wished for comfort from Terika, who stood behind the throne, dressed in a fashionable but demure brown hoop skirt. Seeing her brought him nothing but pain. She wouldn't meet his gaze, but his eyes wouldn't steer away from her. He still couldn't believe she'd used him, in spite of the mountain of indisputable evidence. Even though she'd argued to save his life, he wasn't sure the King wouldn't open Giele's throat right there in the Throne Room. He tried to think of the moments of loving, but instead all he remembered was Terika throwing him away like night soil.

He would never forgive that.

The King waved a finger and the guards stepped aside to leave Giele swaying before him. Courtiers in their fanciful robes and extravagant jewelry lined both sides of the room and whispered as they stared at his shuddering form in distaste. The spectacle would give them stories to share for years.

Teirol spoke but all Giele heard was buzzing in his ears.

"What?" he asked before realizing he'd spoken out of turn.

A guard slapped him across the face. His head snapped back and he found himself focusing upon the ceiling. The blow seemed to have helped his addled senses. He lowered his head to face the King once more, this time with a clear mind.

"At first," said Teirol without preamble. "I decided to simply put you to death. It would have eased my mind considerably."

The deferential whispers of the courtiers stopped as they paid close attention to the King's words.

"It would be an acceptable punishment for a traitor such as you," continued the King. "Don't you agree, Stillwater?"

Giele stood mute. The fever from the infection in his wounds had sapped whatever defiance he might have mustered. Shaky and weakened, he just wanted the King to get on with whatever he was going to do.

Teirol stood and took a step closer to Giele. The Palace Guards tensed but nobody made a move toward a weapon. As old as he was, the King was strong enough to take out a man half his age, particularly one weakened by illness. "But in deference to my daughter's request, I will not renege on my word." He spun on his heel to deliver his next sentence to Terika. "Although it would do you well to remember that I may at any time, because it's my right to do so." He turned back to Giele, descended the steps, and began to circle him. "So I considered what might be a fate worse than death for a traitor. And I believe I have hit upon exactly that. Iago, if you please."

The Court Mage stepped forward, his robes rustling against the smooth floor. Giele wanted to shrink back from him and his infernal power, but wouldn't give him the satisfaction of showing fear. "This will be . . . *uncomfortable*," he whispered in Giele's ear.

Iago chanted guttural words of ancient power and pain wracked through Giele's chest as if he were being flayed to the bone. He gasped at the searing agony as it moved downward to fill his belly like hot tar. Nausea took hold of him. He collapsed to his hands and knees and vomited. Instead of the bile and blood he might have expected, a jet of dark fluid splashed onto the carpet. A taste like sour metal filled his mouth and nose. His entire body turned frigid and he was wracked with uncontrollable shivers. He would have welcomed Death if it would mean the end of his misery.

"I'm sorry about the mess, my Lord," said Iago. "The ink will undoubtedly stain the carpet."

The King's lip curled in distaste, but even so, Giele saw an odd light of satisfaction in his red-rimmed eyes. "No matter. I'll have it burned and replaced since this traitor's feet have despoiled it." His face contorted into a smile of dark pleasure. "Continue."

Giele realized that Iago had stripped his military tattoo right from his flesh with his magic. It seemed such a minor thing, and yet that act cut deeper than if he'd been beheaded by the executioner's blade. Tears of dismay spilled from his eyes. The ink may as well have been his blood the way it pained him to have it taken away. He had no strength left to stand and hunched on his knees over the stinking mess that had been the pride of his two decades in the King's service. Behind Teirol, he saw Terika's jaw clenched as she watched his humiliation, but she betrayed no other sign of compassion, her lineage evident at last. He prayed this was the worst that would happen, but Teirol had just begun his tormenting.

A scribe presented the King with a document, and Teirol signed it with a flourish, then sprinkled Iago's magical powder upon it to fix the signature permanently. "Let it be known," said the King, who spoke faster and with greater passion as he warmed to the subject of Giele's ruination. "That I have taken away this man's rank and commission. No longer is he a member of my Army. Furthermore, I hereby strip him of his family name. No longer shall he be known as Stillwater, and all rights and assignations due him because of it are null and void. Thus, his property transfers to the state."

Gasps echoed among the courtiers. Family heritage was a vital part of Elven culture. Families passed everything from generation to generation: land, wealth, positions of power. That right no longer applied. Giele's family name would die with him. The small property in the King's Forest left him by his parents upon their deaths reverted to the King. Shame after shame heaped upon him. If he could have moved, he would have grabbed a guard's weapon and plunged it into his own breast, or even flung himself at Teirol to die pierced by arrows and bullets.

"I'm not finished." Teirol smirked. "Doctor Shaison, I require your services now."

Six burly men stepped forward, followed by the Court Physician. One of them held a branding iron and another carried a brazier filled with hot coals.

"I have created a mark which will identify you to all as a traitor to Aelfland and an outcast. You may find it difficult to survive when people fear you as a bad omen." A predatory smile carried all the weight of his menacing rage. Never in Giele's life had he felt as hated and loathed as he did there before the King. Teirol's voice dropped to a low hiss. "Hold his head still."

Giele's eyes grew wide as he realized the King's intent. He had no strength to scream, but a moan of pure terror escaped from his lips. He bucked and struggled against his captors, but in his weakened state, it was futile. The four men held him with ease. Another wrenched his head to the left so he couldn't quite see the King as he took the branding iron and buried it in the hot coals of the brazier.

"Iago has treated this iron to leave a permanent mark." Teirol spoke in a husky voice, as if to a lover. "No amount of healing, medical or magical, will remove it. It will remain marked even upon your bones after your death. You will be known forever by this mark."

He withdrew the iron from the brazier. The tip glowed cherry red. Giele had branded his share of horses and cattle in the Army, and knew it had to be excruciating from the way they screamed when the red hot metal was applied to their haunches.

The King approached Giele with the brand outstretched in both his hands. Giele shrank back from it but the guards held him fast. It had a strange, sweet smell, a far cry from the stink of the forges. Even out of the corner of his eyes, he saw the glowing brand's curved shape. A crescent moon. The Elven sign of evil. The King chose a symbol that would mark him forever as evil, and it would be displayed where all could see it. He would be reduced to an outcast, loathed and spit upon.

A pariah.

"Please . . ." Giele found his voice at last. Hoarse, full of shame and contrition, he swallowed his pride to plead. "Mercy, my King. I beg of you."

"I am merciful. I have acceded to my daughter's plea to spare your life. This wound will not be fatal." He paused for effect. None of the courtiers even dared to breathe, lest the sound of inhalation cause offense. "At least, not directly."

Teirol drew in close to Giele. Giele's vision narrowed, and the glowing iron crescent filled his world. He tried to struggle, to flee, but the guards held him even tighter. He couldn't look away.

"You shall spend the remainder of your life wishing I'd killed you," Teirol hissed, and drove the brand into Giele's cheek.

Pain!

Giele screamed a primal cry of anguish, certain the King had pushed the red hot iron all the way through his mouth and out the other side. As he drew breath to scream again, the smoke from the wound filled his lungs and made him choke. In three wars, he had been cut by swords, shot by arrows, captured by enemies and tortured to within a whisper of death. None of those wounds came close to the blinding white-hot torment of the brand. He couldn't see, couldn't think, his senses filled with the sickening tang of roasted flesh. The guards hurled him to the floor and Giele shrieked and sobbed. He wanted to dash his brains out against the cool marble, but didn't have the presence of mind to move.

"See to him, Doctor." Teirol let the iron fall to the floor with a clang that echoed throughout the chamber. Nobody else dared move.

Giele blubbered like a baby as Dr. Shaison's cool hands touched his face.

The King turned his back to Giele, no longer willing to tolerate his presence. "Get this pathetic thing out of my sight forever."

Something cloying and sweet puffed into his face and Giele sank into a den of nightmares.

Chapter Five

Rough hands threw Giele into a puddle of cold rainwater. The palace gates slammed behind him with a resounding *clang* that echoed down the cobblestone street. Rivulets ran between the stones as they sought the fastest route to the river and the sea. The buildings along the road had all shuttered their windows against the cold autumn storm, which left everything a dark, uniform gray. Even the ubiquitous trees had turned into grim specters towering over the single- and double-story square. Inviting bits of light leaked around the edges of doorways and windows, promising the warmth of fireplaces and steam radiators, of gaslight and companionship, but he found no comfort in that thought. He crawled to a drier patch of ground under a rain-soaked poplar and sat up, still wearing the ragged robe in which he'd been brought to see the King.

Only a maddening burning itch remained of the pain he'd endured at the King's hands. After the agony of the wounding, he couldn't believe it didn't hurt more. Dr. Shaison's potions and ministrations must have worked wonders while he laid unconscious, however many days or weeks that might have been. He reached up with tentative fingers to explore the wound on his face. His fingers found the hard edges and smooth surface of scar tissue. Pain shocked him when he touched it, but the scar otherwise subsided to a dull throb.

He had to see it.

He staggered over to the nearest building, a private bank, and gazed upon his reflection in the large, expensive plate glass window. He lurched back in horror at the angry, crescent-shaped patch of mottled flesh that adorned his face. God's Blood, it stretched from his cheekbone down to the edge of his jaw line. Nobody would ever see anything of him again but that scar. He'd never thought himself a handsome man, but now he was horrific.

A monster.

He started at a tap on the window and looked past his own reflection to see a bank guard inside. He tapped the window again and motioned for Giele to move along, his lips pulled back in a telltale expression of disgust at Giele's scarred, soggy visage.

Brokenhearted at his plight, Giele staggered downhill, following the drainage streams through Morningstar City until he reached the seafront to the south of the harbor, in a neighborhood populated by working-folk, laborers, and craftsmen. Waves dashed against the stone seawall which protected Lower Morningstar neighborhoods from storm surges. The turbulent gray sea matched the dismay in his soul. It would be so simple to take one more step, to let the water swallow him into the harbor. The ocean cared not about scars or traitorous acts or kings. One step, and he would find peace. He inched closer to the edge. Terika's betrayal loomed large in his heart. Oblivion called to him, but then he realized it was with someone else's voice.

"Go on, get out of here, you rutting bum!" A city watchman stood nearby under an umbrella. He held a large truncheon in his other hand and looked like he would enjoy swinging it against Giele's ribs.

In the space of one heartbeat, Giele changed his mind. His death would give the King great satisfaction, but he wouldn't let Morningstar win after the way he'd taken away everything else that Giele had called his own. Of course Teirol wanted Giele to die; the King had marked him forever in the hopes that it would seal his fate. Teirol Morningstar may have taken away everything else, but Giele still had his life, and would do something with it, although he had no idea what. He growled at the watchman.

The man took a step back, aghast at Giele's sudden aggression. "God's Blood!" he cried in horror as Giele turned and displayed the angry red scar upon his cheek.

Giele hunched over and ran away from the watchman, leaving behind the siren call of the sea to escape back into the labyrinth of city streets. He settled underneath a wooden overhang in a narrow alley. Rainwater flowed past his bare feet as he sat and shivered, but at least no more icy drops pelted onto his skin.

He had no money, no home left, and no prospects for the future. He was even worse off than he had been as a prisoner of the Jigans. At least after they had almost pulled him in half on their elaborate stretching machine, they'd fed him watery gruel.

He sat in the growing darkness, shivering, and wondered what the morning might bring if he didn't freeze to death overnight. The temperature had plummeted, and he was still wet through. Desperate for warmth, he knew he had no choice; he would turn to thievery.

He used a loose cobblestone to break into a garment store through the glass of the rear door. He squashed the pang of what little honor he had left as the shards rained down among the puddles. Before the owner staggered down the stairs from his slumber, Giele decamped with wool trousers, a silk shirt, a heavy oilskin overcoat, socks and boots, and a wide-brimmed hat, which he pulled low to hide his face. He fled down the alley with the angry voice of the shop's owner burning in his ears. He had been reduced to stealing. Would this be all he had left? He found a dark corner to pull on the stolen clothes. Each piece pained him as if it were a lash. Such was the punishment meted out by the King, and it cut Giele deeper than if he'd been run through with a blade.

The idea of remaining in Morningstar City as a thief sickened him. He wouldn't find any work here. Within days, he would be unwelcome throughout the country as the news spread. He was a pariah. A hundred years ago, he might have disappeared to live in the woods as a solitary hermit and hunter, living off his woodcraft and skill with a bow. But civilization was now encroaching upon even the wildest remaining parts of Aelfland. The great wildernesses were being roped off into parks and preserves, patrolled by the King's Army, and he would not find safety or solace there.

Giele would have to leave Aelfland, perhaps forever.

Frigid Jiga lay to the south. He knew the people there, because of the time he'd spent among them as a combatant. Despite differences in some basic philosophies and politics from Aelfland, Jigans were still Elves and would respond poorly to the mark upon him. They might welcome him for the information he brought, but it would be used to overrun Aelfland. Giele held no grudges against the Army who held the line along the border, and he was unwilling to put them in danger by turning coat. It galled him that in his desperation he'd even considered the notion. The King may have called him a traitor, but Giele would never call himself one.

He couldn't go to the Dewar Archipelago to the east, but for a different reason. The Dwarves were Aelfland's closest allies, and he wouldn't be any more welcome there than he would be if he remained in his homeland. The rocky, mountainous territory there was treacherous to those who hadn't been raised within it, and he doubted he would live a week in the untamed parts of the Dwarven homeland. So many Elves inhabited the Dwarven cities that Giele would be as much a pariah there as he would be if he remained among his own people.

To the west lay impenetrable mountain ranges and great glacial fields. Other nations existed beyond them, but it might be years before Dwarven engineers built roads, tunnels, and bridges to reach them. Giele knew their names from seeing them on maps, but knew nothing more of their people or cultures. He would have even less success traveling in that direction than he would across Aelfland to Dewar.

The remaining alternative he saw would be to cross the Aeresic Ocean to the north, and start a life anew in the Colonies. The courageous seafarer Captain Verig Riverbank had discovered the continent of Verigo when Giele was but a child. He had returned to Aelfland a hero, having claimed the great northern continent in the name of Teirol Morningstar. The southern coast of Verigo lay within tropical climes, and farmers had relocated to cultivate the wonderful citrus fruits and sugarcane, which grew wild on its shores. The silkworm ranchers too found it an excellent locale for production, and in fifty years more silk came from across the ocean than from within Aelfland itself.

North of the coast, Verigo stretched out into great rolling prairies suitable for farming grain and raising cattle, sheep, and creatures called Greatdeer, which made the stags of Aelfland's forests look like saplings beside towering oaks. At first, it had been thought that Verigo was uninhabited, but a pre-civilized race of barbarians had been discovered. The horse-faced nomads were called Horks. Explorers brought a few back home for display, but Giele had never seen one.

In Verigo, he might be able to make some sort of living. There wasn't much call for warriors in a land without wars, but he was resourceful if nothing else. He could find some kind of work, even if it was herding cattle or cutting sugarcane.

To travel across the ocean would present its own challenges, the first of which was the question of fare. He had no money, and no nautical skills to barter for working passage, provided he even found a crew that would take him aboard. Sailors were notorious as a superstitious lot—even more so than soldiers—and his scar would be seen as a bad omen. His best bet would be to buy passage, and to pay enough to overcome a captain's fears. For that, he needed a sum of money, and he could think of just one place where he might obtain it without stealing. The desperation of his circumstances overcame his fear of running across those from his prior life.

The next evening found Giele lurking outside the garrison as a crescent moon the same shape as his scar shone in the sky overhead. Pale clouds over the ocean suggested another Autumn storm was brewing, but wouldn't arrive for hours. The long, low blockhouse of the 136th had been old when Giele was still a Leaf Archer. It was at the far end of the garrison, which made an unseen approach easier. He'd circled around the garrison hours ago, careful to keep hidden from posted watches, climbed up into an elm tree overlooking his old unit's barracks, and settled in to wait. A bugler sounded the call to bunks. Gaslights and lanterns were extinguished, leaving the garrison bathed in darkness.

In the waning days of Giele's command, the new class of Leaf Archers had graduated from basic training and many of the fresh young faces had been assigned to fill out the ranks of the 136th. Giele would never get to know those young soldiers now. It hurt to see his old home and know it had been forever denied to him. He finished the last piece of bread from a loaf of bread he'd stolen earlier from a window where it had been left to cool and gazed down upon the building from his vantage point.

Newly-promoted Grove Colonel Kiler was a man of habit. After the call to bunks, he slipped outside with his pipe and his customary bag of Tencho leaf. Although Giele didn't smoke, he and Kiler had often sat up late and discussed strategy, tactics, or shared stories with one another. Kiler had been the most logical candidate to replace Giele with his sharp mind and good rapport with the Elves and Dwarves under him. Giele recalled a nighttime battle in the last Jigan War when he'd been pierced by three arrows and Kiler had hauled him back from the front lines despite a bullet wound in his own leg.

Kiler was the closest thing Giele might have to an ally.

He slipped unnoticed into camp. He'd have to remind Kiler that watches shouldn't be shoddy simply because the 136th sat deep in friendly territory. To Kiler's credit, he didn't jump or reach for his sidearm when Giele stepped around the corner of the building where he sat and smoked his pipe.

"Hello, Kiler." Giele kept his voice low and muscles tensed, ready for action. He didn't know how Kiler would react to his presence. He hoped his old friend wouldn't sound the alarm, or slay him on sight.

"Giele. I rather expected I might see you." His calm, studied face betrayed no threat.

Giele shrugged. "Here I am. Congratulations on your promotion. The 136th is in good hands."

Kiler blew out a lungful of smoke. "Not how I'd have chosen to earn it, but thanks." He tapped ashes from the bowl of his pipe. Kiler was deliberate and patient with everything, including his conversation. Giele couldn't rush him or he'd balk. "Can I see it?"

For a moment Giele didn't understand what Kiler meant, but then he pushed up the brim of his hat and raised his head to the moonlight.

Kiler whistled. "God's Blood, I bet that hurt."

Giele nodded. "Worse than that barbed shaft I took in Three Hills. Worse than anything."

"So what is your plan?"

"I'll head for Verigo."

Kiler nodded. "I thought you might. I couldn't see anyplace else you'd go."

"You know me well enough."

He shrugged. "You were the best commander I ever had. You saved my life more times than I can remember. That counts for a lot. And that goes for all of us."

Hooded lanterns flared in the darkness. Giele realized too late that Kiler's watchmen hadn't been lax after all. It looked like the entire 136th had turned out. He stiffened, ready to flee, but none of them held weapons, and many of them were smiling.

"What is this?" Giele asked Kiler.

"The King may have stripped you of your rank," said Kiler, his eyes bright, "but as far as we're concerned, you'll always be our leader. And we wanted to wish you farewell and good luck in your journey."

For the next hour, one at a time, each Elf and Dwarf in the 136th came up to Giele, shook his hand, and thanked him for his service, for leading them, for saving their lives. Many of them pressed crown bills into his hand, in spite of his protests. He felt overwhelmed at their gratitude. The other Bole Majors thanked him at the end of the line. One presented Giele with a brand new fletching kit and said he heard there was good wood in the northern continent. The Dwarven Bole Major gave him a heavy fighting knife with a secret compartment in the handle. Kiler shook his hand last and pressed his pearl-handled pistol and gun belt upon Giele.

"No, I can't take that," Giele said.

"You have to," he said. "Your name is on it."

Giele looked, and in the flickering light from the lanterns, he saw etching on the handle. It read *Giele Stillwater, Grove Colonel, 136th Regiment.*

His throat tightened as he realized it might be the last time he ever saw his family name, and it took him a moment to speak. "Thank you. Thank you all. I'll carry this with me in memory of the greatest soldiers it has ever been my privilege to serve with."

Under different circumstances, the men would have sent up a rousing cheer, but that would have been inappropriate at a time like this. Instead, to a man, they all doffed their caps in a display of deference and honor. Giele didn't feel he deserved such treatment, but it lifted his heart the way the sunrise will after a stormy night.

"If you ever need us, send word. We'll find a way to help." Kiler clasped Giele's hand in friendship.

One of the watchmen raised an alarm, hooting like a night owl. The unexpected gathering must have caught the attention of another unit commander.

"You should go, sir," said Kiler. "Good luck, and be careful. The King has criers out all over town. They're hanging posters. Everyone's going to know your face and that mark upon it."

The entire 136th saluted Giele. He returned it, his fist clenched tight over his heart, and then turned to disappear into the darkness.

The lantern light must have been far too bright, for Giele's eyes kept watering as he slipped away from the camp.

CHAPTER SIX

The boys of the 136th had given Giele a truly obscene amount of crowns. Seeing Teirol's face on the printed bills galled him, but they represented his chance to get away from the King forever. His former soldiers must have each given up a good chunk of their weekly pay. He vowed their money would not go to waste and would make sure he left no other debts behind him in Aelfland. A newsstand vendor at the bazaar outside the city walls sold him an envelope and overcharged him for it. As Giele left, he overheard passers-by chastising the vendor for selling to him at all. "What? His money spends like anyone else's," said the man.

Giele placed a ten-crown bill into the envelope and sealed it. It took him five wheels—a full half crown—before he recruited a young lad who wasn't frightened off by his face. He sent the boy to deliver the envelope to the clothing merchant whose shop he'd robbed. The amount was more than sufficient to cover the cost of his stolen clothing and the damages he'd done in the break-in.

Convincing the street vendors to sell him food was more difficult and costly, but he found one whose greed outweighed his disgust of Giele's scarred face. He bought three round artisan loaves at a price more than twice what was fair, and left them on the windowsill where he'd stolen one the night before.

Having discharged those personal obligations, Giele wondered if perhaps the world owed him a bit of good luck, and went to the docks. There he learned once more the universe has little place in it for those who require luck for their success. Captain after captain refused to grant him passage aboard their square-sailed and steam-driven ships, even when he offered to pay three times the standard fare for oceanic passage. He knew why they turned him away, but by the time he'd approached the tenth man, a long-legged old crow of an Elf with silver rings at the tops of his ear points, he had grown frustrated and that translated into surliness. "You won't take my money either, longshanks? Business must be booming."

The captain spat at Giele's feet. "You're marked with evil. Get off my ship."

Giele gave up on passenger vessels and tried his luck with cargo carriers. He found them to be, if anything, even more superstitious. One such captain, an Elvish brute with arms like casks of wine and carefully-combed mustaches that dangled Dwarf-style from the corners of his mouth, had two of his deckhands grab Giele the moment he set foot upon the gangplank and hurl him back to the dock.

"Yer type ain't welcome here. Ye won't sully the deck of the *Loria Darkwood* with yer treacherous feet!" He waved a crossbow speargun at Giele. "I'll spit ye right where ye stand!"

Giele didn't wait for him to take a shot, and ran up the pier with one hand holding his hat on his head. The captain's parting words rang in his ears long after he was out of range. "Run, Pariah!"

Rejected by, it seemed, every boat in the docks, Giele slouched upon a broken crate that stank of fish and pondered his next move.

With a fluttering of gossamer silken wings, an insectile *whirly* landed beside him like some kind of brass and aluminum grasshopper. Whirlies were toys the rich used to deliver messages. Fear, greed, whores, or strong drink often diverted traditional messengers, but the mechanical whirlies were guided by magic, and located their targets without fail. The one that had sought and found him now rested on three articulated legs. It ticked like a clock as its spring-wound motor idled.

A small scroll sealed with a familiar sigil was tied to the whirly's tail section, which it pointed toward Giele. *Terika.* He couldn't understand why she would have reached out to him now. Hadn't she done enough to destroy him? He turned away from the whirly. It hopped around and pushed the scroll at him once more. The poor, dumb machine would keep up its vain attempts until it ran out of fuel. Numb, he reached out and untied the delicate ribbon. Sometimes a whirly would await a return message, but as soon as he had the scroll, this one's wings blurred into motion and it flew away, leaving behind an acrid chemical stink of burned oil and flash powder.

For a long moment, Giele didn't have the heart to move. He stared at the scroll lying in his hands, thinking he should crumple it up, unread, and hurl it into the Aeresic. More than once, he raised his arm to do just that, and each time he lowered it. Longshoremen hurried past him, wrestling shipping crates full of everything from wine to wool, syrup to spices, and bundles of cut timber. Life went on in a blur while Giele stayed frozen in thought. In spite of his anger toward her, he had to know what Terika had thought so important to tell him now. Finally, he broke the seal. With trembling fingers, he unrolled the small piece of parchment and read Terika's note.

Dearest Giele,

I know you must hate me now, but I didn't want you to leave without knowing why I used you as I did.

To forge an alliance with the Jigans, my father promised me to the Imperius of Goei. I pleaded with father to withdraw the marriage contract—the Imperius is a lecherous old goat who's already buried three wives—but my father would not be moved.

I thought my fate was sealed, until I found you. I knew that the Imperius would reject me if I was despoiled, and you were so sweet, and strong. I could find no one better to take my virginity from me and save me from my father's plans.

Doctor Shaison's work to restore my maidenhood will not hold up to the Jigan's inevitable examination before marriage. I will forever bear the mark you left upon me, and for that I thank you.

I am sorry you bore such cruel punishment on my behalf, and wish it could have been resolved some other way. I had no idea my father would take such extreme measures. I argued for your life and at least won that battle for you. Please know that everything I said to you I meant in truth. Perhaps someday, when I ascend to the throne of Aelfland, we may meet again under better circumstances. If so, I hope you can find it in your heart to forgive me.

Take care, dear Giele, wherever you go in this life.
Terika

Giele blinked and read the message through a second time. She'd used him, and yet still claimed to have meant it when she told him her heart sang for him. More confused than ever, he sat unmoving on the crate as dumbfounded as a raw recruit after his first battle. As he turned over her words again and again in his mind, his temper grew. How dare she plead for his forgiveness now? His teeth ground together and he crumpled the note between his fingers. Everything she said to him was true? Impossible. Lying, rutting whore. He'd let her use him for the simple pleasure of her body, and she'd played him for a fool. He hurled the note into the ocean for real. He wouldn't waste another thought on the Princess of Aelfland.

"Here, now, littering is a crime, mister."

Giele looked up to see a City Watchman's badge pinned to the chest of an imposing Elf who stood half a head taller than him. His eyes widened as he saw the mark on Giele's face. "Pariah!" He reached for his truncheon.

Giele had had enough. He drove his fist upward into the watchman's belly with a wordless roar of fury. He gasped and staggered back, and Giele followed it with another blow to the point of his chin. The watchman tumbled backward off the dock to splash into the water.

Strong arms grabbed Giele from behind. He drove his head backward hard, breaking the nose of whoever held him. He glanced down and saw a tattoo of an anchor on the muscular forearm. Anchor Man's grip loosened a little and Giele hit him on his broken nose with his head again. He let Giele go and Giele whirled around to slam his foot into the side of Anchor Man's knee. He crumpled as another couple of dock workers charged at Giele. One swung a gaff at his ribs. Giele took the shot against the muscles of his forearm. They would bruise but it was better than broken ribs. He whipped his arm over around around the gaff, trapping it against his side.

The other worker tried to throw a punch but Giele kicked high and hard, catching him square in the chest. He fell one way and Giele fell the other, snapping the gaff out of the other man's grip. In a moment Giele was back up on his feet, spinning the gaff around hard enough to make it whistle.

Their faces fell in dismay when they realized they weren't facing a drunken, scarred vagrant, but someone with military hand-to-hand combat training. They glanced at each other, reached an unspoken agreement, and ran away. Giele took a half dozen steps after them; his blood was pumping hot and it felt good to cut loose with some unschooled brawling. He had a weapon, and a lot of anger to work out; he'd clear the docks until somebody took him down.

A voice interrupted his pursuit and brought him up short. "You're the fella offerin' triple rates to cross the Aeresic?"

Giele turned to regard an old sea dog of a Dwarf. His whiskers had gone white and his bald pate had seen so much sun and salty sea air that it looked more like the leather armor Giele had worn in the Army. He walked with a cane and had an iron shod hardwood foot on one leg. Sea salt collected in the crevices of his forehead and cheeks, and his prodigious nose looked like the gnarled aftermath of a battle between it and a determined sea bird. He raised his cane and pointed it at Giele.

"If you're going to swing that toothpick at Ole Fisk, get on with it. I've got a departure deadline. But I'm the only one likely to give you what you need."

Giele dropped the gaff, feeling foolish for even considering to attack the old man. The Dwarf was tall for a member of his race, the top of his head reaching up to Giele's chest. He stared at Giele with eyes darkened from years of squinting through sunlight reflected off the waves.

"Them other fellas say you're bad luck to have aboard, but I don't take no truck with that." He stuck a proud thumb against his chest. "Captain Fiskelius makes his own luck for bad or good, and that's me. So the question is, are you willing to pay me the same as them other fellas?"

Giele nodded. "I am."

"Well bugger me for a monkey's uncle. For triple fare I'll take you to the moon if you ask me to."

Giele gave him a wry smile; he couldn't manage much better than that with the brand marring his cheek. "And you're not worried about bad omens?"

The derisive Dwarf spat onto the dock beside him. "I already told you, Scarface, Ole Fisk don't believe in that bilge. I'm more worried about the Blue you knocked in the bay. Them sons of whores don't take kindly to such abuse. Although I know him by reputation." Fiskelius grinned. "Ruttin' bastard deserved a bath, as he was about a year overdue, and that's God's own truth." He frowned for a moment. "I've got a Padre aboard for this trip. He'll see to any bad omens if you bring them aboard the *Allusi.*"

"That's your ship?"

"Aye, named after my dear sweet mother. I'm Captain Fiskelius Deadmarsh, owner and operator, and for triple fare I'll take you to any port in Verigo, long as it's Golden Sands."

Giele managed a laugh. The Dwarf's demeanor had a way of disarming his suspicions. "Golden Sands is fine, Captain Deadmarsh."

"Aye, call me Fisk. That formal bilge is only for merchant houses."

"Fisk, then. When do you ship out?"

"Soon as you get your lanky shanks aboard, lubber. Have you got valises or cargo? If Ole Fisk is going to collect triple, he may as well give you some space in the hold."

Giele shook his head. "Just me."

Fisk sniffed in doubt. "You ever been aboard a ship before, lubber?"

"No, sir, I have not."

"Sea salt's powerful rough on clothing, and although I don't know your personal preferences, I'm awful sure the Verigans won't take kindly to you walkin' into town bare-assed. I'll give you the time you need to fill a bag if you want."

"That's kind of you, Ole Fisk, but nobody will sell me anything."

"Bugger me sticky, why not?" He seemed perplexed. "Money's money, ain't it?"

"The locals seem to think mine is tainted by my bad omen. Because of this." Giele pointed to his cheek.

Fisk spat on the dock again. "Weed-eatin' sons of whores. Here's Ole Fisk with a foot clean bit off by a buggerin' shark and a nose like a freighter's prow and all you got is that scar and nobody's takin' your money." He pounded the tip of his cane on his wooden foot for emphasis. "Maybe the Padre would help you out. Them churchgoing types tend to want to help those in need. And I'd say you're about as needful a bastard as I've seen in many months. Come with me back to the *Allusi* and I'll have the boys sling you a bunk while we get you sorted out with some gear." He paused as if remembering something important. "Uh, maybe you'd better show Ole Fisk the color of your money."

Giele handed him a sheaf of a thousand crowns.

The aged Dwarf pounded his thigh and laughed. "The moon, you said? We'll depart within the hour. Put up your cash, lad. Flashing a wad like that here on the docks is like as not to get you rolled and dumped into the drink. Although . . ." He thumped his cane again. "Ole Fisk would pay a percentage to see anyone try."

He led Giele to the far end of the docks, where the least-fashionable boats docked. Men yelled to one another over the noise of steam cranes, livestock, and the constant thrum of the incoming tide. More than once, they had to step aside as trains of ox-drawn carts trundled down the dock, laden with piles of crates and barrels or mountains of grain bags or bolts of silk. The air was redolent with the stench of fish, lubricants, and salt. Gull dung decorated every horizontal surface as the birds dove after edible cargo again and again. Junior longshoremen set after them with paddles, sending the indignant scavengers squawking back into the sky without prizes.

The *Allusi* fit every definition Giele had ever heard of a tramp freighter, from the scuffed timbers that made up the hull to the discolored patches on the sails to the oversized paddle wheels on either side which looked more like afterthoughts than original construction. Once on board, Giele realized the haphazard appearance could be an intentional deceit. The deck shone from many layers of lacquer and resin, so smooth that not a splinter poked up anywhere. The ropes were all coiled in neat stacks and well-oiled with military precision. The small crew of sweaty Elves and Dwarves worked in a line to load the forward cargo hold with bags of beans, tea, and other consumables.

"Ho, Beltius," called Captain Fisk. "One more passenger for the trip north. See that he gets a berth."

A strapping young Dwarf with impressive slabs of muscle on his stocky frame gave Fisk a smart salute. "Aye, Cap'n."

"Mate Beltius O'Coaston. He runs the ship when Ole Fisk is in a kip or on the drunk," said Fisk.

Beltius extended his hand to Giele. "Welcome aboard, mister." If he noticed Giele's scar, he had the courtesy not to question or stare. Dwarves wouldn't see the mark on him the same way Elves would, for their eyes tended to look to the earth instead of the sky for inspiration and omens. Even so, none of Fisk's Elven crewmen gave Giele more than a cursory glance before returning to their work.

Beltius turned to the Captain. "We're ninety percent loaded, Cap'n. Just waiting for Wexel to get back with outgoing post."

"Fine, carry on."

"You carry mail?" Giele asked in surprise. He had always thought Naval vessels handled that as part of the King's mandate.

Fisk grinned, showing several gaps in his teeth. "Aye, lad. Quicker than the Navy to boot. Me business philosophy is that people will pay extra for speed of service. We'll deliver our cargo ahead of that behemoth over there . . ." He pointed out a huge steamship near the main freight terminal. "Them sons of whores would love to see me beneath the waves because I cut my chunks right out of their profits. Sure, she carries twenty times what the *Allusi* can, but because we'll arrive before her, my cargo will fetch a premium price. Them colonists do love their little tastes of home." He opened a door in the forecastle. "You'll berth up here with the Padre. Oh, here he is now. Padre, your bunkmate for the voyage north."

A handsome young Elf in simple homespun beige robes looked up at Giele over wire-framed glasses. His sandy hair hung around his face so only the points of his ears poked out from it. Despite his soft hands, Giele saw the strong muscles of physical labor under his robes. No weak scholar, this one. Perhaps he'd carried many heavy books, or learned some esoteric fighting arts, or done more than his fair share of calisthenics. He placed a tassel in his book and closed it. "Hello, I'm Padre Tarvy at your service, sir."

"Giele."

"Buggerin' wonderful, we can all be friends." Fisk clomped away.

CHAPTER SEVEN

Traveling on the *Allusi* proved to be one of the more memorable non-combat experiences Giele had in his life. He'd never been out to sea before, instead sticking to riverboats. Seafaring travel was much different; it took him three days to recover from his seasickness and two more after that to get his sea legs. Tarvy took care of Giele during his illness, bringing him water when he could stomach it and a bucket when he couldn't. When Giele emerged blinking into the sunlight for the first time and felt the wind on his face with no sign of Aelfland anywhere, he knew he'd made the right choice.

Captain Fiskelius ran a tight ship with one eye always directed at his bottom line. When the wind blew the right direction, his crew lifted the steam-driven outrigger paddle wheels clear of the water to reduce drag and spread the sails wide. When the wind blew the wrong way, sails were stowed and the steam boiler sent the paddles whirring into noisy motion. And when the air was becalmed, it became Piprel's job to provide suitable gusts.

Piprel was a wizard who'd signed on as contract labor for the *Allusi* in return for transport to Verigo. Well, first and foremost he was a drunk, and somehow it became Giele's job on board to keep control of him and to monitor his wine intake. Giele had seen men in the Army who were trying to kill themselves with drink, and more than a few who succeeded. Piprel had many of the same characteristics about him of the combat-shocked soldier. Whatever he was running from in Aelfland gave him nightmares that he softened through the frequent application of booze. Giele's first night on board, deep in the throes of his own seasickness-induced misery, Piprel screamed himself awake in the early low bells, slapping away at things apparent to him alone. Delirium took him at random, where he would curse or scream at the visions from his pickled mind. Thus Giele spent much of the voyage keeping an eye on him and calming him through soothing words or, more often, another sip of grog.

"What's the matter with your face?" he'd asked Giele in his slurred voice when they first met. He made no gestures to ward off evil, nor did he spit or hiss. "Looks kind of like a waxing moon." His own face wasn't much improved over Giele's: far too slender, framed by unkempt hair that was stringy and greasy, with the ruddy nose and cheeks and rheumy eyes of the perpetual drunkard. Despite his prodigious appetite, most of what he ate wound up vomited into the Aeresic, so his bones stuck out like he was starving. He eschewed most clothing on shipboard, preferring to bake away under the merciless sun in short pants and nothing else. His skin burned, then peeled, only to burn again.

Until his offhand remark, it hadn't occurred to Giele that the moon was crescent not just when waning, but on its way toward fullness. Perhaps he was himself waxing now, returning from the darkness of the new moon. He squeezed Piprel's shoulder. Piprel belched sour wine in Giele's face, and the moment ended.

Tarvy had purchased some supplies on Giele's behalf, and had returned to the *Allusi* shortly before the Captain raised anchor and headed out to sea on a puff of steam. He'd selected a hardy mix of clothing that would last for months, maybe even years with careful laundering.

The Padre had been to Verigo once before on a mission, and was returning after a year's sojourn in Aelfland. He intended to travel to the frontier and bring the Word to those Elves and Dwarves who lived at the very edge of civilization. He and Giele spoke at length about life in the new world, and to a lesser extent about his faith.

Giele never had much use for the Church of Aelfland. The extent of his relationship with the Elven God was the occasional epithet. He didn't pray, attend services, or participate in any of the Full Moon rituals which formed the cornerstone of Elven faith. Seeing young soldiers impaled on spears, poisoned by their own excrement, screaming with every breath, tended to shake one's faith in the existence of a higher power. He told as much to Tarvy.

"I understand," said the Padre. "Other soldiers have expressed similar sentiments to me. They want to know how God can allow such atrocities to take place when they are taught from birth that God loves us."

"Well? Do you have an answer for that?"

Tarvy smiled and adjusted his glasses. "I do not. It is foolish for us to consider that we might understand the motives, whims, and wishes of our creator, any more than a stalk of wheat may understand us, its planter."

"But we harvest wheat, and wheat doesn't think."

"Doesn't it? Perhaps Elfkind is a field of wheat, tended by God. We must likewise be harvested, and rotated with other crops in order to provide better sustenance."

"Now God is a farmer, cutting us down and threshing us to be baked into bread?" Giele smiled. "You're making me hungry."

A week into the voyage, Giele discussed his history in the Army and the nature of his own journey with Tarvy. Since by his own admission he didn't keep up very well with current events, Tarvy had heard none of the criers detailing Giele's punishment at the King's hands nor seen any of the posters. "Your scar isn't a mark of evil," he said. "It's a weight upon your soul. Like any muscle, the more weight it carries over time, the stronger it becomes."

"It's a weight I wish I could put down."

"The weights we cannot drop are those which bring us the most strength."

Giele found an odd comfort in that statement.

To his credit, Tarvy did not proselytize or flaunt his beliefs beyond the occasional mild theological discussion, which he filled with so many metaphors that Giele often fell asleep more confused than ever. Tarvy made for an agreeable roommate in the tiny cabin they shared.

They spent most of their time on the deck, careful to stay out of the way of the sailors. So far, they had enjoyed a pleasant voyage under skies filled with fluffy white clouds that chased one another in gentle spiral patterns. Every day was warmer than the last as the *Allusi* crossed into the tropical climes.

Like the sailors, Tarvy and Giele had taken to wearing naught but trousers, letting the sun bake the autumnal chill from their bones. Every once in awhile Giele would glance down at his chest and wonder whose it was, for his should have been decorated with an elaborate tattoo. Then he'd grow so melancholy that even Piprel would offer him a sip from his bottle. Giele always refused; that was a road upon which he didn't wish to take the first step. The three passengers were an oddly-mismatched bunch. Piprel's body had wasted under the spell of constant alcohol, and his skin showed many burst veins beneath its surface. Giele's own skin had drawn tight from a reduced appetite and what little winter fat stores he'd built up had vanished, leaving him as wiry as ever. Tarvy, on the other hand, had muscles which even made sailors' eyes widen. The young Padre delighted in helping with the physical aspects of sailing from coiling ropes to folding sails.

"How does a man of faith develop such strength?" Giele asked him one day after observing him lift a coil of rope that had taken two of Fisk's sailors to move.

"God has seen fit to bless me with this body. Far be it from me to reject God's gifts. Besides, womenfolk find it appealing." He chuckled.

Giele knew some of the younger Padres didn't hold with the notion of celibacy. Tarvy subscribed to that philosophy as well. Giele smiled. He guessed that Tarvy would explain it as another of God's gifts that he didn't reject.

"Is it this hot in Verigo?" Giele took his hat off and flapped some of the stifling hot and moist air at his face with it.

"It is," said Tarvy. "Although as you move further inland the air becomes much drier and quite a bit more tolerable. You'll want to wear a hat to keep the sun off your head. I've seen more than one tourist faint from the constant heat. Besides, when it rains, you'll be glad of the extra protection."

Beltius paused as he passed by them on some errand. "Rain, eh? Best you get ready for some. Storm's a-comin'." He pointed to a smudge of clouds on the horizon.

"What is it you'll require from us, Mate Beltius?" Giele asked.

"Stay out of the way, mostly," Beltius said. "And you might get some tea into the mage. We'll probably need him before the day is done."

Giele looked over to his cabin where Piprel was sleeping off the previous evening's drink. Giele had questioned Captain Fiskelius about the wisdom of providing the mage with so much alcohol during the trip, but had received a stony glare and a "bugger off" in return.

"Shall I awaken the poor fellow?" asked Tarvy.

"No, I'll do it. He already doesn't like me and I'm used to dealing with recalcitrance."

Piprel lay on the floor alongside the bunks where the motion of the *Allusi* must have tossed him out at some point. He wore naught but rough-spun breeches. His dark, unkempt hair stuck out like the tuft of a thistle. The cabin stank of the grog which sweated from his very pores. Giele kicked at the soles of Piprel's bare feet as he snored on the wooden deck. He muttered in his sleep and curled up into a ball. Impatient with the mage's slumber, Giele bent down until he was right beside him and bawled in his ear. "On your feet, soldier! Duty calls!"

"God's Blood!" He clapped his hands over his ears. "What'd you do that for?"

"Time to work, Mage." Giele hauled Piprel to his feet. Giele's nose wrinkled at the sour odors of Piprel's unwashed body and stale vomit on his breath.

The mage gasped at the sudden motion, and then staggered over to the rail to drain his bladder into the Aeresic. "How about a li'l drink of something? It appears I'm empty again."

"Nothing but tea for you. Mate Beltius says a storm is coming and they'll need your services. Time to sober up."

"Bugger that, rut face."

Giele sighed as Piprel staggered for the aft cabin where the cook stored the wine. Some men couldn't be reasoned with, and for those times Giele had learned a few tricks. Before Piprel opened the galley door, Giele snaked his arm underneath the mage's, angled it up behind his head, and gave a firm pinch to one of Piprel's earlobes. Piprel shrieked.

Keeping hold of his ear, Giele hauled him over to the mainmast and slammed him up against it. He cursed Giele, his lineage, the ship, the ship's lineage, the Captain, the ocean, and the bloody great Universe of Buggering Mystery as Giele lashed him to the mast and proceeded to fling bucket after bucket of seawater in his face. Eventually his protests died down and Giele fed him tea and hardtack until he reached a level of lucid drunkenness.

Over the next two hours, the sea grew choppy and great towering thunderheads rushed in towards the ship. The wind shifted direction and the Captain ordered all sails lowered. Beltius and his crew dropped the paddle wheels and for awhile they made good time, keeping ahead of the storm. The *Allusi*'s boilers hissed as the Captain ordered full speed ahead. The wheels kicked up great sprays higher even than the foamy crests of waves as the *Allusi* dove into troughs and climbed mountains of water. Soon, though, the angry blasts of thunder became audible even over the roaring of the steam engine and the wind.

"It's no good," shouted Fisk. "I hoped we'd outrun the bugger, but it looks like we're in for it, lubbers." He bellowed at the crew to lock down the paddle wheels. As outriggers, they'd help keep the small ship afloat as the rough waters increased. "You ready to earn your passage?" This last was directed at Piprel, who glared from where Giele had lashed him to the mast.

The mage nodded as he gazed, terrified, at the waves crashing around the *Allusi*. "I can't work like this. I need freedom of movement."

"Untie him," said Fisk. "You'll have to at least keep a line about your waist, mage."

"Very well. God's Blood, I need a drink."

Giele removed the ropes that bound Piprel and secured a new rope around his waist to the mast. "Good enough?"

Fisk nodded. "Keep the ship upright and on a northerly heading, however you can." He turned to look at Giele. "You better get to your berth, Scarface."

"Captain, I'll stay on deck with Piprel. He might need help."

"I will stay as well," said Tarvy. "Your men will be busy with the ship, Captain. We will attend to Piprel's needs."

"Damned fool lubbers, this is a storm, not a buggerin' stroll through a garden!"

"The risk is ours to assume, Captain," Giele said.

"Fine, do what you want. But don't ask me to jump in the bloody drink when you get washed overboard." Fisk stalked up toward the poop deck where he could best keep watch over his ship as it braved the storm.

Rain drove in their faces as they lashed themselves to the mainmast. Tarvy and Giele bound themselves to Piprel by a short length of rope, allowing enough slack that Piprel could traverse the length and breadth of the main deck as needed with the other two Elves staying beside him. Giele reasoned that if the main mast went, the ship was already lost and it wouldn't matter much what they were tied to at that point. "What do you need us to do?" he shouted over the gale.

"Help me to stand," said Piprel. "If I lose my footing, I may lose the boat."

Giele didn't understand the explanation, but he could keep Piprel on his feet. With Tarvy supporting him on one side and Giele on the other, Piprel began to chant an incantation. Bluish green energy flowed down his body from his upraised hands and out his feet where it spread across the deck in concentric circles.

Giele had not spent a lot of time around mages. Some Army units had magic specialists, but the 136th never did. Most mages abhorred combat and preferred to remain safe, ensconced in their studies surrounded by texts and people more cultured than soldiers were. Being around one made Giele feel uncomfortable, for he had no comprehension of magic, and as a soldier, anything he didn't understand was a potential threat.

The *Allusi* lurched and shuddered as Piprel's magic tried to wrest it from the storm's grip. Piprel stood amidships, his thin arms over his head as if daring the storm to do its worst. He chanted nonstop and the energy ebbed and flowed from him, making his hair stand on end even as it was whipped by the gale. He seemed stronger now that the power had taken hold, and Tarvy and Giele could brace him instead of outright supporting him. The deck shuddered in a peculiar way that made the hair on Giele's neck stand up. The bobbing of the small ship ceased as an strange and different motion took hold of it. A giant, invisible hand plucked it right out of the water and the *Allusi* rose up into the air above the tallest waves. Giele saw foam splashing the hull on all sides, shaped like fingers. Two massive columns of water like arms rose from the waves and held the *Allusi* aloft. The ferocious wind whipped Giele's hat off into the darkness. The ship spun around in a slow, graceful circle as Piprel sought his direction.

"North, blast you!" bawled Captain Fisk from the poop deck, barely audible over the whistling of the rigging. He pointed to starboard. "That way!"

Piprel's eyes were glassy and his face already showed strain. Giele didn't know how long the half-drunken mage could keep up his chanting. Tarvy's eyes were closed and his lips moved in silence, perhaps in prayer. Between them, they kept Piprel upright with his feet planted on the deck. Then the *Allusi* stopped spinning and on its great columns of seawater, began to plow forward against the driving rain as if it were a balloon held by a child. Giele squinted into the storm for any sign of relief, but only saw blue lighting painting angry arcs against the swirling gray clouds.

A pulley broke loose from its mooring on the yardarm and swung down toward the three Elves in a lethal *whoosh*. "Watch out!" Giele pushed Piprel aside. As Piprel stumbled out of the way, the heavy pulley caught a glancing blow on Giele's arm and spun him around. The water columns supporting the *Allusi* swayed and the ship took on a dangerous list to starboard. Piprel and Tarvy staggered and just as fast the ship tilted portside, flinging them all to the deck. The energy which Piprel had been emitting dissipated and his eyes grew wide as he lost his chant. Giele realized what that meant and wrapped his arms around the deck railing.

With a shuddering roar, the magical columns of water crashed back down into the swirling sea and the *Allusi* dropped beneath them. Giele crashed against her deck as she impacted the sea, snapping both paddlewheels off as if they weighed nothing at all. She came close to capsizing, but then popped back out of the water once more. Crewmen went flying as waves crashed over the deck. The small ship listed to port, dashing Giele hard against the deck railing. Timbers snapped and one whirling board came close to taking his head off. Part of the mizzenmast came loose and swung down right into the pilot's wheel. The rope holding him in place broke and Fiskelius flew off the poop deck, bellowing in fear and fury, to bounce onto the heaving deck.

Giele didn't hesitate as he drew his heavy knife and slashed it through the rope binding him to Piprel. Giele dove after Fisk, hoping to reach him before either the captain slid off the deck or the rope connecting Giele to the mainmast fetched up and drew taut. Giele caught Fisk's stubby fingers just as he ran out of line, but then a gargantuan wave slopped over the deck and Fisk slid from Giele's grasp. Another crewman leaped to his captain's rescue but lost his own footing. Both were going to go over and in these rough seas, they'd be lost forever.

Giele cut the remaining rope from his waist and jumped, knife held high over his head. As he hit the deck, he pounded the knife tip down as hard as he could into the decking. The blade dug deep into a floorboard and held fast as he lashed out with his free hand and grabbed the sailor's wrist before he went overboard. Giele winced as both his arms threatened to rip themselves from his shoulders.

Fisk dangled from the sailor's grasp, and they dangled like a living daisy chain over the side of the *Allusi*, desperate to seek a handhold. The grim sailor hung on to Giele's wrist with one hand and his Captain with the other, and the only thing supporting all three of them was Giele's hold on a knife of Dwarven mosaic steel embedded in the ship's deck. Then Tarvy crashed down next to him, pulling on the sailor with his powerful muscles. More crew joined him and helped pull all three of them back to safety. They sprawled on the deck, exhausted and soaked to the bone.

Piprel, white-faced and shaking, staggered to his feet. He looked like he might collapse, but he spread his legs in a wide stance and the energy flowed from him once more. He raised the damaged *Allusi* above the waves and steered for a brief sliver of blue sky, direction be damned. He didn't falter again, and within minutes they floated in calming seas in the storm's wake.

"Well done, my friend, well done." Tarvy clapped a hand on Piprel's shoulder.

Piprel fainted dead away.

CHAPTER EIGHT

Several hours after the storm, Giele met with Captain Fiskelius in his cabin. The old dwarf sat on his bunk, nursing a large lump on his head with a hunk of questionable meat wrapped in a filthy handkerchief. "You sure you don't want to sign on with me? Ole Fisk could use a quick-witted bugger like you on me crew. Not like them other blocks of wood," grunted Fisk.

Giele laughed. "I'm afraid if I don't see another ship again, it may be too soon, Captain."

"Then you can bloody well bugger off my boat once we hit port." He looked at the Elf and twitched his mustaches for ferocious emphasis. Then his mood lightened and he opened his strongbox. "Savin' Ole Fisk from the bottom of the ocean is worth free passage." He pulled a sheaf of bills out and thrust it at Giele.

"Nonsense. I'm no freeloader."

"Now don't go and get all honorable on me, lubber. Captain's prerogative."

"Fisk, I insist on paying my way."

"Huh." Fisk eyed him from under the gory parcel he held to soothe his head. "Too much time around the Padre, I'd wager. Or else that scar's addled the cold oatmeal you call a brain. Tell you what . . . Since you're so bloody insistent on spending your money, I suppose I'll have to take it." He thumbed through the stack and removed a third. "But I won't accept one wheel more than what's fair passage."

Giele made no move to reach for the remainder. "Captain, I won't take it back."

"It's a day's and night's sailing to Golden Sands from here. Ole Fisk thinks it's rather a longer swim, and you're about to find out." Nevertheless, his eyes sparkled under his thick brows.

Giele took his money back and with a salute, left Fisk's cabin. Once out of the Captain's earshot, he slipped the remainder back to Mate Beltius and asked him to use it toward fixing the *Allusi*. Despite his new-found dislike of ocean traveling, he knew he'd always keep a fondness in his heart for the sturdy little vessel and would feel better knowing she was back out cruising the waves as quickly as possible. With that debt settled, he went to check on the Padre and the mage.

Piprel still slept from the exhaustion of his spellcasting. His breathing was peaceful and for once didn't smell of wine or grog. Tarvy sat in Piprel's cabin and read, ready to assist the mage if he required it upon waking. Satisfied that things were set as right as they could be in his unofficial command, Giele retired to his cabin at last.

The next morning, the *Allusi* limped into Golden Sands' harbor and Giele had his first look at Verigan civilization. They'd been able to see the continent since the dawn, a long smudge along the horizon that resolved into rocky cliffs and gentle rising hills. Golden Sands was at the mouth of a river that emptied into a deep inlet surrounded by cliffs of red sandstone. The alluvial plain was a shocking shade of yellow sand, which gave sharp contrast to the red of the cliffs and the sparkling blue of the water and gave the port its name.

Giele was shocked to see so much land without trees. Back in Aelfland, ancient forests covered most of the country, and clearings were the exception. He looked at the land surrounding the bay where Golden Sands lay, and spotted a few strange, stunted trees—

nothing which could even be construed as a copse or grove, much less a forest.

"A treeless land," he murmured.

"It's not quite as severe as that," said Tarvy. "There are trees along the river, and occasionally one will rise up from the prairie."

"Prairie?"

"Like a grassy clearing, except it goes on for miles and miles."

Giele felt his guts twist as he realized just how strange Verigo would be compared to the familiarity of Aelfland.

He returned his attention to Golden Sands as the *Allusi* coasted in toward the stonework harbor. He noticed upon further inspection that very little wood was evident in construction throughout the city. Most buildings were clay-covered brick and stone, and matched the color of the surrounding cliffs. Instead of the lofty, high-peaked roofs of Morningstar and other Aelfland cities—a necessity in the winter and spring when heavy, wet snows would collapse flat-roofed buildings—Golden Sands' structures were blocky with rounded corners. Many had rooftop gazebos and canopies that flapped in the breeze from out of the canyon carved by the mighty river.

Elves and Dwarves swarmed around the harbor town on various errands. Despite the sweltering hot climate, most of them covered their arms and legs with light-colored long shirts and trousers, and either wore peaked, wide-brimmed hats or had masses of cloth wrapped around their heads—even the women, which surprised Giele. He saw very few hoop skirts and parasols, such as Terika and the other courtiers fancied.

Strange, wonderful smells assailed him as the *Allusi* reached an open spot along the harbor, guided into place by gentle swells under Piprel's control. Smoke with an appetizing odor of grilled meat and flatbread emerged from mud-and-stone chimneys of several waterfront buildings which must have been restaurants. The odor of citrus wafted on the breeze. Sharp smelling oil coated the machinery of elevators as they lifted people and cargo up the sides of the cliffs to whatever facilities sat out of view above.

"Are they safe?" Giele indicated the lifts to Tarvy as they stood on the deck.

"To my knowledge, yes," he said. "Tell me, Giele, what plans have you now that we've arrived in Verigo?"

"I have no idea."

"Would you care to come with me to the frontier? I'm taking on a mission in a town at the northern edge of the civilized lands."

"Is it a large town like this?"

"Hardly. Golden Sands has a large church presence. It is, after all, the first place anyone from Aelfland generally stops. You might as well consider my destination to be the last place anyone would stop. The end of the railroad line. It will just be me and a small chapel. The town is called Goose Creek Crossing."

"Is there work out that way?"

"There are railroad jobs there, surely. You'll find ranchers and farmers who would likely overlook a blemish in favor of a strong back or skilled rider." Tarvy squeezed Giele's arm. "And it's nice to have friends when one is in a strange place."

Tarvy had an extra hat in his belongings and he gave it to Giele to replace the one lost to the storm. The high-crowned hat of woven straw provided immediate relief to cool his head and protect his eyes from the glaring sun. Worn low, it also shielded his face from the gaze of passers-by. Giele slung his bag over his shoulder, as did Tarvy with his. They agreed to steer Piprel clear of taverns until they got him to the company where a job awaited him.

The mage's face looked drawn tight, but he was cheerful about being off the boat at last. Giele looked back at the *Allusi* one last time as they stepped onto the brick and mortar dock. Captain Fisk saluted the three Elves as they left, and Giele returned the farewell. Fisk nodded once in acknowledgment before turning to his crew and bellowing orders to unload the buggerin' cargo before it spoiled.

The Elves set off through the crowded streets of the port, heading toward the elevators.

Golden Sands was divided into two distinct portions: the port and the town. The port sat on the alluvial plain, with warehouses, shops, shipping offices, and businesses that catered to sailors, passengers, and longshoremen. Up the elevators, atop the cliff was where the townspeople lived and worked. It was, as Tarvy said, where the more civilized folks stayed. Giele kept his hat pulled low and his head down, unsure how the locals would react to his mark. People who saw it muttered and women pulled their children closer out of fear that perhaps he might reach out, snag and eat one. Tarvy pointed out a newspaper someone was reading with an artist's impression of Giele. Giele sighed and bowed his head a little lower, knowing then the news of his expulsion had reached Verigo ahead of them by trans-Aeresic tele-spell. Those mages who specialized in spells of communication were in high demand for long distance information dissemination. Giele wondered if Piprel knew spells like that. It disappointed him to learn that the King could still harm him even from half a world away.

"Cheer up, my friend," said Tarvy. "Once we move away from the coast, I'm sure things will not seem so bad."

More than once Tarvy and Giele had to steer Piprel away from an open and inviting tavern door despite his protests that he was *thirsty*. Sometimes he didn't even realize he was heading for one until they drew him away.

"Why do you do that to yourself?" asked Tarvy.

"When I drink, I don't have to think." Piprel puffed up his chest with pride.

"When you drink, you stink," Giele said.

"What is it you fear? What do you retreat from?" Tarvy asked, but Piprel wouldn't answer. Tarvy sighed in exasperation. Sodden mages, it appeared, tested even the patience of a Padre.

They arrived at an elevator platform, built from sturdy imported timber sheathed with riveted iron bands. If a storm washed the entire port away, it would still leave the elevators intact. A dozen or so patient people waited in line for the blue-painted iron cage to return to port level. Nobody seemed impatient or out of sorts; apparently it was normal to stand in silence and read a book or speak with one's neighbor while the carriage-sized steam boiler beside the elevator framework hissed and the pipes rattled and groaned. The attendant rushed about and squirted fresh oil onto the cable and gears. As the elevator touched down to the platform, the sweating attendant tapped a gauge on the boiler, frowned, and then cranked a handle that rang a brass bell. Passengers emerged from the car and headed down a ramp. People in line grumbled a bit at the additional delay as the attendant rang the bell once again.

A woman in heavy coveralls arrived at the platform. Her hair was either cut short or tucked up inside the shapeless floppy hat she wore. She pulled thick gloves onto her hands, which she then placed on the boiler. She chanted an incantation and her hands glowed white hot. The gauge on the boiler leaped up out of the red zone. When she pulled her hands back from the tank, they left behind two spots that glowed ruddy like metal in a forge.

As the mage hurried away, heading for the platform offices, Piprel said to Giele, "That's what I'm going to do. Boiler mage. Good money on the rails."

Giele shrugged. "I guess that's good enough, but I've seen what you can do with your power. Why waste it just to heat water? Any low-grade mage can do as much."

"It's all I want to do, all right?" Piprel's voice echoed enough to cause people to turn and stare.

"Hush," said Tarvy. "Be at peace, my friend."

Piprel glared and shrank back into himself once more.

Giele wondered what demons ate away at the mage. "Why don't you come with us, Piprel?"

"Where?"

They packed onto the elevator car with several other people. One man saw Giele's face and pushed his way back off the car. "I ain't ridin' with no marked man," he announced.

Piprel squinted at him, pursed his lips, and blew out a gentle breath. A gust of wind rose out of nowhere and sent the man's hat flying all the way across the port to disappear in the harbor. The man shouted, jumping for his lost hat in vain. Giele met Tarvy's gaze. Something significant had just transpired with Piprel leaping to his defense, even in such an unobtrusive way. Neither of them called attention to it for fear of embarrassing Piprel.

The cable groaned and with a jerk, the car lifted clear of the platform and rattled up the side of the cliff with a lurching unsteady motion that reminded Giele of his recent seafaring voyage. The elevator squeaked and made rhythmic clacks as it rose through the framework.

"Tell me about this town you're taking me to, Tarvy." said Giele.

"Goose Creek Crossing. I don't know much about it except that it's currently where the railroad ends."

Piprel pricked up his pointed ears. "Taverns there?"

Tarvy turned to him with a sad smile. "I presume so, my friend."

"Well, maybe I'll come work out there then."

"I would enjoy your company on the journey." The young Padre rubbed his jaw in deep thought. "Perhaps we might discuss more useful applications of your magic than boilers and freeing hats from the oppression of swollen heads.

It took a moment for Tarvy's joke to penetrate the fog in Piprel's brain, after which the mage giggled like a

Leaf Archer visiting a bordello for the first time and gave Giele a look of embarrassment. Giele clapped his hand on Piprel's shoulder in silent thanks for his chivalrous act. For a moment, Giele saw a spark of pride which had been buried deep within the drunkard. Given time, perhaps he could nurture it.

The elevator lurched to the side, and Giele grabbed the nearest rail to keep from bumping Tarvy, Piprel, or any of the other passengers, even though they were packed tight. Giele yearned for a measure of freedom and distance from other people. The way people had piled into this elevator, almost on top of one another, reminded him of the way men huddled in the trenches and behind fortifications, sometimes for days at a time during a siege.

Giele no longer wished to huddle.

He looked out at the red cliffs that went on as far as he could see in either direction. "I suppose I'll see what's available and who'll hire a marked man like me."

It took another few minutes for the slow-moving elevator to reach the platform at the cliff top. It ground to a halt and Giele looked down, dizzy when he saw how far they'd come. The Aeresic stretched out to the southern horizon. One of those tiny specks of sail out there might be the *Allusi*, already making for Aelfland with Ole Fisk eager to steal yet another profit from the big companies. The breeze blew from the north, carrying the sweet scents of grain fields and citrus orchards, and it was dry, unlike the moist wind down at harbor level. The attendant rolled two heavy beams into collars on either side of the elevator to lock it in place. At last he slid open the grate and the passengers spilled out onto the wooden platform, which was covered by a thatched straw canopy.

Giele was glad to be on solid ground again. The other passengers hurried away from him, several muttering about his cursed face. He sighed. He would have to get a lot further away from Aelfland than this before he might find people who'd accept him despite his mark.

The platform was adjacent to a rail depot. Several empty cars sat on a siding, but he saw no engine. Tarvy led Piprel and Giele across the platform to the station house, where he inquired about the arrival of the next engine bound for Goose Creek Crossing and was told it should arrive within six hours, but if they missed it they'd have to wait a full week for the next train.

"Our luck holds." Tarvy looked relieved. "We have pleased God."

"Six hours." Piprel smacked his lips. "Plenty of time for a taste of local wine."

"Go ahead," Giele said. "I'm going to have a look around."

"Be cautious," said Tarvy. "People here are well-informed and know about you, Giele."

Giele pulled his hat down low and slouched to keep the scar hidden. "How's that?"

"As good as can be, I suppose. Do you wish me to accompany you?"

"No, you'd better stay with Piprel. Try to keep him out of trouble."

Piprel snorted. "I'm not a troublemaker. I'm a very peaceful, quiet drunk."

They headed for the small pub attached to the station house. Giele watched them leave and smiled. He'd grown fond of these two Elves even though they had nothing in common. Religion and magic were so esoteric to him, well beyond the boundaries of his weapons of wood and steel.

He walked around the station house and looked out at the rest of Golden Sands.

Few people appeared to live on this side of the canyon, for a sturdy bridge of oiled wood and iron rivets stretched across the gap to where he saw numerous residences and shops. He was tempted to wander across and look, but he had no doubts that he'd run across more people who'd recognize his scar, and that could lead to trouble. He'd stay on the side of industry and farming. Near the train station, he found long blockhouses covered with clay surfacing. They looked almost identical to the barracks in which he'd lived while in the Army. He surmised these to be where the railroad workers lived. A small factory belched steam and smoke into the sky. The name over the door—*Judsi's*—gave him no indication of what was made there. He saw a silk farm beyond the factory. He fancied he could almost hear the contended worms chewing upon the imported trees as workers wandered the aisles, harvesting the silk. Past the silk farm lay the citrus orchards, the railroad tracks disappearing between ordered rows of orange and lemon trees. The sharp scent of the fruit made his eyes water, and the reality of his arrival hit him. He was free for the first time in his life to do whatever he chose, to go wherever he pleased, beholden to no man, King, or nation.

Such freedom frightened him, but gave him a glimmer of hope when all around him had been darkness for far too long.

CHAPTER NINE

Verigo was a beautiful country.

Seeing it from the comfort of a steam-driven, mage-powered railway car gave Giele an appreciation he'd never had when on the march back in Aelfland. The King disapproved of rail travel because of how many trees would have to be cut down in his forests, so railroads on the main continent stopped at the Dewar border. Elves had to ride or walk everywhere they went within their own lands. Traveling by rail felt fast and luxurious to Giele. Once they passed out of the orchards, the rails ran straight north. The plateau sloped downward at a gentle rate until the train caught up to the river and followed alongside it. Tarvy called it the Pendant River, so named because it ended at the brilliant medallion of Golden Sands. It was some twenty yards wide and so clear that Giele saw the shadows of large fish as they darted to and fro along the bottom. Lush green grass grew tall and waved in the breeze, with an occasional bright flower cresting above the fuzzy grass tips, surrounded by honeybees and hummingbirds.

"Beautiful countryside, even without trees," said Giele. "Don't more people live here?"

"There are homesteaders out in the fields," said Tarvy, "but this isn't Aelfland. People here tend to spread out quite a bit. It can be a day's ride or more between neighbors."

Unlike the majestic, ancient forests of Aelfland, trees in Verigo were scarce—solitary titans sturdy enough to brave the strong winds and dig deep roots in the dry soil. Most of the trees Giele saw clustered right alongside of the river. He understood why Verigans built from stone, brick, clay and other materials accessible along the riverbanks. He saw one stand of trees which hugged the river, slender trunks and branches covered with white bark and round leaves of such light green they were almost yellow. He wondered what kind of bow they would make. None of the plants seemed familiar to him. Even the few odd pine trees he saw were stunted with widely-spaced branches and sparse needles, unlike the towering majestic pines of Aelfland.

After two hours, the train reached a small hamlet and stopped to take on water and recharge the boiler. The three Elves stepped out of the coach to stretch their legs and enjoy the fresh air with the strange, smoky tang that came from bushes with olive green bark and tiny leaves.

"Giele, do you have any crowns?" Piprel's hands flapped around him like birds, as if he had no idea where to put them.

"Yes, why?"

"I was going to go into the store, maybe to get something to eat or to drink, but my purse is gone. I think somebody filched it in Golden Sands. I didn't have much in it, but it was mine, and now I've got nothing at all!"

Giele realized the mage was on the verge of hysterical tears. He put a hand on Piprel's shoulder. "Would a bit of wine help that?" Giele knew he shouldn't help the mage continue his drinking, but he pitied the poor fellow.

Piprel sniffled. "You're a saint, Giele. A prince."

Giele bought a small bottle of wine for the mage in the tiny general store attached to the depot. The proprietor gave a nervous glance at his scar but took his money and didn't overcharge him. He was surprised and pleased that the man didn't have a stronger negative reaction. Piprel grabbed the bottle from Giele's hand and upended it into his mouth as if it were medicine for a dying man. Dribbles of the dark liquid ran down his chin.

Giele believed the Padre was correct in his assessment of the drink-addled mage. Something terrible had happened to him—something so devastating he needed to dull all his senses with alcohol. Giele's scar was skin-deep; Piprel's wound marred his soul.

The train continued deeper into the north. Giele saw sporadic farms with Elves and Dwarves tending their crops in the heat of the afternoon. The work of growing things looked the same here as it did in Aelfland, and the familiarity helped him feel more comfortable. As the miles passed, cultivated fields gave way to more prairie grasses, and they took on an olive hue as the air grew even drier. Some plants had no leaves at all, but instead were thick, puffy stalks with spines. Giele asked Tarvy about them. He said Horks called them *cacti* and that they stored water within their soft flesh. "Be careful if you touch one," said the Padre. "The spines are incredibly sharp, and barbed as well. They're like porcupines back in Aelfland. You'll be hours digging them out if you get a handful of them."

The train stopped twice more in small towns; the last of these—called Last Chance—represented the edge of the civilized lands. Goose Creek Crossing lay another seventy-five miles to the north, an isolated outpost past the wild country. In Aelfland, when people talked about the wilderness, they meant forests and foothills more than a day's ride away from the nearest town. Often as not, when one was several hours out of one town, another lay but a few hours away. In Verigo, the wilderness was untamed, with no hints of civilization at all. Giele looked out across the living desert, with its scrub plants, broadleaf grasses, tall cacti and red rocks jutting up into the sky, and see no sign of development all the way to the horizon save for the railroad tracks carving a neat line across the terrain.

"Why is Goose Creek so far away from everything else?" he asked Tarvy.

"Gold. Prospectors found quite a bit of it in Goose Creek, and where gold is, towns grow in Verigo."

"Do I understand you were in Goose Creek last time you were here?"

Tarvy laughed. "Oh, no. I was an acolyte in the Golden Sands chapel. Goose Creek was only a campsite when I returned to Aelfland to complete my schooling."

"I see." Giele turned to look out the window at the landscape as it passed by. As the train ate up the miles, the arid, dusty plain gave way to more flowing waves of tall grasses. He saw more stands of trees—none of familiar breed, but the very sight of them made him feel almost happy.

Movement caught his eye. A herd of Greatdeer wandered through the fields. He'd seen photographs of the creatures, but the grainy sepia-toned images did no justice to the magnificent beasts. The adults were as tall as a full-grown Elf at the shoulder. Their racks of antlers featured twelve, fourteen, and on one massive buck who must have been the alpha male, eighteen points atop a mountain of thick muscle.

Giele whistled in appreciation. Tarvy and Piprel crowded in next to him to see what had earned his attention. Piprel's stomach rumbled loud enough for Giele to hear over the clatter of the coach's wheels. "They good eating?"

Tarvy nodded. "They are quite delicious. Some people here ranch them, although the Horks disapprove. They prefer to use the animals as mounts and pack beasts. I've heard that when they do kill a Greatdeer, they use every bit of it. Meat, hide, bone, sinew. They've found a use for it all."

"Sounds efficient," said Giele. The notion of fully-utilizing a resource appealed to the military mind within him.

"Sounds wasteful. I could eat that big fellow there and pick my teeth clean with those horns." Piprel gave a deep, wistful sigh. Giele passed him a tin of crackers and a small round cheese covered with a thick layer of wax.

"Tell me more about the Horks," said Giele. "What kind of people are they?"

Tarvy pushed his glasses up his nose. He took a cracker before Piprel demolished the entire bunch and ate it with slow deliberation. "Horks are a curious lot. Very different from us. They're short and stout like Dwarves, but that's where the similarities end. Instead of whiskers on their cheeks and chins, they have smooth skin with a mane of fine, dark hair like a horse's tail. They even look kind of like horses with their protruding noses and jaws."

"They sound ugly." Piprel wiped cracker crumbs from his lips.

"They're not pretty. They're nomadic hunters and gatherers that follow the Greatdeer herds across the plains. Savages, for the most part."

"How so?" Giele asked.

"They don't believe in God. They don't smelt metal or use magic. They don't even bathe or bury their dead."

"Their camps must stink," said Piprel.

"Jigans don't bury their dead either," said Giele. "They burn them. Maybe the Horks do that."

"I think they just drag them away and leave them to be eaten by scavengers. It's certainly not a very civilized way to honor the dead. I don't know much more than that," said Tarvy, "but the few Horks I encountered when I was in Golden Sands before could have knocked a buzzard off an outhouse with their reek."

Piprel burst out laughing.

"They almost never came to Golden Sands when I lived there. Too far south for their liking, and probably too civilized. We may meet more of them in Goose Creek Crossing. That's in their territory. Maybe I'll get the chance to talk to a shaman about their complicated polytheistic beliefs." He smiled at the expression on Piprel's face as the mage tried to decipher the phrase. "Perhaps I could even convert a few of them to a real set of beliefs."

Giele searched for signs of zealotry in Tarvy's eyes, but all he saw was honest excitement about his missionary work. "Who's to say their beliefs are any less legitimate than yours?"

"Interesting point." Tarvy sat back on the seat and rested his chin on one hand in deep thought.

Giele turned back to look at the Greatdeer herd again. He spotted one animal off to the side all by itself. At first he thought perhaps it had strayed, or might have expelled by the herd leader. Then he noticed the faint blue and red colored spiral lines under the creature's eyes. He realized what he thought had been a stump or rock beside it was a being with a mane of shining black hair. He pointed and exclaimed, "There, is that a Hork?"

The train moved on as Tarvy squinted in the direction Giele indicated. "I don't know. I never saw it clearly. You have good eyesight, Giele."

Two hours later, the train rolled to a stop on a siding at Goose Creek Crossing. Giele grabbed his bag, impatient to be off the train, but the passengers weren't allowed to disembark until the engineer and brakeman disconnected the engine from the coaches. The creek, which gave the town its name, was a mere trickle through a mostly-dry stream bed. Giele wondered if that was due to a lack of rain or a dam somewhere upstream. The town was a collection of buildings arranged in traditional Elven fashion—radial streets leading to a large open clearing in the center. In Aelfland towns, the clearing was often a sculpted park or beautiful garden, but in Goose Creek it was just a grassy field with young saplings around its edges and a well in the center. The daubed mud, which covered the brickwork of the buildings, had dried to a brilliant off-white that gleamed in the sun as it dropped low over the plains.

The train must have arrived around the time of the evening meal, for the streets were just about empty. A handful of citizens ambled along the packed-earth streets. They regarded the train passengers with detached interest. A station attendant pumped water from an underground source into a bucket and splashed it into an outhouse, following the flushing with a generous handful of lime. The breeze kicked up small dust devils, whipping them between buildings until they dissipated. The air smelled different than it had in Golden Sands—more primal, and it made Giele want to run straight off into the sunset and leave all civilization behind him to become one with the world.

He reined in his fanciful thoughts as he followed Tarvy from the station into town. This far out on the frontier, attire had grown even more casual and utilitarian. Men wore heavy cotton trousers, dyed in shades of blue or brown. These contrasted with the printed lightweight silken shirts. Women wore simple cotton dresses or trousers and silk shirts like the men. Most people had hats or bonnets. Giele heard the shouts of laughter and snippets of song from a bright tavern. Piprel lurched toward it, as if yanked by an invisible rope. Tarvy and Giele each grabbed his arms and steered him away.

"Come on, cut a fellow a break," said Piprel. "It was a long train ride. I'm dry as a bone."

"You should stay that way," said Giele. "I'll have a hard enough time finding an innkeeper to rent one to me with this face. If I have a drunk wizard in tow, I may as well sleep in a stable, so long as the horses will have me as a guest."

"Nonsense," said Tarvy. "You two will stay in the Mission tonight. Tomorrow you can seek more permanent residency and employment."

The church wasn't far from the railroad tracks. It looked the same as most of the other buildings in Goose Creek, although a tower on its roof housed a bronze bell. A small parsonage sat behind the house of worship, and it was here that Tarvy led the others. As they reached the front door, he withdrew an envelope from his robes and slit it open. A small silver key fell from it into his hand. He fitted it into the door lock and they entered the Padre's new home.

Small, cozy, with a dirt floor and a single window that let in the last of the waning light, the one-room parsonage was still less cramped than some barracks Giele had lived in. "Ah," said Tarvy after an uncomfortable pause. "I'd hoped it might be a bit more spacious. We'll be packed in here. I shall sleep in the church tonight."

"Nonsense," said Giele. "Take your cot, Padre. I for one will gladly sleep upon the dirt. I have many nights before. It's as comfortable as anything when nobody is firing arrows at you."

Piprel explored the tiny cupboard and the containers on the shelf above the iron stove but found nothing except a few dead weevils, which he swept out into his hand to show to Giele.

"What's troubling you about some dead insects?" asked Giele.

"Poor fellows probably starved to death," said Piprel. "They needn't have died here. There's plenty for bugs to eat outdoors."

"Then they shouldn't have been in here in the first place," said Giele.

Piprel looked up at Giele with a spark of something in his eyes. Fury, perhaps? It flashed but for an instant before his expression returned to dismay once more.

"Sometimes things happen beyond your control." His voice was soft and haunted.

Tarvy gave a sharp glance to Giele and shook his head. Now was not the time to pry into Piprel's past.

"Alas, I fear the parsonage has been empty for some time," said Tarvy. "If you will rest here, I will fetch some provisions from the store and perhaps the tavern."

"Hurry, Padre." Piprel sat down on the cot with his head in his hands and moaned. "I don't feel well."

"Approaching sobriety," said Giele. "How long has Goose Creek been without a Padre?"

"Some months," said Tarvy. "Ever since the previous Padre was lost."

"Lost?"

"Yes, lost. He disappeared out into the wilds to the north and never returned. Many people said he must have been killed by Horks." Tarvy made a dismissive gesture.

"But you don't believe that?"

"Horks may be unschooled savages, but they're not murderers. He most likely ran afoul of a great cat or wolf pack. They hunt on the plains."

"Sounds wonderful." Piprel perked up a bit. "Can you eat a wolf? Or a great cat? I'm game to try."

Tarvy laughed. "Very well, my friend. I shall return with haste." He gathered up an empty basket and departed into the looming dusk.

Piprel paced back and forth, stopping every few minutes to look out the window. At first Giele found the rhythm of his feet padding on the parsonage floor soothing, but after a quarter of an hour it had grown tiresome.

"Piprel, sit down. You're so unsettled you're making me feel the same way."

The mage flopped down onto the cot, pushing his limp hair back from his face. Underneath his tan, he looked pale and drawn, exhausted from more than just their travels. "I'm sorry, Giele. I'm not used to feeling so lucid."

"Why? What's so terrible that you have to run from it?" Giele raised his head enough so Piprel could see the scar on his cheek in the waning light. "What's worse than this?"

For a minute, Giele thought the mage might be ready to open up, to share what had been haunting him from the minute they'd first met. Instead, he sprawled on the cot, turned away from Giele, and began to snore right away.

"Whenever you're ready, my friend, I'll listen," whispered Giele.

Left alone with his thoughts, Giele shut his eyes to consider his next move, but didn't get far before thoughts of his future swirled into darkness and he drifted off into a fitful sleep where a dancing, laughing Terika tormented him while the impassive King's court watched and the King himself stoked a brazier with a pike over and over again, saying it wasn't quite hot enough yet, but soon . . . soon . . .

CHAPTER TEN

Giele awakened to the smell of eggs frying and coffee simmering. Tarvy whistled a merry tune as he cooked. Giele yawned, stretched, and worked out the stiffness of sleep. Sunlight streamed in through the small window, giving the parsonage a comfortable, homey atmosphere. It made him feel at peace for the first time in weeks. Tarvy noticed Giele's movement and smiled. "Good morning, my friend. You were sound asleep and I didn't want to awaken you last night. I have fresh bread, eggs, and coffee. Did you sleep well?"

Giele nodded and rubbed the last bits of the Sandman's dust from his eyes. Piprel still slept, curled up into a ball at the foot of Tarvy's cot. He twitched and moaned a bit, haunted by whatever demons pursued him beyond the bottle.

"Alas, I hope he finds peace out here at the edge of the world." Tarvy scooped a mass of scrambled eggs onto a tin plate, stuck a lump of brown bread beside them, and proffered it to Giele, who accepted it with grace. A moment later, he pressed a clay mug of coffee into Giele's hands.

"You are an amazingly cheerful person, Padre," said Giele. "Does anything ever bother you?"

Tarvy set aside a plate for the mage, and then served himself up the remainder. "Of course things bother me. Men do evil things to one another, and every day I pray they see the folly of their ways and change for the better." Tarvy sipped at his coffee, his eyes alight behind his glasses. "God teaches that despair pollutes the soul. Spreading joy and good cheer is an important part of my work, which I gladly accept. I've found that happiness spreads like a benevolent fever. If I can make someone else feel even the slightest bit happier because of my own optimism, then the world will be a better place."

A cloud passed before the sun and dimmed the light through the window for a moment. The momentary shadow matched the one in Giele's heart. He'd seen too much evil to believe such noble simplicity. If he closed his eyes, he saw King Teirol's terrible grimace of joy as he lowered the brand. "Some wounds cannot be healed by laughter."

"Perhaps not. But nobody ever complained about a good laugh or an honest smile from a stranger."

That gave Giele pause, and he finished his breakfast in silence.

Tarvy left Giele to his thoughts and cleaned up their plates. As he wiped the dishes dry with a clean cloth, he said over his shoulder, "While I was at the market, I met a Dwarfmistress whose monsignor is an important person at the railroad. She gave me his name. You may wish to speak to him for possible employment. She also mentioned he needs more mages on staff. So if nothing else, you might take Piprel with you, whenever the poor sod finally awakens, that is."

"I'm awake. God's Blood, how can a body sleep with you two gabbing like a couple of fishwives? Ugh. I feel ill." Piprel clenched his hands over his stomach.

"Not used to awakening sober?" asked Giele.

"Good morning, merry sunshine," said Tarvy. "Would you care for some breakfast before you leave?"

Piprel's eyes grew wide and his complexion turned green. He rushed out of the small parsonage and was ill in the weeds.

"Sometimes, I'll admit, it's a bit more difficult to remain positive," said Tarvy.

Giele laughed. "Pray for rain."

Later, with the Padre's laughter still echoing in their ears, Piprel and Giele strolled through Goose Creek Crossing, heading for the railroad offices beyond the turntable. The small town bustled with people attending to their morning errands.

A barber snapped his laundered towels and hung them across the rail outside his shop to dry. With a straw broom, a Dwarf mistress swept the boardwalk outside a shoe store. Giele smelled the sweet syrups and sharp tang of chemicals from a drugstore. Children chased each other through the streets on their way to the school building near the center of town. Women gossiped. Men argued and laughed. A few people glanced toward Piprel and Giele, but a couple of elderly women glared at the angry red scar upon Giele's cheek and whispered to each other like conspirators. Despite their distaste, Giele found himself growing more confident as more and more people ignored his mark to go about their own business. It seemed that here on the Frontier, he'd found a place where people might at least tolerate him.

Crockery and glassware clinked inside a saloon with swinging doors. Piprel made a beeline for the entrance.

Giele grabbed one of Piprel's arms and twisted it behind him until he gasped in pain. "It's not even midday yet. Breath and Bones, Piprel, if you're so rutting hot to kill yourself, I'll hand you my pistol and you can save us all the trouble of minding you."

Piprel struggled. "Let me go, you fatherless son!"

"No chance of that," Giele hissed in his ear. "Talk to me, friend. What troubles you?"

He tried to drive his elbow into Giele's side; the fire in his soul hadn't burned all the way out. "Still some fight left in you yet. Good, we'll start there if we have to." Giele muscled Piprel into the space between two buildings.

"We're not on the rutting boat anymore. You're not my keeper. I can do as I please."

Giele threw him against the wall, hard enough to rattle the mage's teeth and perhaps to jar some sense into him. "God's Blood, you want to go into the tavern? You'll have to get past me first, and I just don't think you're man enough to do it . . . *coward*."

An unseen force hurled Giele against the wall of the opposite building. Dust from between the boards drifted down around him as the energy pushed him upward until his feet left the ground. Piprel gritted his teeth as he directed the magic that pinned Giele fast, like a bug on a card in a museum display. Yellow energy crackled around his hands and encircled Giele, pricking his skin like barbed wire. His movement had been so quick, he took Giele by surprise.

Breath and Bones! He'd meant to provoke Piprel, but must have pushed him a bit too hard. This wasn't the Piprel he knew. The desperate, half-crazed mage seemed ready to rip Giele apart with his power.

Giele didn't dare show any fear. "That's all you've got? I'm just your friend, Piprel. You kill me, I'll be gone, and you'll still have whatever it is driving you mad. God's Blood, either talk to me or slay me!"

Piprel's power tightened around Giele and he gasped for breath. It felt as if a thousand nails were being jabbed into his skin all at once. "You mustn't tell. Not ever," hissed Piprel.

"I won't."

"Swear."

"God's Blood, I swear not to repeat whatever it is you're going to tell me."

As fast as Giele had been pinned to the wall, the force vanished and Piprel lowered his shaking hand. Giele fell to his knees. Piprel loomed over him the way Teirol had weeks ago. The similarity made Giele want to flee. Nevertheless, he climbed back to his feet and stood still, barely even daring to breathe.

Piprel hesitated. Giele saw the struggle in his face as Piprel overcame the last of his reticence. "I wasn't always like this. I was once important—a court mage."

"Where?"

"It doesn't matter. A province in Aelfland. I was the Baron's confidant and adviser. He trusted me with affairs requiring magical intervention. He trusted me with . . . with so much."

"Go on."

"He'd planned a b-birthday celebration for his youngest son." His eyes became shadowed as he spoke. "I loved his children. I loved his whole family. They were good people, and so kind to me and to those around them." He shut his eyes as if he couldn't bear to see whatever horror he was reliving. "I'd prepared a display of illumination spells—sparks and such to brighten the evening and entertain the boy on the eve of his birthday."

His shoulders shook. Giele didn't know how to comfort the mage. When men in Giele's command had broken down, the unit's Padre had handled them.

"I don't know what happened. I might have misspoken an incantation. I might have transposed a gesture. Or I might just have lost my concentration, but instead of the dancing sparks . . . I conjured a burst of flame."

He sank down with his back to the wall he'd flung Giele against, his head held in his hands. His voice was so choked with pain and self-loathing Giele could barely understand him.

"He was only four. Such a sweet child, always with a smile for me. He laughed and clapped his hands. He thought it was part of my display, but the flames leaped out of my control . . . they . . ."

"Piprel . . ." Giele wished Piprel wouldn't finish his tale, but knowing he needed it to salve his soul and begin healing himself.

His voice became a ghost of itself. "I b-burned him. Burned him right up."

"God's Blood." Giele's losses at the King's hands seemed minuscule. Nothing felt worse for a soldier in war than to slay an uninvolved civilian by accident. One time he'd almost put an arrow through a Jigan woman who surprised him as she walked a battlefield in search of her brother's body. She'd opened her arms as if to embrace the arrow Giele held to his cheek. He would not have forgiven himself had he let it slip from his grasp. Piprel looked like a shell of a man, pathetic and broken. Giele felt guilty about his irritation with the mage, for at last he understood the depth of Piprel's pain and why he retreated from it in a bottle.

Giele decided he'd buy Piprel his next drink.

He knelt down beside the mage and placed his hand on Piprel's arm, speaking in the same voice he used when reassuring men who'd suffered mortal wounds in combat. "Come on, friend. Pull yourself together and we'll stop in the saloon before we visit the railroad offices."

Piprel dashed his hand across his green eyes. "No, I'm all right. Give me a moment and we'll go." Nevertheless, when he stood, he seemed smaller, like he'd folded in on himself. Giele saw a great struggle taking place on his face; Piprel was desperate for a drink, and just as desperate *not* to want one.

Giele squeezed Piprel's shoulder. "All right. We'll go."

He smoothed out his robes and scrubbed his face with a rough cloth before tying it about his head to keep the sun off as it rose higher in the sky. They left the narrow alleyway and continued onward across the small town toward the railroad offices. The temperature rose as the sun crawled toward its zenith. Sweat trickled down Giele's neck and behind his ears.

Giele kept his hat pulled low out of what was becoming a habit. Beside him, Piprel's head was bowed as he trudged along. The most telling change in his demeanor was his hands no longer wandered and flapped like they had minds of their own. Instead, they hung loose at his sides, as if content to remain still.

CHAPTER ELEVEN

The Dwarf Jordinius Blackpool had a habit of shouting, even at those who were in the same room with him. He dressed in an expensive silk shirt and cotton trousers, but his boots had seen many decades of hard labor. His gray mustache and beard was neat, trimmed in a short fashion Giele hadn't seen before on a Dwarven face, and he wore wire-framed spectacles. For the last twenty years, with brute strength and sheer determination, Blackpool and his crews had hammered, dug, blasted, bridged, and laid railway track from Golden Sands to the northernmost point of the colonies at Goose Creek Crossing. Despite his advancing age, he showed no signs of slowing down, and he intended to push much further yet.

Blackpool leaned forward in his office chair and rested his muscular arms on the rough cedar desk in front of him. This was one Dwarf Giele wouldn't want to meet in a fight, even despite his height advantage. "So my mistress met the new Padre at Cianid's yesterday." His voice was loud and gruff as a bellowing bear. "He told her you're ex-military and looking for work."

"That's it, more or less," said Giele.

"What?"

Giele raised his voice to repeat himself; the Dwarf must have been hard of hearing. Out of the corner of his eye, he saw Piprel wincing with every loud word. He hadn't had a drop of alcohol since the night before, and Giele knew the mage was feeling plenty of discomfort.

"And what's the drunkard's story?"

"He's a mage, looking for work on the boilers, sir." Giele felt so out of his depth among civilians, but he wasn't about to show Blackpool any of his insecurity. From the heavy furniture in his office, the chunky iron fixtures, and thick timbers around the windows and door, the Dwarf respected strength above all else.

"Mage, eh? He looks like he couldn't magic his way out of a bottle, and like he's been trying for a good long time."

Piprel raised one of his palms and spoke a single word. A miniature sun bound by coronas and prominences hovered above his hand and added to the already oppressive heat in Blackpool's office. Giele winced as hot air flooded into his lungs.

Blackpool shielded his face from the brilliant rays. "God's Blood, put that away before you roast us all!"

Piprel closed his hand into a fist and the sun winked out in a burst of sour smoke. Flakes of ash fell like snow onto the scuffed wooden floor of the office.

Giele was impressed; that miniature sun showed astonishing power and control. He knew court mages received the best training, apprenticing to master wizards, but to call up so much power with so little effort showed Piprel was a far greater mage than he let on. The sun had been no simple illusion. Giele's face prickled from where he'd been sunburned. The smoke and ash residue from the sun swirled in the slight breeze from the window, and the tang of it lingered in the air. Giele had been thinking Piprel's rescue of the *Allusi* had been more luck than anything else. After this last display, he considered he may have given Piprel an unfair shake. Despite all his flaws, he had control and power which might even have rivaled that of the King's own Court Mage, Iago. For Piprel to reduce his abilities to heating water would be like utilizing the entire 136th to retrieve a kitten stranded in a tree.

If Blackpool was impressed, he didn't show it. "All right, I can always use another boiler mage." He scribbled on a sheet of paper with a quill, then pounded upon it with a rubber stamp. "Take this to Mewele Flattop over in the mage shop. It's at the south end of this lot. He'll assess you and find a job for you somewhere. Standard pay is ten crowns a week, plus bonuses for unusual spell requirements. Come to work drunk or drink while you're on the job and you can pound sand."

Piprel looked at Giele, nervous at the prospect of enforced sobriety.

"You'll be fine," said Giele in an undertone Blackpool wouldn't hear. "I'll have the Padre keep an eye on you if I'm not around."

Blackpool frowned at them. "What's that whispering?"

"Nothing, sir. Just reiterating your directions."

"Oh, all right." He glared at Piprel and shoved the folded paper at him. "Sooner you're out of my office, the happier we'll both be."

Piprel hurried away, ashes straying from his flapping robes as he departed.

Blackpool turned back to Giele. "Now, what to do with you?"

"I'm open to pretty much anything, sir."

"What happened to your face, anyway? It looks like a rutting brand."

Giele didn't feel like recounting his recent life's story to this loudmouthed Dwarf. "I took an arrow in the First Jigan War."

"Breath and Bones. Lucky that one didn't kill you."

The heavy scar tissue on his cheek pulled tight as he gave Blackpool a wry grin. "Yes, I'm quite fortunate."

"Looks kind of like a moon. I bet people give you the stink eye about it all the time."

Giele said nothing.

"And you're ex-military. Been in long?"

"Twenty years."

"So you'd have been, what, a Bole Major?"

"Grove Colonel."

"Ha! I knew it!" Blackpool smote his desk with a well-callused hand. "You would have fought in . . . I think three wars, right?"

"Yes."

"So you probably know your way around when you're on your own, right?"

"On my own?"

"No nearby headquarters. No nearby resources. On your own."

"Yes sir, of course."

"Have I ever got a job for you, if you think you can handle it."

"Try me, sir."

"I need someone to scout the terrain further to the north. The rutting railroad company in Golden Sands is shrieking that we haven't chosen a new expansion route yet and claim they're bleeding crowns in every dispatch they send me. Now, just between you and I, they're not hurting for finances. Rail is the best way to travel and move freight on this continent. The problem is, I can't get any decently skilled outdoorsmen to come in from Aelfland who know anything about rail construction."

"I'm not sure I understand, sir."

"Look, if Elves and Dwarves are going to spread further into the New World, it will be on the iron wheels of mage-powered steam coaches. The rail company understands this, and they'll profit from the increase in fees, fares, and freight tariffs. But people aren't going to expand much past the furthest point on any given line, and Goose Creek isn't exactly a hotbed of growth since the gold rush ended. It's been too long since we laid new tracks, and they're holding my toes to the fire."

He stood and pulled down a rolled-up wall map. It showed details of Verigo's southern coast, and the rail line that ran north from Golden Sands and ended at Goose Creek Crossing.

North of that, the map was blank.

"I need you to explore further to the north, map your travels, and seek out areas which might be good locations for future development either for mining and industry, farming and ranching, or even recreation. Help me fill in this map. Do that and I'll pay to equip you and issue a regular retainer. What do you say?"

"You have nobody to do this now?"

"Sure, I've sent five drippers out there over the past six months. Not a one of them rutters have come back. Either they were thieves or a lot less wilderness-savvy than they told me. Whatever the case, I'm stuck with no information about the region and work crews sitting on their arses. I don't want to start building in a random direction at the pace of a survey crew. Them rutting idiots don't think further than a hundred yards ahead. I need someone who can help me plan the next hundred miles. You might be just the fellow I've needed."

Giele nodded. The idea of spending weeks out in the wilderness, away from prying eyes and fearful glances, seemed mighty appealing to him. "Mr. Blackpool, it sounds exactly like what I came here seeking. I'm your man."

"God's Blood, I bet you are. Next dripper who comes in here probably won't be half as qualified." He extended a hand. Giele leaned across his large desk and clasped it. "Welcome aboard, Giele . . . say, I don't believe I ever got your family name."

Giele forced himself to use a light, jovial tone. "Just Giele is fine."

Blackpool opened a drawer of his desk and withdrew a small silk bag. "All right, then. These are B & R Railroad credit chits. Any merchant here in Goose Creek will accept them for purchases. You pick up what supplies you need and then the bills will come to me."

He smiled. "The saloons and whorehouses won't accept them, so you're on your own there."

Giele shook his head. "No worries, sir."

"Good. I approve of clean living. Now there's just one more thing, and that's the question of your payment. You return once a month and deliver me solid maps with detailed information, I'll pay you five hundred crowns, plus a twenty crown bonus for any site B & R determines we'll run a line to. So, obviously, the better your information, the better you'll get paid." He kicked his feet in their ancient leathery boots up onto his desktop and folded his hands behind his head. "Now if you're thinking about taking your supplies and running away, well, you could do worse than to steal from the largest railroad company on the continent. We can certainly afford the losses. However . . . get greedy on me, and I'll send a hired gun after you. I have a few in my employ. You'll either pay us back full in cash, with interest, or you'll pay us back with your life. Deal?"

Giele thought it seemed a fair offer. "I won't let you down, Mr. Blackpool."

He grinned. "Then I'm looking forward to a long and profitable relationship."

Giele left the railroad offices and headed back into the main part of town. He had a purpose again, a mission to fulfill. The future spread out before him in the form of a world ripe for exploration, and he found himself eager to take those first steps into the unknown.

He tried to do most of his business at Dwarf-run shops, because Dwarves would be far less concerned with the mark on his face. He purchased a good quality mare from the stables—brown with a light tan face and hooves, lightweight but with good muscle tone. She'd carry him for many miles without complaint so long as he kept her well-fed. The Dwarf in charge of horse sales became very cheerful and helpful when he saw Giele's railroad chits. He tried to sell the most expensive saddle in the house, but Giele wouldn't hear of it. Instead, he selected a sturdy saddle with thick straps that had heavy stitching along the edges and hooks for extra bags and slings for rifle and bow.

Tallgrass's Apparel and Tailor Shop provided him with a few changes of clothing, a sewing kit, and a waterproofing rub for his coat and new leather hat, which the proprietor promised Giele would need when the great storms raced across the prairie.

Next, Giele went to the office of the *Goose Creek Crossing Gazette*, in the hopes of purchasing paper and pencils. The man in the sweltering office was a hawk-nosed Elf with sweat stains under the arms of his silk shirt. "You're him," he said in astonishment when Giele entered. "Don't go yet. I want to talk to you. I want to hear your side of the story."

"My side?" Of all the reactions Giele had expected, interest wasn't one of them.

He laughed. "Nothing ever happens out here. I report on tavern brawls and the weather. Occasionally I get news from the homeland if it's interesting enough to send via spell." The newspaper he displayed was a single folded and printed sheet of newsprint. In comparison, the *Morningstar Clarion* back in Aelfland was eight to ten sheets thick. He spun around and dug through a file cabinet with the dexterity of long practice. He whipped out a file folder. Giele's eyes widened as he saw the name on it: *Giele Stillwater*. He held it up for display. "We ran the story here, of course. News is news, but I never thought I'd see you here."

"That's not even valid anymore. The King stripped me of everything. Including my name."

"The point is, I'm giving you a chance to tell your side of the story to me, if in return you give me the opportunity to publish it. Let me tell the people why the King chose to punish you as he did. I'll be fair and honest. Maybe it'll help if folks understand the truth about you. You might not get such harsh treatment."

Giele snorted. "Doubtful. Why would you even do such a thing?"

His eyes got a faraway look in them. "I always wanted to tell a story that would move my readers. Something which they'd remember a week or a month or a year later." His gaze drifted back to Giele. "Your story could do that. I'd bet a lot of crowns that you've got something over the King for him to mark you instead of having you executed."

"Some things are better left undisturbed in the darkness. I'm no folk hero. Don't go and make me into something I'm not."

"Don't go and make yourself into something you're not, either. I can see you have places to go and things to do. Will you promise to talk to me at a later date? There are a lot of people out here who don't know anything more about the King than what they read in the papers and that his name is on the coins they pay in taxes." He paused. "Some of them would look pretty favorably upon you if you made the King look like a fool." He dropped the folder back into the cabinet and slammed the drawer shut, as if that would close the subject.

It was tempting. Giele's tale, sordid though it might be, could sway those who disliked the crown and the man who wore it. The tale was still too close to him, though, and the memory of burning pain in his face very fresh. He shook his head. "I'll be away for several weeks. Perhaps when I return, I'll feel more like talking."

"I'll be here, reporting on the weather."

He sold Giele some paper and pencils, ink and quills, a blank journal, and a large waterproof tube in which to store it all. Giele left the newspaper office and continued on his errands. He obtained an excellent pair of boots from a Dwarven cobbler, far more comfortable than anything he'd ever worn in the Army—soft, with plenty of support inside. The cobbler promised Giele he could walk twenty miles in them and still dance a jig afterward. They would keep his feet cool in the heat, dry in the wet, and warm in the cold. Giele suspected the cobbler would have told him they'd fly if he asked. Nevertheless, they felt very good on his feet, and he took them along with a pair of camp sandals.

The rest of his gear would have to come from Elf-run shops. Giele was no slouch of a bowyer, but would rather not chance his skills with an unknown piece of local wood when he could get a professionally-built or even imported bow. Skria Woodyard's Bowyer and Fletcher was the only seller in Goose Creek. Giele hesitated at the door. Walking into a roomful of weapons when he was marked like he was could be a risk if someone inside took offense at his appearance. Enough people had seen him in town that whispers preceded him wherever he went, and most of the Elves frowned or scowled at him. Giele pushed open the door, causing a bell to ring. There would be no sneaking inside this shop.

Skria wore a leather apron over a sleeveless tunic, and eschewed the typical heavy trousers in favor of light cotton drawstring pants. He turned his head when Giele entered and said "just a minute, sir." The elderly Elf hunched over his worktable, a fine sheen of sweat on his balding head. He had broad shoulders from a lifetime of drawing bowstrings to cheek. He finished sanding a great bow and ran his careful fingers along the wood to check for rough spots or irregularities. When he turned, Giele saw that milky cataracts covered his eyes and he was blind. "How may I help you today?"

"I need a bow."

"Of course. You're recently from Aelfland? The Army?"

"Yes. How did you know?"

"I can hear the accent in your voice. You don't slur and drawl the way locals do. You walk with a measured, regular gait and when you stopped, you stood completely still. If not military, you're unusually well-controlled with your motions."

It was a good thing Skria was blind, or he would have seen Giele's mouth hanging open like an idiot. "That's astonishing. I didn't believe a blind man could be an effective bowyer, but now I see that's a possibility."

Skria smiled. "Just because I can never see a target to shoot at doesn't mean I don't appreciate the fine grain of yew, the scent of hickory, the feel of teak. I warranty every bow that leaves my shop for the lifetime of the purchaser."

"Very well. I need one of thirty-eight and one-quarter inches, with a pull of eighty pounds. How soon can you have one for me?"

"I have four of those in stock. Two are imported from Tyuther's in Morningstar, one I built from imported teakwood. The last I built from a local hardwood which comes from the coastal jungle to the south and west."

"May I see that one?"

He found it without any fumbling about in his shop. Giele examined the bow. Built from a single piece of wood with straight grains, he found no blemishes along its length and smiled at the traditional design. This longbow was beautiful and sturdy, without the laminated extenders that added range and reduced pull for civilians, but made the weapon more fragile.

Giele tested the draw, pulling the bowstring back to his cheek. His arms and shoulders complained at the stress; he was out of shape. The bow bent in smooth silence, without any creaking. That more than anything convinced him of the superior workmanship. In twenty years in the Army, he'd seen more than one ambush spoiled by the inopportune sound of a bow being pulled taut.

"This is an outstanding weapon. Will you accept a B & R Railroad chit for this?"

"Of course. Will you be needing a quiver to go with it?"

Skria sold Giele a quiver of twenty-five arrows with a fletching kit built into its base and two spare bowstrings. Giele gave him the chit, and hoped Blackpool wouldn't have a paroxysm when he saw the bill. He'd have paid a hundred crowns for a bow like that one. Skria would be a fool to charge much less than that.

"Best of luck to you in your travels, marked man," Skria said as Giele turned to leave.

Giele froze. "What did you say?"

"Are you not the exile? With the brand upon your face?"

"Yes. But how did you know?" Giele's blood thundered in his ears. He wondered if he had fallen into a trap of some kind.

He shrugged. "Word travels quickly in a small town like Goose Creek. It seemed a likely guess."

"It doesn't bother you? The waning moon?"

"I've never seen the moon." He tilted his head upward, as if straining to find the silvery orb in the sky by the feel of its rays upon his skin. "I hear it's very beautiful, though. I suspect it is even when slipping into shadow. You should remember that when your own dark times come."

Giele snorted. "Doubtful I'll find darker times than I did in Aelfland."

He returned to his work. "I pray to God you are right."

Giele's insides rumbled. He knew he should return to the parsonage to eat in solitude, without the prying eyes of the locals judging his every move, but it seemed a long way across town when he had a few crowns in his pocket and the smell of roasting pork coming from the saloon nearby. It might be a long time before he tasted prepared food again. He decided to chance it.

It was the same saloon which Giele had stopped Piprel from entering before. Rarik's Retreat, said the sign over the door. Several horses and mules were tied to the wooden bar along the deck. Giele found a place for his newly-bought horse, pulled his hat down low, and walked in through the swinging doors.

It took his eyes a few seconds to adjust from the bright sun to the dim gaslight within. Elves and Dwarves sat at tables, eating, drinking, and playing cards. A Dwarf with garters on his sleeves behind the bar tapped kegs of ale and whiskey and set the glasses on the bar, where serving women collected them to deliver to tables. Conversations died down as the patrons noticed Giele, or rather, noticed his mark. Several of them glanced up to the second floor loft, where a man in shadows stood, surveying the scene in the bar below. Giele could make out no details about him, except that he wore a long coat and to see him make a brushing-off gesture with one hand.

The bartender whistled for attention and pointed at Giele. "You. Out. We don't serve marked men here."

"I've got money," said Giele, knowing deep down that he could have a wagon-load of gold and it wouldn't be enough.

"Out," repeated the Dwarf.

Giele turned, angry, and stalked out of the bar. He wondered if he ought to head straight back to the newspaper office. Oh, he could give a scathing account of the King that would forever mark Teirol the villain in these people's minds, but such a victory would still feel hollow when all Giele wanted was a hot meal. He untied his horse, whipping around the leather straps like they were lashes.

"Mister?" A tentative, feminine voice interrupted his thoughts.

Giele turned to see a woman, who seemed young but whose face was obscured by a silken veil. Only her dark eyes flashed between veil and bonnet. "What?" he snapped, and then was sorry for it by the way she flinched.

"I'm sorry, I just thought that maybe I could buy something for you. If you wanted me to."

"Why?" She didn't present herself with any guile beyond her veiled face, but Giele was learning to become suspicious of everyone.

"I work here. They'll serve me even if they won't serve you. I'll bring you a plate and a bottle of whatever you like if you want."

Giele considered it. She wouldn't meet his gaze. A breeze floated past and moved her veil, which she readjusted in a motion that seemed habitual. He hadn't seen any other covered faces besides hers and wanted to ask her about it, but instead handed her four crowns. "Keep two, and with the other two get me whatever they'll give you."

She nodded. "I'll meet you 'round the side of the building. It won't do any good if they see me."

He suspected he'd just given away four crowns to a thief, but he needed to calm himself down anyway, and waited at the side of Rarik's where Piprel had spilled his guts. Giele passed the time prying dirt from under his nails with a knife. A few minutes later, the veiled woman rounded the corner. She had a plate covered with a napkin and a plain brown glass bottle with her. As Giele sat in the dust with his back to the building, she knelt beside him.

"Thank you," said Giele, smelling the roasted pork with unusual but appetizing spices rubbed into the crust and steamed vegetables with fresh butter melting atop them. "What's your name, Miss?"

"Shali."

"What do you do here?" The pork was juicy and delicious, and he almost groaned at how good it tasted.

She bowed her head. "I serve drinks, and sometimes I . . . I serve customers too."

"I see." He swallowed the first bite and cut another. "Do they like you to wear a veil?"

She reached up to touch it. "Most of them don't like me at all. Rarik—the owner—he keeps me here for . . ." she sniffled a little. "For the ugly men." She pulled down the veil.

A ragged scar stretched from the corner of her mouth across one cheek, with bumpy raised scar tissue discoloring the flesh along either side of the badly-healed wound. Giele couldn't fathom how someone had been so incensed as to disfigure her alabaster skin. It was one thing for the King to brand Giele, but to mark a woman like this . . . Even the women of the bordellos and the camp whores back in Aelfland were treated with greater respect. Something like this was unthinkable cruelty. Shali covered her face once more.

"What happened?" asked Giele, aghast.

"I wouldn't . . . do something for him. He said he'd make it easier for me. He took his knife . . ."

The food wasn't as appetizing as it had been a moment ago. Giele set the plate beside him. "He cut you. God's Blood."

"I saw you earlier today. They said you were marked by the King, that you're a traitor."

"Is that what they're saying now?" He took a drink from the bottle. It was bitter, but even peach nectar would have tasted sour to him at that moment.

"I felt bad for you." Shali hugged her knees to her chest. "Nobody helped me when I was marked. I thought God would want me to help someone else who'd been marked."

"You're an honorable girl, Shali. Not many people have your kind of integrity."

She shook her head. "I'm just a whore, mister, and not a very good one."

Giele touched her hand. She had such a vulnerability about her, unlike Terika, who only put on a facade. Shali saw him not as a monster—or a pawn—but as someone in genuine need of help. She set aside her own disfigurement to help him because of his. It astonished him. After being used by Terika, here was a woman who was the complete opposite. Giele reached up and moved the veil down. She stiffened, but didn't stop him.

The ugly scar couldn't hide this girl's goodness, and Giele realized that the marks they bore didn't have to go below the surface.

"Your boss may have cut your face, but he didn't nick your soul in the least. My friend Tarvy would say that. He's the new Padre. You should go talk to him. He has a remarkable way of making anybody feel good about themselves."

"I will." Shali pulled her veil back up. "I try to do the right thing. If you want to, you know, visit me, you can."

"I'll keep that in mind." Carnal pleasure was a low priority for Giele at the moment, but perhaps he might feel different another time. With the crescent moon on his face, it seemed unlikely he would find many willing partners in the future. "But for now, I have a job to do. I'll check on you when I return to town."

He heard the smile in her voice. "Thanks, Mister."

"Giele."

"Thanks, Mister Giele. I better get back inside. Rarik will wonder where I've gone." She stood up and hurried back to the corner of the building.

"Rarik. He's your boss? The one who cut you?" He called after her.

Shali looked back at him once. She didn't answer Giele, but something about her expression confirmed his question.

Rarik. Giele would remember that name.

CHAPTER TWELVE

With the spices from the pork competing with the bitter aftertaste of the ale Shali had brought him, Giele headed off to his last supply stop. It would be where he spent the most time, and would doubtless encounter many other Elves: the general store. Cianid's Trading Post had a recently-painted sign, as if it had just changed ownership or titles. It was on Goose Creek's innermost street, the one that formed the boundary around the open field in the town's center. Unlike many of the other buildings sandwiched between the radial streets that spread out into the rest of the town, Cianid's shared no walls with adjacent businesses; it was large enough to warrant an entire block itself.

The general store was busy with shoppers. Whispers were already beginning to reach Giele's ears as he tied the mare to the rail. He unbuckled his saddlebags and slung them over his shoulder, a habit he'd learned early on in the Army. He steeled himself, lowered his hat, and entered the store.

He had never been in a store like it before. The warm glow of overhead gaslights filled the interior, adding to the natural illumination that came in through the large picture windows in the front. Tables had been arranged end to end to create aisles, and the merchandise piled on them was in quantities large enough to fill individual shops in an Aelflandic city.

One aisle was devoted to foodstuffs—bags of flour, beans, coffee, and tea. Tins of crackers shared space with fresh vegetables and fruits, arranged in colorful patterns. Paper bags were in neat stacks next to barrels of salt and sugar that had polished wooden scoops sticking out of them. Crocks of lard sat beside jars of jellies and jams, all sealed with paper and tied with twine. Another aisle held bolts of cloth, blankets, cured hides, and tools of all sorts. Giele could have outfitted the entire 136th for a month with everything they'd require from this store's inventory.

A young man in a white apron and a broom in his hands bumped into Giele. Dropping his broom, he jumped back, crossed his arms in front of his face, and hissed like a threatened cat. Giele fell back a step in shock. In Verigo, people had whispered about him, had even pulled their children aside, but this was the first time anyone had made a blatant sign to ward off evil.

Giele's hope for a quiet shopping experience evaporated. "Please don't."

"Begone, Moon-Eater."

"I—what?"

He hissed at Giele again. Others in the store glanced in their direction.

"Foul creature! Destroyer of the light!" he shrieked.

People in the store backed away from Giele. Many left their purchases on tabletops as they retreated. Most held their arms up in the sign to ward off evil. In a few seconds, Giele stood alone in the shop, temples throbbing and ears burning. If he hadn't been too shocked to move, he'd have fled the store,

"I hope you're intending to spend a lot of money, stranger," said a strident, feminine voice. "Because you've just cost me a morning's business."

Giele turned to see an Elf woman standing several feet away with her arms folded in front of her—not to ward off evil, but to indicate displeasure. She wore a white apron over a simple printed silk. She was slender and at least ten years his junior, with black hair caught up in a bun held in place with polished ivory pins and eyes that sparked with disapproval.

Giele raised his hands in supplication. "I apologize, ma'am. I just came here to buy supplies and then I'll be leaving."

"You're the one everyone's been talking about. The man with the moon-mark." Her voice was stern.

"Giele." He offered his hand, in the hope it might make him seem less a threat.

"I'm Cianid. This is my store." She nodded her head to the front windows where people had gathered in curious knots and stared in through the windows. "Those are my customers out there, afraid to come in because of your face."

Giele's temper rose. "I'd cover it if I could. You think I like being a marked man? You think this is the life I chose for myself?"

She sniffed with disdain. "You see? You're just a man like any other. No evil spirits here." She stalked to the door. "Either come in to spend your money or get lost!"

The groups outside broke up and dissipated. Nobody returned to the store.

"Breath and Bones. Superstitious idiots." She spun around, picked up the discarded broom, and started sweeping the front aisle in vicious strokes now that it was devoid of customers.

"I'm sorry. I'll leave."

She rounded on Giele. "Where are you going to go? This is the only general store in town. Pick out what you need and get out of here. I won't have you disrupt my business twice in one day by coming back later." She stamped her heel like an angry mare.

He bowed his head. "Your pardon."

"What do you need?"

"Camp supplies for a month."

On her counter, Cianid laid out a bedroll, tin cookware, a spool of wool string, and a pouch of waterproof matches. Giele added a telescope that caught his fancy, a canteen, and a military-style pup tent. He picked out a selection of useful tools—hatchet, hammer, shovel, and a small saw. She piled up bags of flour, dry beans, dehydrated vegetables and fruits, and salted meat. On top of that went a small pouch containing salt, sugar, and other spices. A tin of coffee joined the pile, and atop it all a coil of sturdy rawhide rope. He dropped his saddlebags down beside it, ready to start packing away his new supplies.

"Will that be all?" Cianid glared at him as if he might start asking for chocolates, lace handkerchiefs, and perfume next.

"Yes, thank you." Giele handed her a railroad chit.

She looked at it in askance. "You don't look like any railroad worker I've ever seen."

"I'm a surveyor," said Giele, enjoying the feel of the new career designation as it rolled around his mouth.

"So Blackpool finally found himself someone who isn't afraid of the Horks. I'd wish you good luck, mister, but it looks like the luck which follows you around isn't of the good sort."

"I thought the Horks were savages." He started to gather up his new purchases. "Barely better than animals."

"That doesn't mean they won't kill you given the chance. Spawns of darkness will kill you and eat your horse. Use your skin to patch up their tents."

"You seem well-informed."

She raised her head with the kind of defiant strength Giele had once showed to Jigan torturers. Her eyes were bright with tears, but she wouldn't permit them to spill forth in front of him. "Horks killed my husband two years past."

"I'm sorry."

"Don't be. He was a mean son of a boar and got free with his hands when he drank, but he loved me and I him. He went down fighting like a man. Honorable." Her eyes moved to something behind Giele. "More than I can say for this lot."

He heard a rustle and footsteps behind him and turned to see three men—two Elves and a Dwarf with an eye patch —had entered the store. One Elf and the Dwarf split up and headed toward different aisles. Giele's hackles raised; he knew a flanking maneuver when he saw it. The third man, tall and broad-shouldered, ducked to avoid a low-hanging collection of lanterns and smiled without humor at Cianid. He wore a hat with a shallow brim and a quail feather stuck in the band. His blond hair fell about his shoulders, framing a handsome face that spoke of good breeding. Over a blue silk shirt, his soft leather vest had been dyed black but for the decorative fringe work, which was the color of dried blood. He rolled a match back and forth in his teeth and walked with a bully's swagger.

In spite of the heat of the day, he sported a long, dark coat.

He wore a single pistol on a belt across his waist, riding high for what must have been a cross-body draw. The pistol's grip was well-polished and the edges of the holster were scuffed from use.

"Howdy, Cianid. You havin' trouble with this stranger?" He ducked to avoid a low-hanging collection of lanterns and smiled without a trace of humor. His drawl was much stronger than most of those Giele had heard so far in Verigo.

A muscle twitched in Cianid's jaw. She had history with this man, and not of a pleasant sort, from what Giele could infer. "He's just a customer, Rarik."

Rarik. So this was the man who'd been so free with his knife upon Shali. The slow burn of righteous fury started to spread outward from Giele's heart to the tips of his fingers and toes.

Rarik plucked an apple from a bin and polished it on the sleeve of his blue silk shirt. "And so am I. How much?" He jingled his purse as he took a bite.

The other Elf and Dwarf had moved into positions where they could attack Giele without being caught in each other's crossfire if they chose to do so. They all wore pistols, but Giele's was in one of his saddlebags, and his bow in its case outside with his horse. All he had on him was the knife given to him by the 136th. He winced at the irony. They often joked in the Army about the futility of bringing a sword to an archery battle, and here he had brought a knife to a gunfight.

"On the house, Rarik." Cianid's clenched jaw stood out in sharp relief.

His eyes widened in mock surprise. "Oh ho, so you're giving things away, are you?" He stepped toward her. "What else is free today?"

"Easy, Scarface." The Dwarf cocked his pistol and pointed it at Giele when he started to move. Giele never even saw him draw it. "This ain't none of your business."

Cianid stood her ground as Rarik circled her, looking her up and down in appreciation. His eyes lingered upon her like a hungry cat regarding a pigeon. "I've told you before and I'll tell you again. No."

"Come on, little filly. I ain't gonna hurt you. I just thought maybe we could get to know each other a little better is all." He took another bite of apple and wiped juice from his chin with the back of his hand.

"I'm not one of your whores." She put on a brave face but the quiver in her voice betrayed her fear of him. Giele shifted his weight onto the balls of his feet.

He stopped behind her. She stiffened as he leaned forward to speak into her ear. "Ah, but you should be, with a face and a body like yours. You could be one of my high-priced attractions. Don't you agree, boys? Wouldn't you pay real crowns for a piece of this ass?" He slapped her rear and she jumped away as if scalded by his touch.

The other two thugs murmured their agreement. Giele's fingers found the iron handle of the heavy cooking pan where it rested amid his pile of supplies—a poor weapon, but better than nothing. He hadn't moved his hand more than an inch since the men first entered the store. He moved it another inch.

"Get out of my store, Rarik. I want no part of your business," Cianid growled.

"But I want part of yours." He leered at her and licked his lips. "And I always get what I want."

"The lady asked you to leave, friend," said Giele. "Perhaps it would be best if you did."

Rarik spun to face him and took another bite of apple. He chewed for a moment and then spat it back in Giele's face. "You're that feller everyone's raisin' a stink about. The marked man. I already done threw you out of my place today. I'd be doin' this town a favor if I shot you where you stand."

Giele made no move to wipe the fragments of apple from his face, but tightened his grip on the iron handle. "Seems rather like I could say the same thing about you." He kept his voice low.

"What was that? What did you say, you boar-rutting moon-faced son of a diseased whore?"

He took one more step toward Giele, and that was close enough.

Giele whipped the pan out, up, and across Rarik's face. It rang with the impact of iron on bone as Rarik flew backward into the middle of the aisle. Giele whirled around as the Dwarf shouted and fired his pistol. The bullet hit the pan with such force it almost twisted the handle from Giele's grasp. His hand went numb from the vibration of the metal. He glanced down and saw the bullet embedded in the pan's bottom. God's Blood! It had almost burst through the thick iron and into his chest.

The one-eyed Dwarf aimed again, pistol raised up toward Giele's head. He hurled the pan at the Dwarf. He tried to duck, but the iron edge caught him behind his right ear. He went down as fast as if Giele had shot him.

Giele yanked his knife from the scabbard strapped against the small of his back just as Cianid brought a jar of preserves down on the other Elf's head. His eyes rolled back and he dropped, bleeding blood and raspberries.

"Nicely done." Giele sheathed the blade again.

"Idiot. I had things under control until you got involved. Does trouble follow you everywhere or do you have to seek it out?"

Giele couldn't formulate a response, because she was right; ever since he'd fallen in love with Princess Terika, his life had been one calamity after another. Leaving Goose Creek Crossing to disappear in the wilderness for a few weeks was sounding more and more like a good strategy.

Two more Elves appeared in the doorway with their pistols drawn and pointed at the ceiling. Giele saw the tin stars pinned to their shirts and raised his hands. Here, at last, was the Law. They kept their guns at the ready, but Giele was glad to see they hadn't yet decided to target him.

"Cianid, what's going on here? This blow-through causing trouble?" One of the Elves, a heavy fellow with dark shoulder-length curls, pushed his hat back and crouched down to check on Rarik.

"He was just buying supplies, Deputy Sheksi. He's got railroad chits so his money's good. Rarik came in here hassling me again."

"Cianid, you know that boy ain't never gonna leave you alone," said Sheksi. "Not until you get yourself a new husband who's bigger'n he is. And maybe not even then."

The other deputy was slender as a whip with a long, brown braid hanging out from under his hat. He kept one eye on Giele as he went to check on the one-eyed Dwarf. He found the pan, picked it up, and fingered the flattened bullet out from the dimple it had created. "You fire this bullet, stranger?"

"No, sir. My pistol's in my saddlebags." Giele kept his head down and his demeanor deferential. He raised his hands to show he didn't even have a holster on his belt.

"Damn fool of you not to keep it on you out here on the Frontier, but in this case it means you ain't gonna spend the night in jail for disturbing the peace." He broke open the cylinder in the Dwarf's pistol, counted the shells, and then tucked it into his own belt. "Unlike this dripper here. How's Rarik?"

"Well, he ain't dead, but he ain't gonna be too happy when he wakes up, neither." Sheksi looked up at Giele. "You messed his face up pretty good, Mister. What'd you hit him with?"

Giele nodded toward the thin deputy with the braid who held the skillet. "That pan. He was going to attack me. Self defense, officer."

"Lemme get this straight." Sheksi ticked off the points on his fingers. "This one here was gonna attack you, so you hit him with the pan. Then that feller there shot you and you caught the bullet in the pan and then hit him with it?"

It sounded ludicrous the way he laid it out. Giele winced to himself. "That's what happened."

"Can you corroborate that, Cianid? And what happened to that feller over there?"

"I hit him with a jar," she said. "He was reaching for his gun. I told you, Sheksi, they were here hassling me and the blow-through there stood up for me."

Officer Sheksi lifted his hat and tucked some errant curls back underneath it and turned to Giele. "Breath and Bones, I wish I'd seen all that happen. You in town long?"

"No, sir. Just collecting some supplies then striking out to survey for the railroad."

"Better you leave soon. This feller here, he's from a powerful family outside of town. They run half the businesses here-abouts. Not the sort of folks you want to make enemies of."

"Yes, sir." Giele opened his saddlebags and started to pack away his new supplies with practiced military efficiency. The sooner he was out of sight of these lawmen, the better.

Sheksi went behind the counter and brought back a bucket of water and a dipper. The Dwarf and Elf each got a dipperful of cold water to the face. As they spluttered back to consciousness, the deputies hauled them to their feet. The Dwarf groaned something about wanting Giele arrested.

"Get on out of here," said Sheksi. "You're lucky I don't lock you two up for your goings-on. I figure the headaches are punishment enough." His partner with the braid helped Rarik out the door. The bully's blue silk shirt was streaked red with blood from his shattered nose and missing front teeth.

Sheksi turned to Giele. "As for you, blow-through, you're lucky none of those drippers are dead or you'd swing in the morning. I'd prefer you're long gone by the time the sun rises tomorrow."

"Count on it."

Giele set what cash money he had left from the 136th on the counter.

Cianid's eyes narrowed and she nodded toward the money. "What's that for?"

"Payment for damages and to replace your stock. The railroad won't cover that, but I will."

Giele slipped outside and untied his horse before Cianid pressed the argument further.

He was done with Goose Creek Crossing for awhile.

CHAPTER THIRTEEN

Padre Tarvy had spent the morning cleaning up the small chapel and was sweeping it out when Giele rode up. "Giele," he said as Giele dismounted. "You look ready to depart. I take it the railroad offered you a position to your liking?"

"They did. I came by to thank you for your hospitality and kindness."

Tarvy shook his head, his kind face creased with that gentle smile of his that always warmed Giele. "Nonsense, my friend. God teaches us that service to others is divine. It brings joy to me. I guess you could say I'm being selfish that way, making myself feel good."

Giele laughed aloud at the idea of Tarvy being selfish. As quickly as they began, his chuckles died off as he considered his recent encounter in Cianid's. "I wonder what your God would think of women being impressed into servitude against their wills, or having their faces carved up when they won't perform favors for men. Not quite as divine, perhaps."

Tarvy pushed his glasses back up his nose. "What do you mean?"

Giele told him what happened in the store.

Tarvy's sigh was heavy, as if the weight of the world had settled upon his broad shoulders. "If ever there was a town in need of spiritual guidance, this is it." He leaned on his broom, his eyes already far away as he began composing a sermon. "I'll conduct evening service tonight. Will you stay for it, at least?"

Giele shook his head. "I don't think that would be wise. Cianid said Rarik is from a powerful local family, and I don't want my presence to bring violence to your church."

Tarvy nodded. "That's what I like most about you, Giele. You may not worship God as I do, but you carry His teachings in your heart anyway. Traveling with you has been an honor and a pleasure. I'm glad to call you my friend."

He clasped Giele's hand in a grip that could have bent steel. Giele's eyes almost watered in pain, but he grinned at Tarvy nevertheless, wishing he could borrow some of the Padre's prodigious strength.

"Likewise, Padre. Keep an eye on Cianid for me. I suspect she'll see more trouble from Rarik and his thugs." Giele paused. "There's also that girl named Shali. Wears a veil to hide a scar. She's a good person, and I think she could use your spiritual guidance. I told her to come see you. She needs to find faith, I guess."

"Of course. It's why I'm here, my friend."

"Farewell, Tarvy. I'll return in a month."

"I'll burn a candle for you."

Giele nodded, and then mounted the mare. They wheeled around and rode north and he didn't look back.

He wasn't sorry to leave Goose Creek Crossing. He'd hoped that being the furthest point away from Aelfland might lessen the burden of his scar, but news travels fast in the modern world, and even at the edge of the civilized world he'd be forever marked as evil. It weighed on him, like a cloud always obscuring the sun. Or the moon.

As Goose Creek disappeared behind him, the tightness in his shoulders eased up. He hadn't realized he was carrying so much anxiety. He began even to enjoy himself.

This part of Verigo was as beautiful and unspoiled as every other place he'd been. The air smelled clean, heady with the sweet plains grasses and tangy wildflowers. To be safe, he checked his trail numerous times over the next two hours, but detected no sign of pursuit. Perhaps he could pass the next month in relaxing solitude. It reminded him of the times when he'd ride away from the 136th for a few days of roughing it and solitary hunting instead of the bureaucracy of military life. Those were good times, and he recalled them with great fondness, even though one had led to Terika and to his branding. He'd treat this new job the same way, becoming a part of the land and the creatures that lived over, under, and in it. He'd learn all about Verigo and perhaps along the way, he might forget his own problems for awhile.

Giele found a high hill from where he could see the town at a distance and the whole of the Goose Creek Valley. He broke out the ink and paper and began to work on his first map. He labored over it for more than an hour, estimating distances with his archer's eye and marking spots as landmarks. He saw little in the way of points of interest for the railroad. The terrain ran to gentle rolling hills covered with ubiquitous grasses and occasional tall flowers or small bushes. Few trees marked the landscape. Far to the north, he saw the snow-capped peaks of great mountains. With his first foray on the railroad's behalf, he would explore toward them. In Aelfland, mountains defined the edge of the Jigan front lines, and he'd spent many days wandering the game trails and climbing the rocky outcroppings for the sheer pleasure of it during the periods when the 136th wasn't engaged in active maneuvers. He wondered what kind of animals inhabited the high mountains of Verigo. Great cats? Bears? Something unimaginable?

He would be the first to come back and report upon them. The more time he spent out among the wild of Verigo, the more he ached to see a greater amount of the country. Spending a lifetime as an explorer, surveyor, naturalist . . . he could think of far worse ways to pass his remaining days in the world.

He sat atop the hill for several hours, skipping lunch to take nourishment in the form of hot summer sunlight baking the toxins from his bones. He was content to let his horse graze upon the wild grasses while he tried his hand at sketching some of the various plants he saw nearby. One in particular with spiny leaves like sword blades and white flowers atop a tall central stalk appealed to his aesthetic sensibilities, and he tried to capture its look upon the page. He'd never drawn anything more complicated than a scribbled map in Army planning sessions, and learned that sketching took far more effort than he'd ever thought. When he regarded most of his attempts, he called them clumsy and vowed not to share them with anyone. The last two—a pair of wildflowers with a spider web slung between them and a quick scribble of a ground squirrel—were good enough for him to feel proud. He started to sign his name to them as artists are supposed to do, but then paused after *Giele*. Officially, he no longer had a last name since King Teirol had abolished his. Adding *Stillwater* to the signature would have felt hollow and dishonest. He wasn't that man any longer. An inspiration struck and he scrawled *Pariah* as a last name. A pariah he had been made, so a Pariah he would be henceforth. Perhaps someday he could make it mean something more than just *outcast*.

Insects of all sorts wandered and raced through the tall grass—ants, beetles, and spiders all performed an intricate ballet. Bees and wasps darted amid the tall golden and blue flowers while a dozen varieties of colorful butterflies fluttered to and fro. Here and there, shiny dark green dragonflies would dart in to snag aphids or mosquitoes. Giele recognized the basic types of insects, but they were so different from those he was accustomed to seeing in Aelfland. Back home, insects lurked in the shadows of trees and forests, coming out at night to hunt and bite the unsuspecting traveler. Bold Verigan insects went about their business in the bright sunlight, rushing about with fevered intensity that seemed at odds with the peaceful climate.

One bug in particular fascinated him with its overlarge hind legs and bulbous eyes. They lurked amid the grass and would leap away in clouds as he approached. He managed a couple of rough sketches of one that seemed content to sit still for him. Small birds feasted on seeds or on the copious insects. Most of the sleek feathered creatures were dull, drab colors so they could hide amid the plants from the larger hawks and falcons that spiraled overhead. Ground squirrels and rabbits popped out of the grass near him on occasion. They startled when he moved and disappeared again so fast it was like he'd imagined them. Once he barely dared to breathe as a mottled brown and tan snake as thick as two fingers slithered past his boot.

At long last, the sun began to push toward the western horizon, and Giele decided he'd better find someplace to camp. He packed up his gear and made for a small stand of trees he'd spotted earlier by Goose Creek, well upstream of the town. By the time he reached them, the shadows had grown long and the pangs in his belly reminded him that he hadn't eaten for several hours. The trees had olive-hued bark that gave off an appetizing, smoky odor which made his hunger stronger. He picked up a broken stick and touched a lit match to it. When the wood burned, the smoky scent intensified to a heady intensity. It would add its flavor to whatever he cooked over it, and it would be delicious.

He watered the horse and splashed some of the cool stream water on his face. He gathered up enough of the smoke-scented wood for a cooking fire. Soon he had a merry blaze burning with a simmering pot of spiced beans while flatbread wafers cooked on a flat river rock amid the coals. It felt good to have his boots off, to breathe campfire smoke, and to have room to move without jostling neighbors. Despite hours of sketching and mapping, a creative spark within him still burned, and he spent another hour writing down some of his recent experiences in a journal. It helped him to get a better handle on some of the things that had happened over the past month of his life. Sleep beckoned to him as the fire died down to embers and he lay his head on his pack and enjoyed restful sleep for the first time in what felt like years.

The next morning Giele ate before he broke camp and set out to the east. His plan was to work in a back-and-forth pattern, ever extending further outward, with Goose Creek Crossing as the focus.

The day passed without event. He found little in the way of useful B&R real estate, although a distant herd of Greatdeer and a large, tawny cat stalking them piqued his own interests. He estimated the predator was close to Elven size. It took down an elderly Greatdeer specimen that might have outweighed it by two or three hundred pounds. Well-practiced in the art of slaying Greatdeer, the cat ducked under a vicious swipe of the antlers, and then sprang for the hapless creature's throat and bore it down. The cat fed upon its kill, and fought off a small herd of dog-like scavengers. Satisfied at last, it slunk off into the scrub brush to leave the carcass behind. The scavengers and vultures moved in to battle over the remaining gobbets of Greatdeer flesh.

Giele sketched what he could of the creatures, although at the distant range he couldn't see many details. He was relieved that the cat had headed in a different direction. He had no desire to meet a predator like that in his travels. The way it had dodged the Greatdeer's antlers suggested it would be difficult to score a fatal hit with an arrow unless the hunter struck the heart or lungs with the first shot and the monster bled to death.

A bullet would just enrage it.

That evening he wrote more in his journal and organized some of the notes he'd taken before the fire died down. A waning moon mocked him from the skies overhead. This was the moon of Giele's face, the Pariah's moon. Soon, the shadow would overtake the moon, and then, according to Elven legends, evil would walk the lands.

Giele didn't believe that himself, but the myths of the moon cycle had been part of Elven culture for so many thousands of years it was impossible not to think of it. The crescent shape reminded him of Aelfland, and Terika. The memory of her so-called love hurt like peeling the scab off a wound. Even so, his anger toward her had abated somewhat. Time heals all wounds, as the old Dwarven adage went, even those of the soul. Giele could never forgive her for the way she used him, but he didn't have to keep his hatred knotted up in his heart any longer.

In this new life of his, there was no place for her. She wasn't even worth the energy spent upon hatred. He'd be better off to put her out of his thoughts forever.

He wondered what Tarvy would think of his feelings. The Padre would say something of insufferable cheer like, "The moon always comes back, my friend," and then he'd share his gentle laugh. Giele smiled at the notion, and then smiled up at the crescent moon. It would return to full in several days as it always did. The pattern of the moon was one of the first things ancient Elves monitored to create their modern calendar. In that moment, it occurred to Giele how foolish they were to fear its pattern. The cycle always repeated without fail. It had since the world was created and would until the world was destroyed. Why fear something so predictable? The thought amused him and he drifted off to sleep at last.

The next day, Rarik and his men caught up to him.

CHAPTER FOURTEEN

They caught Giele with a simple trick.

Morning had come. He struck camp with typical military precision, burying the remains of the fire and removing as much evidence of his stay as he could. Once he'd packed everything back into the saddlebags, he took out his telescope and scanned the horizon in a slow pan to look for anything that changed overnight.

Some two miles away he saw a solitary horseback rider. Giele couldn't make out many details except that the rider was Elven and wore rough travel clothing. His horse ambled along, reins dangling. Giele wondered if the rider was asleep in the saddle. Then as he watched, the rider slid out of the saddle, drew a pistol, and aimed it at the ground. He saw two muzzle flashes and heard the reports a second later. The rider bent down to pick something out of the tall grass. It looked like a snake the way it dangled in his hand. Then he jumped backward, flinging the creature away from him. He swayed, looking at his hand, and then fell over.

The poor fellow was snakebit. "Breath and Bones," Giele muttered. He knew nothing of the poisonous reptiles of Verigo, but if they were anything at all like those native to Aelfland, the wounded rider was going to need help. He mounted the mare and nudged her sides with his heels. She was no cavalry horse, but her trot broke into a passable gallop and they covered the distance to the fallen man in a few minutes.

He lay on the ground, face down. Giele dismounted, grabbed his canteen, and hurried to his side. "Mister, are you all right? I'm here to help."

Giele rolled the fallen man over and as he did, the rider raised a gun he'd hidden underneath him and pointed it at Giele with a gap-toothed grin.

Giele hadn't expected trouble of that sort, but didn't hesitate to lash out and kick the man's hand. He yelped as his pistol whirled off into the tall grass. Giele's hand dropped to his waist where his own pistol hung, but his fingers slapped empty leather. As he looked down at the vacant holster, he heard the snap of a pistol being cocked behind him.

"Easy there, marked man," grunted a voice. "I won't miss you a second time."

Giele raised his hands.

"Turn around."

Giele did so and his guts twisted into a knot as he recognized Rarik's one-eyed Dwarf companion. His good eye was bruised and swollen from where Giele had hit him. In his hand he held Giele's own pistol. The sly rutter had lifted it right from Giele's side without him noticing. He'd have admired such stealth if it hadn't been used against him. The Dwarf raised his other hand to his lips and uttered a piercing whistle. Heads appeared over the crest of a nearby hill as more Elves approached, all with bows or pistols pointed at Giele. One of them was Rarik, with a bandage about his head. No longer dressed in his fancy blue silk and black leather, he wore dun-colored riding gear that would help him vanish into the tall grass at a moment's notice. The others were attired in similar clothing. It had been a well-executed ambush, and Giele fell right into it like a first-day Leaf Archer.

"Well, well, well, looky what we have here," Rarik gloated through his ruined smile.

Giele said nothing. He knew he had little time. He wouldn't go down without a fight, but Rarik seemed to be of a mood to jaw first.

"Ain't no whore to help you here, boy," said Rarik. "It's just you and me and the Big Empty." He pulled a tin whistle from his pocket and blew a blast on it. Over another crest appeared a lone rider leading several other horses tied together.

"Well, fellas, what do you think we ought to do with him?"

"Shoot him?" suggested one of the others.

Rarik shook his head. "Too quick, too easy."

"Bleed him," said the man who'd feigned being snakebit. He rubbed his hand where Giele had kicked it. Giele hoped he'd broken a finger or two.

Rarik considered that option. "Better. Maybe we'll do that."

"Hey, look at this." One of the Elves who'd been rummaging through Giele's pack held up the sheaf of sketches. "He thinks he's an artist."

"Aw, ain't that sweet?" said the Dwarf.

The others laughed.

Rarik grabbed away the sketches and flipped through them. "*Giele Pariah.*" He sounded out the letters like someone unskilled at reading. "You sure like the animals, huh? You draw enough pictures of them." He crumpled them up and tossed them aside. Each crumple felt like Giele's own skin being torn away. He'd spent hours on those sketches. They might not have been exceptional works of art, but they were his. "I got an idea, fellas. Let's shoot his horse and stake him out next to it and let the scavengers eat him."

The others laughed.

One of them produced a mallet from in his gear while another pulled four ironwood shafts from his quiver. Cold sweat began to dot Giele's brow.

"What's the matter, Rarik?" Giele lowered his head and spread his hands. "You're not man enough to beat me in a fair fight?" If he could impinge upon Rarik's honor, he might relent and give Giele a fighting chance.

But, like all bullies, he wasn't goaded into a conflict he might not win. He chuckled. "Fair like hitting a man across the face with an iron pot when he's unprepared? Fair like interrupting a perfectly legal business transaction with violence?"

"You tell him, Rarik," said one of the Elves.

Rarik had an audience; he was going to give them his best show. He swaggered up to Giele, chest puffed out like a bird, and pointed at his face. "Let me tell you what I think. You're that feller who was in the papers—the one who got exiled from Aelfland for messin' around with the King's daughter. Oh yes, boys, this is him. The Pariah. He even signed his name that way on his ruttin' drawings. They had a picture of you with that brand and everything." He dropped the act and came in even closer.

Giele smelled the whiskey on his breath and saw every tooth he cracked when he smashed Rarik's face with the frying pan. He wished he'd hit him much, much harder.

Rarik's voice was low and dangerous. "I think you were goin' to make a play for that stitch in the general store. Well, let me tell you somethin', outcast." He jabbed his pointing finger into Giele's chest and it took every ounce of willpower Giele had not to grab hold and twist it right off his hand. "She ain't for you. She ain't for nobody but me, and the way I see it, I'm doin' her a favor."

Giele shuffled his feet a little and Rarik glared at him.

"What's the matter, Moon-Face? Got something to say?"

Giele didn't waste his breath on sassy words; he had to act without hesitation if he was going to have any chance to survive this encounter. He flung himself backward and rolled between a horse's legs. It shied away from the sudden movement. Pistols cracked and bullets kicked up dust around him. He grabbed the horse's rider by the ankle and twisted it until it snapped. The rider shrieked and dropped his pistol. Giele leaped up, wrapped his arms around the man's throat, and heaved backward with all his weight. The horse stumbled but the man slipped out of the saddle.

Rarik's face contorted with rage. "Shoot him!" He grabbed two of his men and flung them toward Giele even as he backed away.

Giele didn't dare stop moving and grabbed the fallen pistol.

Bullets and arrows thudded into the horse. The animal screamed and went down, crushing the Elf that Giele just unseated. Giele dove behind the horse and used its body and the dust it kicked up as cover. There were too rutting many of them and he only had six shots. He fired into the crowd of thugs. One of the Elves crumpled. Then a gunshot sounded right next to him and pain lanced through his leg. Giele turned just in time to see the Dwarf's gnarled fist smash into his face with a sickening crack that he felt as well as heard. His nose filled with blood as more blows struck until the entire world spun around him and he couldn't see anything except stars. His eyes swelled up and almost blinded him and he had a painful, bloody gap in his gums where he'd lost a tooth.

Rough hands dragged him across the dirt. Rope tightened around his hands and ankles. They stretched out his limbs and pounded the ironwood shafts into the ground at sharp angles so he couldn't move. The wound in his thigh burned and throbbed and his trousers grew sticky and damp as more and more of his blood leaked from the ragged hole.

"Hey, Rarik, Stubin's in a bad way," said a voice. "I think we ought to get him to the doctor."

"I want to stay and watch him die," said the guttural voice of the Dwarf.

"He probably ain't gonna die from that hole in his leg, Vilnius," said Rarik. "But it'll sure make him smell nice to that cougar what's been hunting the area. Or them coyotes. And none of them will come if we're around. We'll take Stubin to the Sawbones in town and then come back." He paused. "Besides, I want to have another chat with that stitch in the store. My blood's a-pumpin' now and maybe I'll finally make her see things my way."

More laughter resounded around Giele, but it seemed distant compared to the pounding and throbbing in his head.

"Any famous last words, Pariah?" Rarik spat into the dirt beside Giele.

Giele licked his lips. "I'll die soon, but you still have to spend the rest of your life looking at your ugly face in the mirror." He coughed. "And you can't spit straight, either."

A couple of the Elves snorted in amusement and Rarik drove a pointed boot hard into Giele's side, breaking at least one of his ribs.

The sounds of the men and horses receded, leaving Giele alone, stretched out on a hilltop and wondering what would kill him first—blood loss, dehydration, or a hungry animal. The sun was a bright blur overhead, and the light grew until he saw nothing at all.

Sometime later, he awakened to a semblance of consciousness. His lips were swollen and cracked, and his face burned from the sun. The swelling around his eyes had receded a bit, but he could still barely squint. Flies buzzed around his face and he felt them brushing against the wound in his leg like the tiniest kisses. The leg itself throbbed and ached with each beat of his heart and he wondered how much blood he'd lost. His foot didn't feel cold or numb, which was a good sign, but his trousers were soaked from the leaking wound. Breathing was torture; with each inhalation, his broken ribs grated together. Only by taking shallow breaths could he manage that pain, and then only through his mouth, for his nose was blocked from swelling and blood clots.

Dark forms circled in the sky over him. He couldn't see them with any clarity but knew they had to be vultures. Once Rarik and his men had left, the birds dropped down to squabble with another over the horse carcass. Sooner or later Giele knew one would get curious about him and come take a peck at his swollen eyes or the soft tissue of his cheeks. The thought of being eaten alive made him shiver in his bonds. He had no way to drive off the carrion-eaters except by shouting at them, and he couldn't draw breath enough to manage much more than a groan.

So Giele groaned at them.

All the birds around him took to the sky in a sudden mad flurry of squawks and feathers. The insects went silent. He heard a rustling in the grass, turned his head, and found himself face to face with the large tawny cat he'd seen the day before. Observed through a telescope, it had been only another predator. Now Giele stared his death right in the face. The beast was gigantic, like a warhorse. The ground seemed to shiver away from its feet in terror as it stepped forward. The demonic cat licked its lips and Giele heard its tongue rasp across its teeth like a file over a blade. The sound made him twitch with involuntary terror.

It drew back and growled when Giele moved, its ears laid back and its teeth bared. If Giele somehow survived this encounter, he knew the rumble of the cat's voice would fill his nightmares forever.

The ironwood shafts held him fast to the ground and he had no leverage to break free. The cat growled again, and circled around to sniff at one of Giele's hands. The animal's well-toned muscles bulged beneath its shiny, straw-colored coat. All Giele had left was his voice, so he hissed at the cat in the hope that he might startle it into running away. It paused, taken aback, but hunger sparked in its green eyes. It reached out to bat at Giele with a curious paw. Its barbed claws hooked in the skin of his arm to open new furrows, making him cry out. He wondered if the monster had laid him open to the bone, tearing muscle and sinew like Giele would skin a rabbit.

The cat sniffed at his arm and then Giele felt the unnerving sensation of a warm, raspy feline tongue as it licked at his wounds. He drew in one deep breath, despite the agony of his ribs, with the intention of screaming at the creature, but all he could manage was a choking sob.

Something whistled past Giele's face and struck the cat's nose. It growled and retreated a few steps with a snarl. Someone was flinging small stones at the animal, and they bounced off its hide with hollow thuds. One hit it right between the eyes with a meaty thunk. It must have decided a meal wasn't worth being pelted in the face. It hissed and yowled in defiance and slunk back into the grasses.

A shadow fell across Giele's face as a figure eclipsed the sun.

CHAPTER FIFTEEN

At first Giele thought it was the Dwarf Vilnius, back to torment him some more. Then he realized that despite the being's diminutive stature, she was no Dwarf. Her face bore the wrinkles of many decades, and her hair was the color of the sky before a snowstorm. Jaw and nose thrust forward, dark eyes set beneath a bony ridge. He'd been found by a Hork. Savage, barbarian, he didn't care. "Please," he rasped. "Water."

The ancient woman bent crouched down to sniff at him. She had a strong musky odor that he might have thought unpleasant were he in a better state. Somehow, the scent fit her, and made her seem like she belonged to the land. Despite his sunburned eyes, he saw she wore a sleeveless leather tunic decorated with beads and braids twisted into spiral patterns. Similar patterns graced the skin on her arms, either painted or tattooed. The haft of a bone knife jutted from a band around her waist, and a leather sling hung from the top of a wooden staff upon which she leaned.

She grunted, less to him than to herself as she squinted at his lanky form staked out on the hilltop.

"Water." Giele licked his lips with a dry tongue before opening his mouth. He couldn't tell if she looked down at him with disgust, compassion, hatred, or disinterest. She disappeared from his view and he wondered if she had left, for he couldn't hear anything. But a moment later, she returned with a leather bag. She loosened the drawstring around one corner and tipped it. Cool water splashed into his mouth. He choked as he gulped it like a greedy child with a sweet drink. She withdrew the bag and looked down at him in curiosity once more.

"Thank you," he mumbled through his swollen lips.

"*Faw.* Why you here, Elf?"

Giele blinked in surprise. "You speak Elvish?"

"Some. Elves here long time."

"Bad men put me here." He hoped he could convey the ideas without using complex terms that might confuse her.

"*Faw.* Why? You bad Elf too?"

Before he could answer, he blacked out.

Insistent poking in his side shifted his broken ribs, and Giele yelped in pain. His eyes flew open and the Horkish woman jumped back. "You fall asleep. Very rude."

"I'm sorry." He gasped to draw breath. Every part of him hurt.

"It all right. Ullu can wake you again." She held up a solemn finger and wiggled it. Then her lips split in a grin that showed straight, yellowed teeth. "Ullu." She beat her palm against her chest. Then she pointed at him.

"Giele." He couldn't tell whether it hurt worse to cough or not to cough.

"*Faw.*" He wondered what the word meant. She seemed to use it like an exclamation. "Why Elf names hard for mouth? Hork names easy. Ul-lu." She exaggerated the simple pronunciation.

"Ullu, please cut me loose. I'll die if you don't."

"Elf may die anyway. Hurt bad."

He took a shuddering breath. He knew she was right. He was dying. "Please," he whispered. "Don't leave me here to die like this."

"Ullu not know. Elf with hard name might be bad."

Giele's exasperation boiled over, and with what little fire he had left, he cried out, "God's Blood, don't leave me here to die like an animal! At least let me face my fate like a man!"

Ullu's eyes grew wide. "Elf speak of blood? Elf know magic?"

He didn't have any idea what she meant, but he'd promise her the sun, moon, and stars if it meant freedom. "Yes, blood! Magic! Anything you like!"

A look of resolution came over her horsey face. "Ullu will free you. Swear on blood you not hurt Ullu."

"Yes, God's Blood, I swear!" Relief washed over him as she pulled her bone knife from her waist. It was as sharp as a forged blade, for it sliced through the ropes as if through paper.

He groaned as tortured muscles seized in his arms and legs from fatigue. Compounded with the bullet wound in his thigh, he knew he wouldn't be able to walk. Nevertheless, he rode out the cramps and tried to sit up. His broken ribs grated and he just about fainted from the pain. Ullu jumped back, her knife held at the ready. He made no threatening moves; he couldn't have even if he'd wanted to. Blood loss and dehydration had made him lightheaded and dizzy.

"Thank you."

"Arms and legs hurt much?"

"Yes. Ribs too."

"Elves too tall. No wonder you hurt. Horks perfect height. *Faw*." She held her hand at the level of her head and grinned.

Giele found Ullu's simple cheerfulness comforting. He gave her a weak smile.

"What you do now?"

As he opened his mouth to answer, consciousness fled him once more and his head hit the hillside.

Sometime later, he awakened to the rocking feel of steady motion. He lay on a piece of leather stretched between two sticks and was being dragged across the ground. He tilted his head around and saw the hindquarters of a Greatdeer. Ullu rode upon it bareback. The travois on which he lay was fastened to a simple harness around the animal's barrel chest.

His thoughts coalesced to form questions he didn't have the energy to ask. Somehow this tiny, ancient Hork had wrestled his battered and bloodied body into a sled and now was towing him somewhere else. He groaned as the travois bumped over a rock.

Ullu looked back at him. "Good, you awake. Ullu have magic for you."

"Magic?"

"Yes, soon now. But first, Ullu must cover tracks before bad Elves return. Even blind Dwarf find our trail. *Faw.* You rest here."

He looked around. They were in a dry gully deep enough to have some shade.

The wound in his leg throbbed and his head buzzed with fever. If he developed a bad infection, Rarik might get his wish anyway. The Greatdeer bowed its head low and Ullu swung down to the ground from its antlers. She placed her water skin beside Giele and withdrew a small brown pellet from a pouch at her waist. Beside it he saw a well-worn leather sling.

"Ullu, did you drive off the cougar? The big cat?"

"Puma too lazy to hunt. Get soft in old age. Like Ullu. Want food tied down. Here, you take this. Chew, then swallow."

"What is it?" He eyed the lumpy brown object with suspicion. It looked like a nugget of dung with seeds and plant fibers mixed into it.

"Magic."

"You mean medicine?"

"Ullu mean magic. Stupid Elf." She pushed the nugget at his lips.

Giele imagined she wasn't going to poison him, but how did she know Horkish medicine would work on an Elf? It didn't matter to him what it was, though. He'd be dead in hours, if not sooner, unless Ullu did something to help him. He allowed her to poke the lump into his mouth.

It didn't taste as vile as he'd feared it would; Elven medicines were notorious for being unpleasant. Actually, he thought as he chewed the sticky, sweet substance, it tasted like it was bound with honey. Tiny seeds and bits of organic matter caught in his throat and he coughed.

"Good magic. Keep you alive. Stop burning. Stop bleeding. Fix you inside. Good magic. *Faw.*"

His lips and tongue went numb and he shuddered as a sudden chill raced through him. "P-poison," he stammered.

"No," she said with cheer, as if speaking to a child. "Magic. Stupid Elf should clean out stuffy pointed ears."

Medicine or magic, he didn't feel any better. If anything, he felt worse as his body temperature seemed to alternately spike or plummet until his muscles ached from the violent shivering. "This is supposed to help?"

She scampered up the side of the gully with a grace that belied her age. "It make you forget pain in leg. Ullu be back soon. Must clear tracks."

He realized that she was correct; he had forgotten the bloody hole in his leg.

"You stay here. Rest. Drink if thirsty but do not eat. Will be messy." She disappeared over the lip of the gully and left Giele alone with his thoughts and the untethered Greatdeer.

With nothing better to do, he studied the Greatdeer as it nibbled the weeds growing in ragged clumps along the gully walls. The animal never took its eyes off him, perhaps waiting for him to make a threatening move. The big buck's antlers had been dyed black and filed to wicked-looking points. As Giele looked closer, he noticed that someone, perhaps Ullu, had carved tiny spirals into them. Yellow and green spirals had been inked on its haunches as well. He'd have to ask Ullu about the markings when she returned.

The mount showed no signs of straying. It was obvious that the beast had been trained well. Perhaps even more so than an Army warhorse. Had any of the colonists ever tried to ride or train any of the huge deer? As attached as Elves were to their horses, Giele thought it unlikely. And the way Piprel had been eyeing them from the train car, Giele suspected his people would regard Greatdeer as nothing more than meat.

Raging thirst took hold of him, as if he'd just eaten a whole tin of dry salted biscuits. With shaking hands, he opened the mouth of the water skin and squeezed blessed sip after blessed sip into his parched mouth. When it was empty, he lay back on the travois and marveled at how the pain throughout his body had ceased—even in his leg, which no longer bled. The fever hum in his head had disappeared and the swelling in his eyes had reduced so much that his vision was no longer affected. When Ullu returned, he was considering the possibility of digging out the bullet with a sharpened stick.

"Good magic, yes?" She slipped down the side of the gully. The sides of her mouth played up in a small grin that told him she was gloating a little.

"Yes, very good magic. I'm in your debt."

"*Faw.* Ullu like having debt to collect."

"How can I repay you for your kindness?"

"Ullu will think of something."

Giele suffered another lengthy ride in the travois, somewhat humiliated because after Ullu's medicine, he felt less like an invalid, but remained immobilized by the bullet in his thigh. She refilled her water skin twice more from small streams that crisscrossed the landscape, and he drained it dry each time.

"Good magic," she said with vindication.

He wasn't about to argue. After the beating Rarik's men had delivered, anything would be an improvement.

That bullet would have to come out, though, and medicine or magic or not, the procedure would be painful and risky. He had neither the strength nor the steadiness of hand to perform the extraction, and so he turned to the ancient Horkish woman who had made him her charge and had been dragging him for miles across the plains toward whatever ultimate destiny she'd selected for him.

He found the opportunity when they broke for camp later that evening. "Ullu, I need your help to get this bullet out of my leg."

"*Faw*." Giele had come to understand it was a general-purpose exclamation, colored by the speaker's intonation and situational context. "Ullu has removed bullets before."

He wondered if she'd removed them from her own people. Cianid had said her husband was killed by the Horks. Giele hated to think that a people who produced someone as kind as Ullu might also produce murderers of Elves. On the other hand, if Ullu had removed bullets, there could be as many murderers of Horks among his own people. Nevertheless, he couldn't dwell on that now. "Will you please do so again? I don't want to continue to be a burden to you."

"Gilly-Elf is no burden to Ullu. See? Ullu not even tired. Smart Hork makes Greatdeer do all work." She selected two long, slender sticks and used her bone knife to strip away the bark from them and to shape them into tips. Then she notched a larger piece of wood, placed it between the sticks, and tied the blunt ends together to form makeshift tongs. She held the tips of the wooden tongs into the coals so they'd become fire-hardened.

Giele borrowed her knife and cut a square patch from his bloodstained trousers to expose the hole in his leg. Blood crusted the edges of the wound, and he noticed the shininess of raw flesh inside. He winced as he felt around the wound, which was swollen and tender. He knew he was in for yet another in what seemed to be an unending series of painful life experiences.

Ullu looked at it. "*Faw*, this going to hurt. Ullu do it?"

"I think you'll have to. I'm pretty weak already."

She directed him to lie on the ground with his leg elevated over a rock the size of a curled-up Hork.

"Why you so far from Elf town?" She crouched down beside him.

He knew she was trying to distract him from the pain to come, and did his best to focus on the answer as she pushed the sharp wooden tongs into his leg. He hissed at the pain, even though he'd expected it. "I was hired . . . *ouch* . . . to make maps for the railroad."

"What is maps?"

"Pictures of the land on paper." He groaned as she poked deeper. It felt like she had the tongs buried up to the hilt in his leg.

"Ullu not understand. Why draw the land? The land is the land. It not change."

Giele yelped as the tongs touched the bullet and sent fresh waves of agony up and down his leg.

Ullu muttered something under her breath in her native tongue. "Ullu sorry. Bullet deep."

"It's all right," said Giele through clenched teeth. "Keep going. I draw maps for people who haven't been in the land yet so they'll know where to go."

"Why they not explore themselves? Land give up secrets to those who in it. Piece of paper have no secrets."

"Not everyone is—Breath and Bones!—an explorer." Giele's flesh pulled and strained as it held tight to the offending bullet, almost like it wanted to keep it. Blood ran down his hip; he was amazed he had any left after he'd lost so much during the day. Ullu's medicine must have helped replenish his blood supply. Perhaps that was why he'd been so thirsty. New blood had to come from something.

"*Faw.*"

"How would you direct someone from here back to the hill where you found me?"

He clung with desperation to the conversation. It was all that kept him from screaming or losing consciousness. He'd been shot with arrows, nicked with swords, and even broken bones in his long tenure with the Army, but this was the first bullet he'd ever taken. He promised himself to avoid ever getting shot again.

"Ullu would say, go to that hill."

"What if he didn't know where the hill was?"

"Ullu would show him." Her tongue poked out of the corner of her mouth in concentration. She tugged on the tongs. The bullet moved a little, which introduced a new batch of agony.

"God's Blood!" groaned Giele.

"Hurt much?"

"Yes!"

"*Faw*. Will hurt more before Ullu done. Bullet not want to come out. Maybe have your name on it."

"What do you mean?"

She didn't answer right away. The elusive bullet held all of her attention. She changed the angle of the tongs and the pain narrowed in its scope across his entire leg but became much more acute. "Ullu have it. Be still."

If he'd had the foresight to put a stick in his jaws ahead of time, Giele would have bitten clean through it. Bright, fresh blood ran from the wound as Ullu crowed with success and held up the small lead slug in her stained fingers.

"This little rock? This cause all your fuss? *Faw*." She tossed it aside, and then looked down at his leg. "How much blood inside Elf body? Not much more than this, Ullu think."

"Oh . . ." he began, but then fainted dead away with a lingering thought that she must not think very highly of Elves.

He awakened later to discover Ullu had moved the entire campsite to another location. She had put some kind of poultice over the leg wound and bandaged it with strips of cloth cut from his trousers. A spongy lump sat on the wound, held down by the bandage. He didn't know what it was, but it made his entire thigh itch. He was thirsty and ravenous, and something smelled delicious.

Ullu had some kind of game spitted on two sticks and was cooking them over a new campfire.

"*Faw*. You slept long enough, Elf?"

"How long have I been out?"

"One day."

"Breath and Bones," he muttered. No wonder he felt so weak. "That smells delicious, Ullu."

"Yes it does. Ullu will enjoy it." Her smile was radiant. "Elf not eat *hachas* tonight. That your food." She pointed to a cunningly-woven bowl of reeds lined with leaves. An unappetizing mush sat in the middle of it.

He looked up at her. "You're joking."

"You sick. Hachas not make you better. Need magic to work inside body." She nodded at the bowl.

"This is magic food?" He looked at the pasty mess.

Ullu removed her hachas from the fire. "It fix you from inside. Ullu fix you from outside. Only way you ever heal all the way."

She did seem to have a way with herbal cures, and she'd done enough work on him that he wanted to honor it by following her directions. He dug two fingers into the bowl and spooned some of the porridge into his mouth. It had a wholesome, grainy flavor, a mixture of sweet and salty at the same time. It seemed to expand as he swallowed it, to the point that he could barely finish the small amount she'd made.

She ate the hachas whole, crunching tiny bones between her teeth or spitting them out if they were too tough. When she finished, she took a small pile of leaves she'd gathered, rolled them up into a tight cylinder, and lit the end of it with a firebrand. She sucked on the roll until the tip glowed cherry red. Giele watched in fascination as she tilted it up and hunched over to breathe the pungent smoke from it.

He recalled watching Kiler smoke his pipe, and he took great pleasure from it. Ullu didn't seem to enjoy this peculiar ritual. From her expression, it looked like she detested the smoke. Medicinal, then, he thought, and asked her about it.

"Ullu has seen many, many turns of the seasons. Smoke help pain in joints. You get old someday, you will need magic smoke too. Although . . . Not if you keep getting shot."

Giele laughed. "I'll do my best to avoid it."

"You need real rest, not on trail. Tomorrow you come to Ullu's village."

He laid back, staring up at the slender crescent moon. Tarvy hadn't said the Horks lived in villages. Maybe he didn't know. Giele suspected there was a lot about Horks the colonists still didn't know that he was about to learn.

Chapter Sixteen

Ullu stopped her Greatdeer atop a hill overlooking a narrow river valley lined on the northern side by tall, reddish cliffs like smaller, less dramatic versions of those which surrounded Golden Sands. Nestled against the base of the bluffs, Giele counted twenty large dome tents made of Greatdeer leather and slender wooden poles. Most of the tents had gardens by them, with vines growing on trellises or neat rows of ground-hugging squashes and gourds. He'd never seen such tents before; Elven tents were cone-shaped. The leather stretched over the frames was inked with colorful geometric patterns, giving each dome a unique appearance. Everywhere he looked, he saw more spirals.

A building of carefully-stacked stone sat at one end of the village, and from the large amount of wood stacked around it and the heavy soot on the stone chimney, it had to be a forge. That meant the Horks knew how to smelt and work metal, and that more than anything convinced Giele that conventional wisdom about them was wrong. These were no uncivilized barbarians in the village laid out before him.

The river was neither wide, nor fast-moving; a lazy winding current content to travel the land slower than a horse walked. The Horks had erected a simple wooden bridge over a narrow point, wide enough for two to walk abreast with a single rope rail for balance.

On the opposite bank from the village was a corral with perhaps two dozen Greatdeer enclosed within. Beside the corral, a large cultivated field spread out, filled with regular rows of strange, spindly plants as tall as an Elf. Each stalk sported odd, tasseled growths that Giele thought might be fruit of some kind.

Several stone ovens were scattered through the village, either for baking bread or for firing the ubiquitous clay pots. Bowlegged Horkish children ran through the village, laughing and screaming. Most of them could have run between his legs without having to duck. Domesticated foxes ran with the children and nipped at their heels from time to time. Women tended their gardens or kneaded dough for bread on large flat stones beside the ovens. Men cleaned hides or fished in the river.

Despite the temporary look of the tents, the village had a definite permanence about it. This was not a group of savage hunter-gatherers, following the herds across the plains. This was a fully-realized agricultural society. If Giele were to show Tarvy the village, the Padre would be shocked and pleased, and above all, amused.

"*Faw.*" The word seemed to fit Giele's feelings.

"This Ullu's home." She looked proud.

Earlier in the day, he'd asked to borrow her sharp bone knife and cut a slender tree bole. He peeled and twisted the bark to make an improvised cord, and then used it to put some cross-braces on the trunk. After a couple hours' work, he had a serviceable crutch.

Ullu had been impressed with his workmanship. "You sure you not have Hork blood in you?"

His pride, what of it he had left, wouldn't let him ride into the village on the travois. He wanted to at least show he was trying to be a visitor, not a burden. Ullu insisted he was being a stupid Elf, but he knew first impressions were important. He didn't want her fellow villagers to watch her drag him into town like a prize kill.

He didn't take into account just how weakened he was. After a dozen or so steps, sweat poured off him and his leg burned like it was on fire. He told hims he'd felt worse and marched with a full kit of combat gear when in the Army. Never mind that he hadn't had an injured leg. Never mind that he'd been twenty years younger then.

"Stupid Elf. Stop being a hero. Get back on travois. Ullu only woman here to impress. Ullu not impressed."

So despite his best efforts to the contrary, Giele wound up being towed into the village. Horks looked up from their work as Ullu rode in. Children cheered as they saw that she'd captured an Elf, and soon it seemed the entire village had turned out to witness the spectacle of his arrival.

A constant jabber of Horkish language assailed his ears, mixed in with plenty of *Faw*s and laughter. The tame foxes rushed over to sniff at him in curiosity before jumping back out of reach. Some of the braver children reached out to touch him before their mothers and fathers grabbed them away with words of anger and caution. The children wore very little beyond loincloths and their manes stuck out in all directions. A few had short hair and Giele learned later that the worst misbehavior warranted a haircut—the direst of punishments for children. The adults wore leather or woven tunics of a variety of colors and cuts. Most had spiral tattoos and designs upon their clothes and skin. Males wore their hair in matted dreadlocks with brightly-colored feathers and other geegaws stuck in them. Females brushed and teased their manes up and out until they resembled fountains sprouting from their heads. Ullu's own look was quite tame and utilitarian compared to that of her neighbors. The air was heady with their natural musky scent, but Giele didn't find it to be unpleasant. He imagined it might be different were they crammed inside a building.

Ullu stopped her Greatdeer in front of the largest tent. A cluster of elder men and women gathered before it, with graying hair and skin wrinkled just like Ullu's. They looked unhappy about Giele's presence. One of them, a crabby old man who leaned on a staff painted bright red and decorated with ribbons and feathers, stepped forward and proceeded to berate Ullu, pointing at Giele, at the hills, at the river, and at the sky. He must have been blaming every single bad thing that could ever happen on the Elf's presence. Giele didn't for a minute think it was because of the mark on his face, but because he was an Elf. The realization made him feel more at ease. If they were intolerant because they knew nothing about him, he could repair that given time.

Ullu touched her deer on the side of its head. As it bent forward, she grabbed hold of its magnificent antlers and swung down to the ground. She spoke in rapid-fire Horkish to the group, who seemed alarmed and all talked at once, gesticulating like the man with the staff. Giele guessed they were the village elders from their cliquish behavior and automatic distrust of anything new and different. He wondered why Ullu didn't fall in line with them, but then decided that Ullu must follow her own path and didn't care much what anyone else thought. The one with the staff must have been a chieftain. He thumped the staff on the ground and the villagers fell silent.

Giele struggled to his feet with the help of his crutch and stood at attention. He wanted to give this man the respect he deserved by not lying helpless on the travois while he spoke.

As he spoke—some long-winded proclamation in Horkish—Giele recognized the smooth tones of a career politician. When finished, he thumped his staff on the ground twice more. Most of the villagers returned to their fields and tents and shot occasional curious glances at Giele. The children, with no other responsibilities, stood around and gaped up at him. Most of them weren't more than knee-high.

One brave little charmer in particular popped his thumb out of his mouth and tugged on the hem of Giele's trousers. He knelt down to regard the child. The boy said something to him, but the only word Giele understood was *Faw*. He looked at Ullu, helpless.

Ullu snorted in amusement. "He say he want to be as tall as you someday."

Giele smiled at the boy. "Tell him to eat all his meals and work hard."

Ullu smiled at that too and relayed some version of what he'd said to the boy. His eyes grew wide and his thumb went straight back into his mouth. The others exclaimed and poked each other with excitement.

"The chieftain want to speak to you," said Ullu. "Ullu will tell you what he says."

She paused and listened to the man with the staff. His face was impassive and his voice rose up and down the scale. Now that his initial shock at Giele's appearance had worn off, the chieftain spoke in lengthy phrases and made grand, sweeping gestures, full of his own importance. "He say you welcome to stay here as a guest. He say we ask no payment in return. This matter of good will."

"Please thank him for his hospitality, and tell him I want to repay the kindness you and your village have showed me however I can."

Giele wanted to trust this man. Ullu had been nothing but honest from the moment she met the Elf. He didn't sense any ulterior motives in the chieftain, although to be fair, Giele's experience with Horks was limited.

"He's not going to have me killed in my sleep, is he?" Giele asked Ullu, careful to keep a smile frozen on his face in case the chieftain was looking for a reason to do him harm.

Ullu snorted. "Chieftain Leyolo like his own sleep too much to bother yours. If anyone going to kill you in sleep, it will be Ullu. Your nose all wrong shape, stupid Elf. Make you snore. Keep Ullu awake at night."

She turned back to speak to Leyolo and the other elders. Whatever she said must have settled any of their doubts, for Leyolo flashed a gap-toothed smile at Giele and clasped his hand. The elders took their cue from him and like the children before them, acted very impressed and excited about Giele. Then the chieftain nodded to Giele and the elders bowed. Giele returned the bow as best as he could with his bad leg.

"You stay with Ullu," said Ullu. "Use magic to fix leg good as new."

She led him across the village toward her tent, pausing often to let him rest and catch his breath. At one stop, she went over, spoke to a woman working in her garden, and then returned with a handful of bright red fruits. "Good magic. You eat these this afternoon."

It occurred to Giele that Ullu explained everything in terms of magic. He wondered if that was common to Hork culture in general or if it was a peculiar quirk of hers. "You know a lot about magic. What is your role here in the village?"

Ullu swelled with some pride. "Ullu is witch doctor. Use plants, animals, even rocks. Mix with magic. Fix hurts. Fix sickness."

They stopped outside a tent. A young Hork male stood in front of the door flap. His arms were crossed, his stance was wide, and upon seeing Giele his face twisted into a scowl of dismay. His short dreadlocks had curly pinfeathers woven throughout and his cheek boasted a tiny spiral tattoo in the same place where Giele had his brand.

"This Ullu's tent, and this Ullu's grandson Wioo." She looked back at Giele over her shoulder. "He not like you."

Wioo spoke in anger to his grandmother. He had her eyes and jawline, but his was firm with youth and grim determination. His dusky skin shone in the sun, highlighting his wiry muscles.

Ullu said one short sentence to him in reply. His expression darkened and Giele thought for a moment he might attack one of them. Then Wioo whirled on his heel and stalked off toward the river, as if he intended to wash himself clean of the taint from Elven contact.

"Why is he so angry?" asked Giele.

"Wioo hate Elves. Think you spread across world like weeds. Think you look at Horks and see only animals, not people."

"I don't think that. I heard stories when I first came here, but I can see they were either exaggerations or just plain wrong."

"See? Elves lie about Horks. Power in lies like power in truth."

"Maybe I can spread the truth about you."

Ullu shrugged. "You not spread anything if you not eat. Good magic." She held up the red fruits. "Sit. Eat. Rest in sun. Ullu must mix potions."

He sat on the woven rug outside her tent. Most of the village children gathered around him and crowded as close as they dared, watching him and whispering at everything he did. He was very careful to make no threatening moves because even while they worked, the adults watched him.

Giele sniffed at one of the fruits. It had a sharp, bitter odor and he expected it would taste bad. The young Hork who'd tugged on him earlier sat right next to Giele as if he wanted to mirror his every move. Giele offered him one of the small fruits. He took it and bit into it without hesitation. Juice and seeds ran down his chin as he chewed the pulp and smiled at the Elf. Giele shrugged and bit into his own.

Flavor exploded in his mouth. It wasn't a sweet fruit, but savory. The shiny soft skin hid rich, juicy pulp and seeds within. The taste was acidic and salty, but satisfying. Like the child beside him, the juice ran down Giele's chin and the kids all laughed as he wiped it away. He was no chef, but he could imagine a variety of ways to enjoy this vegetable—he could no longer call it a fruit. "Delicious," he said.

"Chamo," said one of the children. Others took up the chant.

"Chamo?" Giele pointed at the vegetable. The children all shouted affirmations. He felt pleased; he'd learned another Hork word besides *Faw*.

That gave him an idea. He pointed to himself and said his name slowly. "Gee . . . eh . . . lee," the children repeated it, and pointed at themselves. "No . . ." He pointed at the chamo. "Chamo." Then he pointed at himself. "Giele."

They understood. He spent the rest of the afternoon learning names. Horks didn't use hard sounds in their names. They reserved the consonants for objects. He wondered what that meant; there was so much to learn about them. He wished he hadn't lost all of his equipment when Rarik's men jumped him.

That gave him another idea. "Ullu?" He poked his head behind the flap, but his request died on his lips at the wondrous scene inside the tent.

CHAPTER SEVENTEEN

Ullu's tent was full of bowls, pouches, and bulbs containing all manner of herbs, minerals, potions, and mixtures. Carefully-made wooden shelves sat on the floor, each one crammed to bursting with ingredients. Bone hooks stuck out of the tent walls and poles, each one bearing a dried plant or dead animal or pouch of some mysterious substance.

Ullu sat in the middle of the tent and performed her magic.

Giele had thought her magic would be mixing of herbs and such in bowls, but she wasn't using mortar and pestle or spoon. She was using real magic.

Seeds and powders swirled through the air around the old woman in an aerial ballet. As he watched in stunned silence, a flask of golden liquid rose from one of the shelves. The flask flew by itself to a large mixing bowl at her feet and emptied itself. Ullu muttered, and several bowls joined the dance. She gestured, like a conductor in front of a symphony, and the ingredients dumped into the bowl in measured sequences. She took a wooden token with a complex symbol inscribed upon it that hung from a loop of leather. Dangling the token by its loop, she touched it into the bowl. With a flash of heat, a swirling mass rose from the bowl to hover before her. It glowed as it coalesced into a pellet similar to the one she'd given him the previous day. She plucked the spinning, steaming pellet out of the air with a pair of tongs and dropped it into a wooden bowl where it joined others like it.

"God's Blood," whispered Giele in awe.

Ullu turned her head. "*Faw.* You not seen magic before?"

"Of course I have. It was just impressive. It's different from Elven magic." He struggled to remember what he knew about the nature of magic like what Piprel used, but had to admit defeat. "Elven mages study for years to become skilled at the art."

"Ullu do magic for years too. Ullu have good blood. Best magic come from good blood. Good Hork blood. Ullu not know if Elf blood any good for magic."

Giele shut his mouth with a snap. He'd still been considering the Horks a simple people, and assumed their magic wouldn't be well-developed. They were challenging his preconceived notions, and he resolved to stop thinking of them as primitives and give them their due.

She snorted. "What you want, Elf? Ullu busy."

"Do you have any paper and ink?"

"Ullu not have paper."

"Skins, then. Parchment. Big leaves. Anything I can write upon."

"Ullu have many inks. You make a map now?"

"No, but I want to take some notes."

"Ullu not have notes either."

"No, I want to . . . never mind. May I use some ink and something I can draw patterns upon?"

Ullu stepped out of her conjuring area and pulled some dried skins from a shelf. She handed them to him along with a small wooden bottle with a cork stopper and a large feather quill. "You not making skin pictures?"

"No, no tattoos."

"Ullu make those. Show you sometime. Give you matching moon for other cheek if you want."

All Giele's words went away at that. He stammered his thanks and backed out of the tent.

He spent the rest of the afternoon developing a lexicon of Horkish words. The children were very curious about what he was doing, and crowded in to watch him. Some of the older ones got the idea when he pointed to chamos and said "chamo" and then pointed to other things and tried to get them to name them. The kids ran all over the village, bringing him things and telling him their names.

At times as he worked, he'd see Wioo pacing in the distance, glaring in his direction. He seemed to be the only one in the village with real antipathy toward Giele. The other adults had more or less accepted the Elf's presence and taught him more of the Horkish language.

By the time evening rolled around, he had established many names for the village residents and its objects. Between that and his other notes, he'd returned to Ullu's tent three times for more ink and skins. "Stupid Elf going to use all Ullu's supplies," she grumbled. He decided to be a little more circumspect in his notes, and began to think of how he might work out a trade.

The Hork families each prepared their own meals, but the village had communal dining. Each family brought their meal to the riverside like a picnic. They spread out woven blankets, sat upon them, and dined on stews, fresh bread, and roasted meats. Adults wandered from blanket to blanket to share stories or discuss whatever was on their minds. Many of them stopped by Ullu's blanket to speak with her and to stare unabashed at the Elf. Wioo didn't join them; he sat with another family some distance away and wouldn't look at Giele.

Giele dipped bread into the thick stew Ullu had prepared. It brimmed with garden vegetables and hacha meat, and it was delicious. Even after just a few hours in this village, it felt to him like a place he could spend a great many days, like a home ought to feel. Perhaps if he never found peace among his own kind, he might find it among the Horks. Sooner or later, someone would have to learn about them and share that knowledge with the colonists. He could be that person, since he already had a good start with his spontaneous dictionary.

He resolved to learn and document everything about the Horkish people, language, and culture.

Seeing a venomous expression from Wioo, Giele also resolved to convince the young Hork not all Elves were bad people. Maybe he could somehow heal the rift of bad blood, but that would be a project for a later time. Giele had plenty of other questions to ask and a willing conversationalist in Ullu.

"Ullu, tell me about the spirals. Why are they so important to Horks?"

"*Faw.* Better to ask why they not so important to Elves. You not have sacred symbols?"

"Well, of course we do. The Holy Circle. It's the full moon, with its pure light. It represents God."

"What is God?"

Giele could have clapped his hand to his head in dismay. She wanted to discuss theology? He wished Tarvy was around with his cheerful smile and willing answers, but since the Padre was many miles away, Giele knew it was up to him to provide. "God is the spirit which some Elves believe is the creator of the Universe."

Ullu squinted at him. "*Faw.* You say some Elves, but not you?"

He shrugged. "Not particularly. I've seen far too much evil in my lifetime to believe there is a benevolent spirit guiding us somewhere. I was a soldier for twenty years. I lost too many friends on the battlefield for me to believe in God. In my experience, prayer doesn't work."

"But if it give Elves hope, what harm in it?"

"There isn't any harm in it, I guess."

"Why Elves use circle for God?"

"We always have. Elves have a close kinship with the moon. We believe it symbolizes that which is good in the world, and when the moon is full, evil things are kept at bay and good is at its strongest."

"*Faw.* moon only full one night out of twenty-eight. One night of good against twenty-seven nights of not good. Stupid Elves. You all hide under blankets in fear but for one night a month?" Ullu snorted in amusement. When she put it in that perspective, Giele had to admit it did sound a little ridiculous.

He sipped some water from a bowl. How had this turned into a discussion about Elven theology? "In our scriptures—that is to say, holy texts—it is written that God promises always to return once a month, to come full circle and bring forth the cleansing light of the full moon." He struggled to remember his early childhood catechisms. "Hence we use the Holy Circle to recall God's promise to us, and to provide us with an image of the moon when it is not full."

Ullu picked at her teeth with a bone needle. "You have crescent moon on your face. Ullu guess it symbol of evil?"

He bowed his head. "Yes. My King marked me and branded me an outcast. And now, few Elves look at me with anything except loathing."

"*Faw.* Stupid Elves. Horks not judge you because of ugly mark. Or ugly face. And you have very ugly face. Horks judge you by how you act. By your spiral."

Giele nodded toward Wioo. "He's judging me because I'm an Elf."

"Wioo young and foolish. Take after his father."

"Your daughter's husband?"

"No. Ullu's son. He was foolish too. Thought Elves were intruders here. Which you are. But that not Ullu's point." She leveled a serious, steady gaze at Giele. "He made Elves angry, made mischief. One day, he come back to village covered with blood. Not his. He say he kill an Elf who tried to hurt him two seasons ago. Next time he leave, he not return. Ullu find remains after a week." She shook her head. "Wioo blame Elves for death of his father, even though his father bring it upon himself. Bad for his spiral."

Giele wondered if Ullu's son was the one who had slain Cianid's husband. The tribe was too close to Goose Creek to be just a coincidence.

Ullu made no move to pack up the food yet. Instead, she tossed some scraps to a couple fox kittens playing rough-and-tumble along the riverbank.

"Tell me more about the spiral. What does it mean to Horks?" The sun dropped below the horizon and he saw the evening star over the distant mountains. He took refuge in its constancy in the upheaval of recent weeks. As long as he could look to the sky, he knew some things would never change.

"Every life start from a point." Ullu drew with her bone needle in the sand. "Every being grows, learns, lives." She started tracing a spiral. "Life not follow circle. It has beginning and end. Beginning not important—it just starting point. End not important either—all things end." She looked at Giele with intensity and tapped the needle against the sand. "This line what is important. What you do with your life. Good things make spiral longer, larger. Always growing."

Giele realized she had just told him something vital to the basic philosophy of the Hork people. "So Horks do good things because it adds more turns, more layers to the spirals of their lives?"

"*Faw.* You not as stupid as you look."

He chuckled. "Is that why you chose to help me? To add to your spiral?"

"Ullu has plenty long spiral. Yours could be longer. Ullu give you chance to make it better."

His head whirled as he tried to wrap his mind around this concept. She hadn't rescued him out of altruism, or even out of some need to tilt her soul further into the balance of good—which is what a loyal follower of the Church of Aelfland would have done. Padres reminded parishioners to *do good deeds and God shall richly reward you in the afterlife*. No, Ullu had rescued him because his life was lacking. She gave him the chance to do something valuable with his life, to *add to his spiral*, as she put it.

What he did with that chance didn't matter so much to her, for the choices he'd make would be his and his alone. It wasn't Ullu Giele needed to avoid disappointing.

It was himself.

CHAPTER EIGHTEEN

A week passed.

Ullu's magic was doing its job. Giele's ribs were sore, but no longer sandpapered together when he moved the wrong way. His leg grew stronger until he could limp from one end of the village to the other with the help of his crutch. After a foray like that, though, he needed to rest for a good long while. He used the down time to learn more about the Horks. He must have filled every dried skin in the village with his notes, and Ullu had to replenish her supply of ink several times. He apologized in the face of her complaints, but knew she was impressed with his dedication to his new-found avocation.

The children never grew tired of him. Everywhere he traveled in the village, he had an audience. He learned to speak some Horkish with the vocabulary and inflection of a toddler, and a few of the children picked up some bits and pieces of the Elven tongue from listening to him and Ullu. Between repetition, a lot of jabbering, and judicious gesturing, they all managed to make themselves more or less understood to each other.

Giele began to think about the future. He wouldn't be fully healed for another month or so, but as soon as he was fit enough, he needed to return to the railroad and speak to Blackpool. He'd done his best to honor his contract by recreating a map of his journey to the Horkish village. He hoped the stacks of information he'd gathered on the Horks would be just as valuable. Perhaps the knowledge of the natives would be even more valuable than simple maps. The Horks themselves might find better routes for the railroad, which would give them opportunities for trade and yet leave their lives undisturbed. As much as he enjoyed seeing the progress of civilization, he didn't see how a rail depot would improve this village at all.

Giele was happy among the Horks, but as the days passed, he began to miss his own kind. Tarvy would be glad to see him, and would be fascinated with the Horkish philosophy—Giele hesitated to call it a religion, for despite what he'd heard, he saw no evidence that they believed in any kind of supreme beings. He even missed Piprel's drunken foolishness and simple wishes. He wondered if the mage was conquering his own demons as Giele was defeating his. He hoped so, and felt the compulsion of duty to check on Piprel. Giele also found his thoughts turning to Cianid, the owner of the general store. He wondered if she'd managed to stay out of Rarik's clutches. Her strength of will wouldn't be broken, and he recalled that she'd dealt with Giele on the level despite his brand.

Such introspection was healthy for him, but might at some point take him back to the dark place where his anger at Terika and hatred for the King resided. To follow that path would lead to further ruin. Instead of self-examination, he threw himself back into the daily routine of the villagers with renewed vigor, and continued to learn all he could.

When they hunted large game, Horks used spears with forged iron tips. They flung them with the aid of slotted wooden spear-throwers which gave them impressive range and force. Giele understood in theory how they worked, but when he tried to use one, the spear kept falling out of the thrower to the great amusement of his young gallery. For small game, Horks specialized in the sling to hurl either small stones or iron bullets. If Giele was hopeless when it came to spear-throwers, he was awful with a sling.

His retinue of children had taken him to the edge of the village where they'd set up targets of bundled grass. They were taking turns flinging stones at them from their leather slings. He'd watched them do this every day and was amazed at the skill shown even by the youngest of them. With cheerful babbles, they pushed a sling into his hand and encouraged him to take a turn. He was game to try anything, but he'd never used a sling before. He quickly discovered it was far more difficult than it appeared. On his first attempt, the stone simply fell out of the pocket, much to the amusement of his young friends. With the second try, he sent the stone careening off into the river, well away from the targets. He felt eyes upon him and turned to see Wioo glaring at him from afar. When the young Hork saw Giele turn, he spat on the ground in derision and stalked away. Giele frowned; the young man's hatred was the one dark spot in the otherwise happy life he'd found among the natives. He tried the sling once more, trying to make heads or tails of the rapid instructions and suggestions the children hurled at him.

His third stone plopped to the ground beside his feet, and he joined the children in their laughter. One of them, an eight-year-old named Aral, took her turn and hit five targets in a row before missing one. She had humbled Giele, but he knew a bow and arrow could salve his dignity.

He decided he needed a break from his scholarly aspirations. He desired to work with his hands, to feel wood and bowstring beneath them. Horks did not use bows, and as near as he could tell had never learned the art. Perhaps it would be something to teach them as repayment for their kindness. Giele had been like a child to them—consuming much and giving back little in return.

The following morning, he limped away from the village toward a small grove of trees by the riverside. Aral and some of her playmates ran over to join him. "What you do?" she asked.

Giele pointed. "I'm going to those trees to look for special wood."

Aral and the others scampered ahead of him. They kept hurrying back to check on his progress, bringing him random pieces of wood and asking, "Like this? Like this?"

It took him an hour to reach the grove. Uninjured, it would have taken but ten minutes. The children were already there, laughing and running circles around him. He felt old and sore, with his heart pounding and his lungs burning from the exertion. Nevertheless, he began to scour the grove for suitable wood to build both bow and arrows. Having the children around helped in ways he wouldn't have imagined as a soldier. Once they saw what kind of wood he sought, they ran back and forth through the grove and collected slender, straight branches that he could form into arrows. While they did that, he tested other bits of wood for springiness and workability.

Soon he had a half dozen pieces he thought would make serviceable bows, and enough for a passel of arrows. He wrapped a length of cloth around the wood to bundle it and began his long trek back to the village.

On the way back, Wioo and a few other hunters rode past Giele's party on Greatdeer. Giele stepped aside to let them pass. The others continued on, but Wioo hesitated long enough to spit two words at him: "*Kaa sree.*"

Giele recognized *sree* as the word for *line*, but the other eluded him. Whatever it meant made the children gasp in surprise. Several of them shouted angry words after Wioo as he rode away. Giele tried to get an explanation from the children, but most of them shook their heads. One of them—a round-faced ten-year-old named Yerri whose hair was always short from regular misbehavior—took a stick and drew in the dust.

First, he drew a spiral. "Spiral," he said as if explaining to a child much younger than he. Then he drew a straight line and said "*Kaa*." Ashamed, he wiped out the straight line with his foot.

"Kaa," Giele repeated, causing the anxious children to murmur amongst themselves. He looked from the spiral to where Yerri had erased the straight line, and realized what Wioo had called him.

Giele was a straight line in Wioo's eyes; someone who had done nothing with his life.

The Elf's pointed ears burned. It hurt to be labeled as an evil wrongdoer. Giele shook his head in disappointment; it was bad enough to be at a disadvantage with his own people. When all the Horks except Wioo had accepted him without question—indeed, without the slightest bit of acrimony—this young Hork's hate made him feel confused and even angry. Giele clenched his teeth as he resolved to give Wioo a reason to think better of him. What would Wioo have to say after Giele crafted some bows for the village?

All the way back to Ullu's tent, Giele tried to quell a seething knot of anger in his belly. The children were much more subdued on the return journey. Aral slipped her tiny hand into Giele's as if lending him her strength. As they reached the edge of the village, the children grew more excitable again. With pride, they held up the wood they'd gathered and chattered to the adults as they passed by.

Giele sat on the rug outside Ullu's tent and laid out the wood to dry in the sun. Aral squatted next to him to watch him work. "Aral help," she announced. He smiled at her. Other children crowded in and she yelled at them until they backed away. Despite being so young, she was the ringleader of the village kids, even bossing around those older than her.

First things first, Giele decided. He carved a small piece of wood into the shape of a broadhead tip, making it as sharp as possible. He handed it to Yerri. "Take this to the smith. Ask him to make me some of these from iron."

Yerri swelled with pride from being given such an important task. He stuck his tongue out at Aral and scampered off toward the low stone building. To any smith, such a chore should be quite simple and take nothing more than an hour or two.

"What you make?" asked Aral.

"Bow and arrows."

"Bow and arrows," she repeated, and told that to everyone who stopped by to see what Giele was doing. "Giele make bow and arrows. He make bow. He make arrows. Make for Aral." The villagers must have been surprised to see him doing something productive instead of resting or writing and their conversations rose and fell so quickly Giele couldn't keep track of the words.

Aral and the other children watched as Giele toiled away with a knife until a rough bow sat in his hands. Then he filled a cloth with sand and worked to smooth out the grain of the wood.

Even Ullu stopped her magic medicine making to check on Giele's progress and utter a typical "*Faw.*"

Her interest amused him, and he held up the bow for her inspection. "What do you think?"

"Pretty stick. Good to see you do something important with your time instead of laying about like lump."

Her disdain was mostly for show as she examined the lines of the unstrung bow and tested the smoothness of the grain. She had to have seen bows before.

After the midday meal, he worked as much tallow into the bow as it would take, and then coated the entire curvature with light resin. He heard a muttered comment and some derisive laughter. Giele looked up to see Wioo and a few other boys his age watching from several yards away, and smiled at them. Wioo spun on his heel and stalked away. The others shrugged and ambled after him.

"Funny looking stick." Yerri scratched his short hair. "What it good for?"

"Not stick. *Bow*." Aral shoved the older boy.

"I'll show you in an hour or two when the smith finishes those tips." Giele tested the flex of the bow and was pleased that it bent with very little creaking. The Verigan wood had soaked up the tallow like a sponge and dried in minutes so it required only a little resin to seal it. He set it aside and turned his attention to the string. *Faw*s echoed among the onlookers. He raised the bow and drew the string to his cheek. His arm muscles trembled at the slow draw, but if the bow were going to fail, it would do so here. Instead of allowing the string to snap back, he let it straighten at the same rate he'd drawn it. Then he repeated the slow pull a couple more times. Satisfied the wood wasn't going to snap, he drew once more, and this time he released the string. The bow twanged and the familiar shock traveled up his arm like an old friend.

The bow had less pull than he was used to, but he had never built many of his own bows, and felt satisfied with his first effort in many years.

"What you make bow for?" asked Ullu.

"I thought perhaps I'd teach anyone here in the village who wanted to learn the fine art of archery."

She canted her head to one side. "He not going to like that."

Giele followed her gaze and once again saw Wioo glaring. "You never know. I think he's pretty interested in it. He's been watching me work on it all day."

"Wioo afraid you replace him as hunter."

Giele snorted. "That's ridiculous. I'm a guest here. I have no intention of taking anybody's job."

"Tell him that."

Giele shrugged. "Wioo," he called.

The young Hork turned away and vanished into a tent. Giele shook his head and returned to his work.

An hour later, he'd fletched ten arrows. With Ullu's help in translation, Giele asked two villagers to prepare him a sturdier target at which to shoot. His arrows would go right through the ones they used for sling practice. The villagers bound a tight bundle of weeds with threads and then pounded a pole through it into the ground. They tied a ratty old Greatdeer hide around it with pockmarked silhouettes of ground squirrels, pheasants, and rabbits upon it.

Giele stood thirty yards back from the target— distant enough that he could block out the target silhouettes with a thumb at arm's length, but close enough to be within his comfort zone. Not all archers were snipers, and he never achieved that level of skill, but even a first-year Leaf Archer could hit targets that size at that range.

He nocked the first arrow to the string and looked toward the distant target ninety feet away. He raised the bow and drew the string to his cheek even as he drew in a breath. Over thirty years, he must have repeated that same motion well over a half million times, ever since that first day his father took him out into the forest with a green stripling bow at the tender age of six. He'd had young Giele practice drawing and releasing it for two hours until the boy cried from the pain in his shoulders and the inside of his forearm was raw and blistered from the bowstring snapping across it. Then his father brought him back to their modest house where he helped Giele's mother mix up a salve for his arm, rubbed Giele's shoulders, and gave him a cookie. Giele remembered that day how proud his father was of him, the way his eyes had shone every time Giele pulled on his bowstring. Both his parents were long gone, dead from a plague that raced through Morningstar City more than a decade ago while Giele was off battling the Jigans.

As he drew the bow again, he could almost hear his father's voice, coaching him on the correct pull. His lessons had put Giele in good stead when he'd joined the Army. All these years later, Giele's muscles still remembered his first lessons. He gauged the distance with long-practiced eyes. He felt the kiss of a breeze on his cheek and adjusted his aim to compensate. The target seemed to pop out at him; how could he miss it? All this occurred in but a second or two. With a gentleness reserved for delicate work, or for a woman, he released the arrow.

The officer in Giele winced at the arrow's awkward flight. His fletching could have been tighter; the tail of the arrow wavered from side to side like a fish. The Horks wouldn't have noticed but to him it smacked of failure. A great shout rose up from the villagers as the arrow struck into the pheasant silhouette. Giele clenched his teeth in disgust. He'd been aiming for the squirrel.

Nevertheless, he adjusted for the bow's slight off-kilter release and the errors in his fletching. The next three arrows went where he'd aimed them, to greater cheers. The children shouted with glee and begged their parents for bows of their own. Aral told everyone who would listen that Giele would make the next one just for her.

He'd give them a bit of a show.

His fourth shot stuck into the post bracing the target. Even Ullu was impressed with that one, uttering a *Faw* of her own. For his fifth shot, he angled the bow upward and sent an arrow whistling all the way across the river to plunk into the far bank some hundred yards away. With a true Elven longbow built by a professional bowyer, he could have doubled that range.

He turned to the villagers. "I will teach any of you who wish to learn to make and use your own bows."

Ullu translated for him and many of the villagers and all of the children raised their hands in excitement. At last, Giele had something to repay their kindness.

Movement across the river caught his attention. He squinted into the distance.

Wioo stood there, his head lowered and his fists clenched. Giele knew that look on his face. He'd seen it before on a Leaf Archer recruit during basic training, right before he attacked a drill officer. That officer had the misfortune to die on the practice field from his wounds, and the recruit swung from the gallows pole for his attack.

Giele hoped neither he nor Wioo would suffer a similar fate.

CHAPTER NINETEEN

A week later, Wioo marched over to where Giele was coaching a group in the art of fletching. He pushed his way past the circle of students and hurled a carved antler at Giele's feet. The Horks muttered in fear and surprise as the Elf picked up the antler to examine it. It was painted red with a fine spiral of notches around it. Each notch was filled in with black ink and surrounded by white symbols. Those closest to the base of the antler were chipped and cracked, as if they were very old. Turning it around in his hands revealed no answers, except that the ink in the last notch was fresh and smeared a little on his fingertip. None of the Horks would meet his gaze or explain this unusual occurrence. Giele looked to Wioo, who stood in defiance with his hands on his hips. The muscles in his jaw stood out in sharp relief from clenching his teeth and he glared at Giele with the cold eyes of a killer. For a moment, Giele thought Wioo was going to kill him when he had nothing in hand but an arrow shaft without a point. The Hork made no further aggressive moves and instead faced Giele as if daring him to make the first move in sullen silence.

"We'll finish the lesson tomorrow," said Giele to the would-be fletchers. He needed answers, and from the looks on their faces, he wouldn't get them from his students. Fed up with Wioo's misplaced anger, Giele strode over to Ullu's tent. She sat outside on a woven mat, mixing up more of her potions with a traditional

IAN THOMAS HEALY

mortar and pestle instead of her magic. Giele thrust the antler at her, waving it under her nose.

"Ullu, what in God's Blood is this?"

A muscle twitched in her cheek and her eyes flashed. She whistled low in surprise. "Ullu not see that since she was a fawn."

He was in no mood for her backward speech. "Breath and Bones, Ullu, what is it for? The villagers are acting like I just grew a third arm from my nose."

"You challenged to duel."

His eyes popped out of his head. A duel?

She held out her hand, and he gave her the antler. She frowned as she studied the markings. Then a muscle fluttered in her cheek. "Wioo." It wasn't a question; she knew the answer before she spoke.

"Yes, he threw it at me just now."

She leaped to her feet with a spryness Giele didn't expect to see. "Wioo!" Ullu's voice rang out over the surprised mutterings of the villagers.

He stalked over to stand before his grandmother the same way he'd faced down Giele moments ago. She shouted at him in fast-paced Horkish. Giele tried to follow along but she was steaming mad and her words blurred together.

He responded with quiet confidence.

Ullu turned back to the Elf. "He issue challenge to you. It within his right to do so."

"He wants to fight me?"

"No," said Wioo. Giele hadn't realized he spoke any Elvish at all. His face twisted as he spoke, as though he found the taste of the Elven language on his tongue obscene. "Test skills. With weapons." He raised his spear to emphasize his point.

"Why?" asked a flabbergasted Giele.

"I win, you leave. You win, you stay and I leave."

A weight settled over Giele's heart. He knew sooner or later he would have to leave the village anyway and return to the railroad, but he'd hoped it would be under his own terms. In the few short weeks he'd stayed among these people, he felt as if he'd found a home among them.

He wasn't prepared to be exiled for a second time.

Giele had also hoped to somehow bridge the rift between him and Wioo. He saw some of his own fiery youth in the Hork hunter. If Giele could just reach him, the two might become friends, although the youthful Hork seemed determined to knock down any such overtures.

"Wioo, if you want me to leave the village, I will. There is no need for this challenge. I am a reasonable man."

"Challenge cannot be withdrawn," said Ullu. "If Wioo back down, he must leave forever, become Seeker. His spiral must start anew. This ancient law."

Giele wanted no part of this. Wioo had taken it too far. "What if I refuse to participate and just leave?"

Ullu's wrinkled face betrayed no emotions. "Then Wioo issued flawed challenge, and must also leave."

"What? This is ridiculous." Giele took Ullu's hands in his own and gave her a desperate, pleading look. "I don't want to be the cause of all this trouble. I've enough trouble with my own people. You welcomed me here and I'm grateful for that. I want to repay you, not be a burden."

Ullu pulled her hands away. "Law is clear. You accept challenge or Wioo leave village forever." Her face was resolute, and Giele saw his future written across it.

He turned to Wioo, who watched with a smoldering gaze. Giele didn't want this at all, but the choice had already been made. "Very well."

Ullu nodded and stepped away. She held up the antler to display it to the villagers. "Challenge accepted."

A gasp went up from the onlookers, followed by a great swell of conversation. Wioo's hunter friends surrounded him like dogs *Faw*ning around an alpha male. They escorted him away. He marched, his shoulders squared back and head held high with pride.

Ullu seemed to fold in upon herself, looking every minute of her advanced age. She hobbled into her tent.

Giele followed her and watched as she threw the challenge wand into the fire. The ancient dry antler blackened as the ink upon it burned away. Her little fire wouldn't be hot enough to destroy it, but she made no move to retrieve it. She sniffled a little. The tiny sound, magnified by her large Horkish nose, made Giele's heart catch in his throat. He felt terrible about the way things were turning out. "I'm so sorry, Ullu. I never wanted this to happen."

She took a clay pot from a shelf, filled it with water from a large basin, and set it on an iron stand in her fire, oblivious to the antler sticking up at an odd angle. "Ullu make tea. You want?"

"He hates me because I'm an Elf and Elves killed his father. Surely he knows all Elves aren't like that."

"Wioo young, full of fire. He like iron fresh from forge. Need to be tempered." She dropped some leaves into the clay pot and a heady, refreshing smell filled the tent.

"He reminds me of myself when I was younger."

Ullu sighed. "Ullu only hope he grow up to be like you then." She turned to him. "You good person. Ullu not want you to leave." She poured tea into a clay mug and pressed it into his hands.

"I don't want to leave either."

"Ullu not want Wioo to leave."

"Then why have this ridiculous challenge at all?"

"The law is the law."

"God's Blood, why do you have to be so inflexible?"

Ullu snorted. "Ullu not know that word." She poked a sharp finger into his side. "Ullu spend too much time fixing you to let you walk away. She smart. She think of something."

"So what does this challenge entail then?"

Ullu sat down with her own cup of tea. "Three parts. Strength, skill, spirit. With weapons. Wioo use spear for sure. Ullu think you should use that." She nodded at the bow beside Giele. He'd forgotten he even carried it inside.

"Go on."

"Strength test to see who have longest range."

"That doesn't sound so hard."

"For skill test, your eyes covered, then you get spun around. Hit three targets."

"Oh." He'd done something like that as part of Basic Training, but it had been many years ago. "What's the test of spirit?"

Ullu sipped her tea. "You and Wioo face each other. Take turns throwing or shooting. Goal not to hit, but to make opponent move. You move, you lose."

He gaped in astonishment. He had to stand frozen in place while Wioo threw spears at him? "What's to stop him from throwing a spear through me?"

"If he hit you, it failure of his spirit, and he lose."

"Which doesn't make me any less dead." Giele had run toward enemy arrows before in the Jigan Wars, but then at least he could move to avoid being hit. He didn't know if he could stand stock still while someone who hated him flung spear after spear at him until either he flinched or took one in the gut.

"Sometimes win, sometimes lose." Ullu sounded like an old soothsayer in Morningstar City.

"Can I throw the competition? Lose on purpose?"

She shook her head no. "If you lose on purpose, Wioo sent away for flawed challenge and you sent away for not trying your best."

"What is it with you people?" Giele's ire rose and he struggled to quell it. Ullu shouldn't bear the brunt of his anger. "Are you so stubborn about this that you're determined one of us will leave the village forever?"

"Laws are laws, stupid Elf."

"They're stupid laws!" he shouted.

Ullu shut her mouth with a snap; he'd insulted her. She set her clay mug down and pushed her way out of the tent.

"Ullu," he called as he limped after her, sick at the way things were turning out. "Stop, please. I'm sorry. I need to tell you something."

"What so important you have to tell stupid Ullu?"

Her biting tone burned like the brand on his face.

"Ullu, I need to tell you why I'm here in Verigo at all. Why my face is marked. Why I was really tied onto that hill."

In spite of her anger, he saw she was curious. "It long story? Ullu could die soon."

"It will take a little while."

"Challenge begin soon. Better talk fast."

He looked toward her tent, where they might have some privacy, but she stood her ground, defiant like her grandson. He was going to have to speak out front in full view of the entire village, so he swallowed his pride. He didn't want to hide himself from these people.

"Talk." Ullu stamped her foot for emphasis.

He told her about Princess Terika, and how he'd been the unwitting stooge for her scheme to avoid an arranged marriage. He explained how the King had taken away his home and his name, how he'd made Giele an outcast with a mark of evil on his face. Then he told her how he'd protected Cianid in the general store in Goose Creek Crossing, and how that had led to Rarik and his men seeking their revenge on him.

When he finished, Ullu looked up at him. He wondered if she intended to speak to him at all. Just when he'd decided she had nothing to say, she spoke. "You want stay here in village."

"Yes. This has become a home for me. Your people have welcomed me. I'd forgotten how nice it is to be liked."

"Then win challenge."

"But don't you see?" Giele raked his hands through his hair. How could he make Ullu understand? "I don't want Wioo to have to be cast out. I know what that's like, and I wouldn't wish it upon my worst enemy." She said nothing. "I hold no ill will toward him. I wish he would give me a chance. I wish we could be friends."

"Ullu understand. Ullu not want Wioo to leave either. He last living relative."

Her words made him more miserable. "How can I take that away from you? He's so young . . . I couldn't face it if I stayed and he was forced to leave."

"It complicated. Ullu understand difficult decision for you." She turned away to head back into her tent, leaving him to his misery.

He wasn't ready to be ignored. He stalked after her and pushed through the curtain into her tent. "Decision?"

She turned to look at him. "You must decide whether you win challenge or not. What give you most peace? What expand your spiral more?"

He didn't have to think that hard. He could live with only one possible outcome, and bowed his head. "Thank you, Ullu. You have been a good friend to me."

"Ullu is still good friend to you. And you good friend to Ullu. Elves stupid, but not all Elves." She poked him in the chest with a delicate brown finger. "You not stupid, even though Ullu say so sometimes."

The village elder poked his head into the tent and burbled something.

Ullu translated for Giele. "Challenge happen tomorrow at dawn."

"I should leave tonight then."

"If you do, Wioo cast out anyway."

Giele growled in the back of his throat. One way or another, the Horks were determined to see this challenge through. All he could do was lie in the tent and wait for morning.

189

CHAPTER TWENTY

Giele was up before the dawn. When the sun first peeked over the horizon, he was sitting on the riverbank, listening to the flow of the water and trying to empty his mind of all the negative thoughts that threatened to overwhelm him. He hadn't felt this lost and miserable since wandering the streets of Morningstar City with a fresh brand upon his face. A tiny hand closed over his shoulder and he turned to see Aral smiling at him. She plopped down on the bank next to him and together they watched the sun come up. As it did, a realization dawned upon him It would be easier for him to return to his status as pariah than to know he'd foisted it upon someone else. He never had a choice; he had to lose the challenge. Giele looked with great fondness at Aral beside him. God's Blood, he'd miss these people.

Perhaps he'd be permitted to come visit.

Behind them, the village came to life and people began to bustle about, preparing for the challenge. Yerri hurried down the gentle slope toward Giele and Aral. "Elder Leyolo say it time."

Aral patted Giele's leg. "Aral believe in you, moon-face." She took his hand and pulled him after her. Somehow, her innocent optimism made him feel like perhaps things would work out in the end after all.

The villagers gathered at the center of town as Elder Leyolo made a short speech. Giele understood enough of it to get the gist. Leyolo reiterated that Wioo had issued a challenge. Two Horks bearing garlands of woven prairie grasses and tiny blue flowers approached Wioo and Giele. The Elf knelt down so they could place the garland around his neck. The young man who hung it on him was barely older than Wioo, and he brushed Giele's hand with his in a gesture of well-wishing. Giele glanced over at Ullu. She gave him the smallest nod of approval as she understood what he planned to do.

The villagers had traced a circle in the ground and gave it a wide birth.

Giele understood enough about their philosophy to know a circle represented a dead end, a life without meaning.

Ullu translated for him. "As challenged, you have right to choose who go first."

"Wioo can begin," said Giele.

Wioo had stripped down to his loincloth. Numerous tattoos decorated his skin. Beneath the patterns, his taut muscles twitched. He gripped the ground with his bare feet as he stepped without fear into the circle and fit a spear into his throwing stick. He crouched down and stared across the river as if visualizing his throw. Then he whirled around once, his dreadlocks flying like a tattered flag, and shouted as he gave a mighty heave. The spear flew out of the thrower like a bird frightened out of the underbrush.

After what seemed like an eternity, the spear plunked down some twenty yards past the far riverbank. Exclamations abounded from the villagers. Giele couldn't blame them; it had been a masterful throw, clearing well past a hundred yards. He watched as a villager on the far side of the marked the spot with a flag on a pole. If Giele had a true Elven longbow, he could have cleared that range, but with his self-built amateurish weapon, perhaps not.

First, though, he'd have to lose the challenge without making it appear like he had.

Enough of the villagers had seen him shoot the bow that they'd know if he didn't pull it to full draw. He decided to alter his launch angle and selected one of his sloppier arrows. It wasn't quite straight, and the fletching wasn't quite centered; he could feel it with his experienced fingertips. He drew back the arrow to his cheek and lowered the angle a few degrees. As it left the string, the arrow wobbled in its flight and curved upward a little to extend its angle on its own.

Giele cursed at his rotten luck as the faulty arrow wavered through the air like a flying fish to strike the ground well past Wioo's throw. Some of the villagers cheered as Giele lowered his bow in dismay, and Aral led her troop of children in a rousing chorus of applause on his behalf. The elder called the victory for the Elf without any hesitation. Giele looked over at Wioo. He stood with his hands hanging helpless at his sides, crestfallen. Their eyes met and his disappointment turned to fury as he whirled and stalked back to his cronies. Even as they patted Wioo on the back and spoke encouraging words to their buddy, Giele could tell by the conflicted, sideways glances they shot his way that their loyalties were divided. They weren't the only ones. Most of the villagers were shouting his name. It shocked him that the Horks would turn on one of their own to cheer for an outsider.

But their support made him feel worse. Aral, who'd appointed herself his second, took his bow with a triumphant grin that he couldn't return. He didn't want to win this.

He'd have to try harder to lose.

Elder Leyolo spoke at length about the test of skill. Giele didn't listen, instead watching as Horks set three clay vases atop short poles. He already knew the gist of the challenge. They had to strike each vase and break it. He felt hopeful; his arrows wouldn't have enough mass to break open the heavy pots.

Giele opted to take his turn first. Just before a villager fastened a thick, woven blindfold over his eyes, Aral pressed three arrows into one of the Elf's hands and his bow into the other. "Good luck, Moon-Face."

He clutched his weapon close to his chest as the villagers began whirling him around until he was so dizzy his ears rang. The chief elder cried "*Welah!*" and Giele knew the time had come to act.

He clamped his teeth down on the three arrow shafts and tore the blindfold from his face. His back was to the target, and he stumbled as he tried to turn around. It took him three tries to nock the first arrow to the string. The world wouldn't hold still and he swayed as he drew to full pull. The three targets had doubled and trebled before him. He picked one at random and loosed his arrow. A hissing sound told him he'd missed. He drew the next arrow and shot before he was ready. It also missed. His last arrow, by sheer dint of fortune, struck a vase and it shattered.

One out of three. Giele's old archery instructors in the Army would have been appalled. Every seventh day of training as Leaf Archers, they'd been required to get roaring drunk before afternoon shoot. If they shot less than seventy-five percent accuracy, they'd have to run laps around the field. Then they'd have to shoot again. If they failed again, it meant more laps. They all became pretty fair shots as drunks after that.

There were always a few archers in every unit who shot better while drunk. Giele never could count himself among them.

Even though his intention had been to fail this test, he was still appalled at just how bad he'd been. He half expected to hear a Bole Major bawl him out and order him to start running.

Giele staggered aside to clear the way for Wioo. He was still so dizzy he plopped down in the dust and concentrated on keeping his eyes still.

Aral bent down to check on him, peering into his face with her soft brown eyes. "You not do so good. Aral still believe in you."

Giele patted her hand and turned his attention to watching Wioo.

The young Hork held two spears in his left hand and one in his right. The blindfold went on and the villagers spun him around until the chief elder called for them to stop.

Wioo used the razor-sharp tip of one spear to push the blindfold away from his eyes. Giele couldn't have done that while sober, much less with the world spinning around him. Wioo flung his spears in quick succession, not even taking the time to breathe between each throw. One, two, three vases shattered into tiny pieces. As soon as the last spear left his grip, Wioo fell to the ground and lay there grinning as the villagers cheered his skill. It made Giele feel good that his people were applauding him.

Silently, Giele cheered for him too. Wioo had given himself a fair chance to win the challenge, impressing Giele with his talent. Elven soldiers hadn't used spears in war or training for at least a hundred years, but Giele doubted any of them had been as good as this angry young Hork.

The villagers arranged themselves into two parallel lines, forming a corridor of bodies. Wioo and Giele met at the center, where Elder Leyolo waited for them. "Final test. You, Giele, win test of strength. You, Wioo, win test of skill. Test of spirit decide winner of challenge." He thumped his staff on the ground. "Listen to spirit, follow turn of spiral."

He sent Wioo and Giele off to opposite ends of the pitch flanked by the villagers. Wioo thrust out his chest and stood tall and proud. Yerri wrapped his arms around little Aral to keep her from running out into the field of fire. Giele was sweating and nervous. Not only did this challenge determine who stayed and who would leave the village, there was a very real chance one of them could be hurt, even killed. Giele had spent thirty years learning to put an arrow into a target; trying to avoid hitting one would require him to overcome long-ingrained reflexes.

Wioo didn't look afraid at all. He stood with his chest thrust out as his friends cheered him on. He gathered up his spears and passed them to one of his comrades. Aral waved at Giele. "Aral hold your arrows, Moon-Face."

The simplest way for him to lose would have been to just put an arrow into Wioo, but he couldn't do that when his entire plan was to allow Wioo to stay. On the other hand, Wioo could kill Giele with ease where he stood, losing the challenge but vindicated in the knowledge he'd slain an Elf.

Leyolo took a straight stick that had one end painted red and the other black. He stood between Wioo and Giele, and looked once at each of them. "He who faces the red act first." He tossed the stick up into the air and backed out of the field of fire. The stick spun end over end in a blur. When it struck the ground, the red end pointed toward Wioo.

He didn't hesitate for even a second. He grabbed a spear from his comrade, balanced on the balls of his feet, and then hurled it at Giele.

The Elf froze. It passed a foot to his left. The crowd murmured.

The look of pure hatred on Wioo's face made Giele wonder if he'd in fact been aiming to kill instead, and missed. Giele's palms started sweating. He could very well die here. Would Ullu use her magic to heal him if Wioo impaled him? He hoped so.

For Giele's turn, the crowd grew silent as he nocked an arrow. He drew the bow to a third pull. He wanted the arrows to travel slow enough that Wioo would have plenty of time to look at them, as well as to do less damage should Giele strike him. He stood, impassive as a statue, as the Elf's arrow flew several inches over the top of his head.

Another cast from Wioo, and it was going to hit Giele, he knew it! Giele clenched all his muscles, bracing for the impact, willing himself to remain still. The spear shot by his head so close that he felt the wind of its passing. Exclamations ran up and down both sides of the villagers. Wioo grinned at Giele without mirth, knowing he'd almost had the Elf then. Then Giele realized Wioo intended to win the challenge within the rule of law. He wouldn't slay Giele; he'd humiliate the Elf by making him lose before the entire village.

Giele's next arrow passed near to Wioo's hip. The Hork stood frozen. Giele's blood pounded in his ears. He'd stood alongside his troops when Jigans charged, he'd faced cannon fire and ballistae bolts that would tear a man in half upon impact. None of those moments came close to his anxiety as Wioo selected his next spear, whirled around in a complete circle, and hurled it right at Giele's belly.

Giele knew Wioo had aimed it to kill, to strike him right in the gut where it would do the most damage. For a fraction of a second, he almost stood and took it, but his sense of self-preservation took hold and he jumped back as the spear passed low through the space between his legs.

A masterful throw, it would have missed even had Giele stayed still.

Giele had lost Wioo's challenge. The time had come for him to leave the Horks.

The crowd of villagers cheered, hoisting Wioo onto their shoulders. Somebody rang the village gong, the cue to start a huge celebratory feast.

Giele stood off to one side, forgotten by all except Ullu, Yerri, and Aral. The little girl looked at him and burst into tears like her heart had broken. She ran off, her face in her hands. Giele sighed. He knew he'd done the right thing, but it still hurt. He looked at Ullu and she nodded her approval.

It didn't make him feel better in the least.

Chapter Twenty-One

Giele had few possessions to collect from Ullu's tent. In his short time as a guest in the village, he'd built a bow and arrows and acquired a tall and narrow woven basket he used for a quiver. His original clothes had been beyond repair, so one of the Hork women sewed him some lightweight clothing, very cool and comfortable against the heat of the summer. Several of the children had given him trinkets—sticks they'd carved, colorful stones; valuable treasures all. It took him longer than it should have to pack. He'd pick something up and then pause while recalling who had given it to him, or how he'd acquired it. He wondered if he should be angry with Wioo for having the temerity to issue the challenge as he had, but instead Giele felt a gnawing sadness in the pit of his stomach. The bright spot was that he'd managed to keep Ullu from losing her grandson.

He wrapped those few belongings in a spare shirt, along with all his notes. With luck, he could parlay some of that information into a second chance for the railroad, assuming he didn't run afoul of Rarik again. He tied the bundle together with a spare bowstring and was about to hang it from his quiver strap when Ullu entered the tent.

"What you doing?" she asked in an accusatory tone.

"Packing." Giele stared down at his bundle without seeing it. "No reason to stick around when I'm no longer welcome." He knew he sounded bitter, but didn't care. It hurt that in one short month he'd been cast out of not just one, but two places he'd dared to call home.

"Stupid Elf." Ullu put her hands on her hips and glared at him. "Where you go? How you get there? What you even eat? You not know what plants to eat for food or medicine."

"I'm sorry. I just don't have the time to learn those things now. I'll figure it out on the way."

"*Faw*. You soft in the head." Ullu grabbed his bundle and tugged on it until he looked at her. "Lucky for you Ullu not soft-headed. You need Greatdeer."

Giele's mouth dropped open in surprise. How could he ride a Greatdeer? They weren't like Elven warhorses. Horks and Greatdeer were bonded by magic. The way he understood it, the horned beasts had a strong streak of independence, and were notorious for being ill-tempered. The Horks had found a unique solution to the problem. When a fawn was a year old, Ullu performed some magic and the yearling became bonded to an individual Hork. The Greatdeer would allow itself to be ridden and protect its rider with its life.

The drawback to this system was that unbonded people like Giele couldn't ride. At the moment, there were no unbonded animals in the village. Even if there was a fawn available, the Elf was twice the height and mass of a Hork. A fawn could no more carry him than a dog could.

"I thought all the Greatdeer were bonded. And besides, I'm too large." He frowned at her.

"Yes, exactly right." Ullu nodded and started to pack supplies into a leather satchel decorated with spiral beading. "You have to find wild one. Fully-grown. Bring it back here. Ullu bond it to you."

"I couldn't. You've already done so much for me already." He raised his hands in protest.

Ullu reached up to slap them down, having to stand on her tiptoes to do so. "Stupid Elf. You give plenty back to village. Bow and arrow. Smiles to children. Ullu know you could have won challenge. You could have stayed and made Wioo leave and you did not. Ullu grateful for that."

She saw Giele's confusion and smiled. "So Ullu talk to Leyolo. He agree to send hunter with you to bring back Greatdeer."

"A hunter?"

"Oh yes. Good hunter. Very skilled." She pushed aside the tent flap and took his hand to lead him outside.

A sullen Wioo stood before the tent. He had a bundle of spears strapped to his back, and a leather satchel like the one Ullu carried hung from his shoulder.

"What is this?" asked Giele.

Ullu nodded at Wioo. "Law clear. You leave village. Not clear when and how. Elders decide to let you leave with your own Greatdeer and full supplies. Wioo promise Ullu to help catch Greatdeer." She gave her grandson a stern look. "And to keep stupid Elf alive. He swear not to kill you in sleep."

"*Faw*," said Giele, feeling the sentiment behind the simple word for the first time.

"You speak Horkish badly. Wioo speak Elvish badly. Great fun. Ullu pleased." She beamed at them.

The village turned out to watch them leave. Wioo marched with his head held high, as if daring anyone to say something to him. As they left, Giele waved to Aral, who'd been like a lieutenant in the company of dutiful Horkish children who'd followed Giele everywhere he went during his recovery. She waved back before burying her face against her mother's chemise. Giele knew he would miss her above all the other villagers. He'd been touched by their goodwill and their acceptance. They'd made him feel good about himself for the first time since before he left Aelfland. He would always think well of them for that.

Wioo ignored Giele as they departed. Once they cleared the valley, the young Hork picked up his pace, perhaps hoping he might leave Giele behind. If the Elf's leg had still bothered him, he'd have struggled to keep up, but his longer legs were an even match for Wioo's quicker strides. The Hork must have been roped into this against his will, but Giele didn't care. This delay in his exile meant he might have a chance to somehow reverse it.

As they left the valley behind, Giele decided that his best hope of getting to return to Valley Village would be to appeal to the youth's better side. He spent a good while considering ways to do just that. He'd dealt with recalcitrant soldiers before during his time in the Army. He needed to apply some of those techniques now.

They traveled north at a brisk pace. Giele let Wioo take the lead since he seemed to prefer being in front. At least that way he didn't have to look at Giele. He wouldn't say a word, even when after several hours of walking they set up a camp and broke out some rations. They'd found neither tracks nor spoor, and Giele wondered how far away the Greatdeer herds ranged from the Horks. He didn't fancy spending weeks on the trail with the sullen youth as his companion.

Giele made a few attempts to start a stilted conversation with Wioo, but received only stony glares in reply. "Do you think we should camp here?"

Nothing.

"Which direction should we head in the morning?"

Silence.

"Suit yourself," Giele said as he laid back against his satchel. Wioo's silence had grown tiresome and the Elf was annoyed when he snapped, "This trip would be a lot more pleasant if you'd be a little civil. I'm sure Ullu would prefer it."

"You no speak her name," came his companion's growl from the darkness.

"She is my friend. If you'd settle down your hate, you might find we could be friends too." Giele glared back at Wioo with as much venom as he'd shown for weeks.

"Never be friends." He flung himself over to turn his back to Giele as the last rays of sunlight darkened into nightfall. "Wioo never friend to Elf."

Giele smiled into the darkness. Getting him to speak, even in anger, had been one small victory. It felt good to win for a change. The Elf leaned back on his sleeping roll and put his hands behind his head. "Good night, Wioo."

The young Hork spat back, "*Che ha'oka spetch.*"

Giele didn't know what it meant, but felt certain he'd just been insulted. Wioo's curses gave strange comfort to Giele, and that thought lulled him to sleep.

Despite his confidence in his own safety, it was still a pleasure for Giele to awaken the following morning without having had his throat cut during the night.

The morning was already warm, with promise of a hot dry day ahead. Despite hard, sandy soil underneath, flattened prairie grass had cushioned Giele's bedroll well enough that he felt rested and free of the customary soreness that had crept into his mornings as he aged. The air smelled wonderful, the sharp tang of grass melding with the smokiness of scrub brush and the occasional floral spike. If scent alone could be a meal, he'd be stuffed. Birds flitted through the air, diving to snatch seeds or insects. A tiny, brave ground squirrel dashed across his bedroll to vanish amid the sward.

Wioo was gone, but his satchel and bedroll had remained behind. Giele suspected he'd gone off to hunt or scout since his spears were gone as well.

Giele decided a little hunting of his own wouldn't be amiss. He gathered up his bow and quiver and found a troupe of rabbits grazing amid early morning dew.

When Wioo tramped over the crest of the hill where they'd camped, Giele had two rabbits cooking on sticks over a fire of the rich, smoke-scented wood common to the area. The young Hork had a wild pig hanging from a spear that rested on his shoulder.

"Good morning, Wioo. I see you had the same idea as me." Giele gestured at the rabbits, which smelled delicious. "One of these is for you. Why not clean that pig and set it cooking? Plenty of fire left."

Wioo hesitated, indecision plain on his face. Giele scooted over to give him more space to work beside the fire. The youth crouched down and began to clean the pig carcass with his bone knife. Soon the smell of sizzling pork competed with the roasted rabbits.

They ate the rabbits and wrapped the cooked and sliced pork in cunning nets of prairie grasses which Wioo wove together. Giele planned for them to eat the pork later for lunch and dinner. More than once, he caught Wioo forgetting to glare at him. The Hork's face showed a relaxed, neutral expression much of the time, and once in awhile he seemed to be about to smile, until he remembered he was supposed to be angry with Giele. His resolve to remain the Elf's enemy was weakening. Perhaps he had found some grudging respect for Giele at last. Or it could be that having a full belly had ameliorated his anger.

Giele broke camp with great care, utilizing all the skills and training he had from the Army to minimize any evidence they'd stayed in that spot. For his own part, Wioo took equal care in breaking his share of the campsite.

"Nice work," said Giele as he used a clump of brush to sweep away their footprints in the dirt.

Giele saw the flash of a smile, but instead of the expected glare of hatred, Wioo's face composed itself into studied neutrality.

It took Giele a moment to realize he'd slipped back into Army training with Wioo. Over the years, he'd encountered young recruits like the Hork and had to become a father figure for them. Although he never had children of his own, Giele liked to think he'd raised hundreds of them to become outstanding soldiers in the Army. Wioo reminded him of some of those boys. He remembered being full of heated blood and rebellion at Wioo's age, and yet still desperate for a father's approval. Perhaps Wioo sought that as well. Despite the challenge which had put him in this predicament, Giele couldn't find it in his heart to dislike Wioo. His resolve to befriend the young Hork grew stronger than ever. This would be his new campaign.

They left the abandoned campsite behind and trekked in an ever-widening spiral around the village for four days. If they'd known where the nearest Greatdeer herd could be found, their journey would have been much abbreviated. Giele was thankful for the additional time, for it gave him a chance to get to know his companion better. Most of the time, Wioo ignored the Elf's gentle efforts to draw him into a conversation, so they traveled in silence—sullen on Wioo's part, studious on Giele's. Giele spent much of the time learning some of the signs of Verigan nature. Back in Aelfland, a stroll through a forested grove would provide enough information to fill a book, from the likeliest places to find game to the health of the trees and even the weather forecast. Like a card player, Verigo had its own tells, and Giele studied them as any gambling opponent would. He learned to spot rabbit feeding areas by the chewed prairie grasses near bushes or swells in the terrain. He saw plants with tiny succulent leaves the animals avoided and discovered it was because of bitter scent and juices that caused itching of his skin. He even learned to tell the temperature by how wide red-and-black flowers opened. He and Wioo hunted, and ate together, and Giele was careful to praise Wioo's prowess and skill without sounding insincere about it.

The fourth day after they'd departed from Valley Village, Wioo stooped down to examine a small pile of droppings. He poked into them with his knife to see how fresh they were inside even though they appeared dry. He lifted a couple pellets and sniffed at them. "Greatdeer. Two, three days old. Spread out, look for tracks."

Giele nodded. "You're the expert." Wioo smiled for a moment at that, and Giele knew he'd just made fresh inroads in the quest to become Wioo's friend.

They worked outward in a spiral, stepping with caution to avoid damaging any faint tracks in the dusty soil and closely-cropped prairie grasses. Wioo found the incoming trail and pointed it out to Giele. A few dainty impressions in an anthill suggested the Greatdeer had approached from the southwest. Once they eliminated that direction, Giele found the outbound tracks—cloven hoof prints in soil dampened by urine. They both scanned the distance in the indicated direction, but saw no Greatdeer. "They cover a lot of distance in two or three days," grumbled Giele, whose leg had begun to ache from the excessive exercise.

"Two days at most. Sun dries droppings too fast." Wioo pointed at the horizon. "Greatdeer stop often. Lazy. We catch them two, three days."

"Lead on, great tracker."

This time Wioo's smile came out and stayed long enough for Giele to return one of his own.

CHAPTER TWENTY-TWO

The following day they saw the Greatdeer against the horizon. The males' large racks of antlers arched against the sky like bare trees in winter. "You think we'll reach them today?" asked Giele.

"No. Too far. By time we catch them, already nightfall. Dangerous to hunt Greatdeer at night," said Wioo.

"Why is that?"

Wioo smiled. "You not see one that stabs you."

"Are the wild Greatdeer that aggressive?"

He shrugged. "*Faw.* Why you think Horks breed them, Elf?"

"Well, you're the expert. What do you think we should do?"

The youth puffed up his chest at being given authority. "Get closer. Maybe hunt tomorrow. Day after for sure."

The two hunters traveled along the prairie. Despite Wioo warming up to Giele a little over the course of the journey, their travels were silent. Neither of them were the sort to converse just for the sake of filling up the emptiness with the sound of their voices. Even so, Giele felt their relationship strengthening, and hoped that they would yet become friends.

By nightfall, with Giele's gentle prodding, Wioo had assumed more of a leadership role in the two-man expedition—exactly what the Elf hoped he would do. "We camp here," Wioo decided after investigating a dry stream bed. "Loose banks. We hear if puma come down sides."

"That's comforting." They'd seen no sign of the large predatory cats and Giele hoped they still wouldn't. He didn't fancy trying to fight one off without a troop of riflemen at his disposal, and he still had an occasional nightmare about being stalked by one.

"You want Wioo to hunt or you?" Wioo began gathering dry wood to build a fire.

"I will." Giele scrambled out of the gully in the waning evening light. It didn't take him long to flush out a family of pheasants who were pecking at insects a dozen yards from the camp. Bringing them down was no trouble at all. As he retrieved the birds, he noticed a flickering orange star in the dusky gloom where none should be. A column of white smoke gleamed against the darkening sky. "Wioo," he called. "Come see."

Wioo scampered up from the stream bed to stand beside Giele and squint into the distance. "Campsite. Between us and Greatdeer herd."

"They have Greatdeer in their camp. Horks?"

"Yes, for sure."

"Should we visit them?"

"*Faw*. We will tomorrow. Not get there until well after dark tonight if we pack and leave now."

"Would they attack us?"

"No. Rude to interrupt their sleep. Horks not fight Horks. Only stupid Elves do that. Killing own kind breaks great spiral. We visit tomorrow." Wioo slid back down the embankment to the camp.

The simple truth in his words troubled Giele, and he fell silent to think over what Wioo said. Elves considered the Horks barbarians, but Elves had been fighting wars against other Elves throughout history. Giele had walked away from many battlefields filled with the corpses of Elves from both Aelfland *and* Jiga. And they called themselves *civilized*, he thought.

He took one more look at the distant camp and followed Wioo. "I wonder what they're doing there."

"Seekers, maybe."

"What are Seekers?"

Wioo struggled to explain, not knowing the right Elven words any more than Giele knew the correct Horkish terms. He said, "Horks without tribe. If Wioo lost challenge, he would become Seeker."

"What are they seeking?"

Wioo paused. "Wioo not know how to explain."

It would be a mystery until he could talk to Ullu further about it. Horks didn't often volunteer to leave their tribes, so Giele surmised Seekers must be outcasts. "I've become a Seeker twice over, now."

Wioo burst out laughing at that. It wasn't malicious laughter, but joyful—as if Giele had just told him a fantastic joke. His mirth spread and soon they both chuckled over their dinner. As they ate, Wioo regarded Giele with an unfamiliar expression on his face: curiosity. It was like he'd never seen the Elf before.

All through dinner, Wioo kept drawing breath as if wanting to say something, but then he'd look away, ashamed at his inability to express himself. Giele stayed quiet to let the young Hork gather his thoughts and find the strength to say what he wanted to. "You not so bad." He picked his teeth with the beak of the pheasant they'd eaten. "Wioo sorry to cause you trouble."

"I understand, and I forgive you." It was as if a huge weight had fallen off Giele's chest. After trying so hard to be a friend to this angry young Hork, Giele had managed to reach him.

Wioo's eyes gaped out as if Giele had said something of monumental importance. "You forgive?"

The Elf nodded, mystified. "Yes, of course."

Wioo sank down beside the fire, his dark eyes shining in his horsey face.

"Nobody but Grandam Ullu forgive Wioo before. Wioo make mistakes. Too many. It why hair still short."

Forgiveness. The word was rife with connotations. Giele's breath caught in his throat as he understood how it pertained to him, like a magical flare illuminating a nighttime battlefield. He'd made one huge mistake in Aelfland, and realized that all this time, he'd just wanted to be forgiven for it. After serving the King for twenty years, only to be branded and exiled as he had been, was painful. He'd been an unwitting pawn in a royal scheme. A more sympathetic lord who ruled from the direction of love more than fear, would have seen that. He would have forgiven Giele. "Everybody should have the chance to be forgiven."

Wioo shook out his dreadlocks and jumped up to his feet. He pulled his bone knife from the leather sheath he kept in the small of his back. Giele tensed up, fearing an attack for some reason. Instead of charging, Wioo drew the blade across his palm and left a thin line of dark blood in its wake. He reversed the blade, offered it to Giele handle first, and held out his cut hand.

"Wioo offer you his blood."

Giele looked at Wioo's hand and the dark Horkish blood, purple in the flickering firelight, and at the extended knife, and realized what the Hork was offering. Horks put great value on blood and the innate power within it. Ullu had explained that blood was the source of all magic, and those with good blood were the best magicians.

Giele took the knife from Wioo. The Hork looked nervous and eager, like a Leaf Archer before his first battle. He licked his lips as Giele raised his other hand and made a quick, decisive cut. The sharpened bone sliced through his skin and Elven blood welled forth. Wioo nodded and held out his wounded hand, palm up, fingers extended. Giele clasped it. Their blood mingled between their palms, pale red Elven and dark red Horkish.

"Blood mix," whispered Wioo. "Always now Wioo carry bit of Elf blood, and you carry bit of Hork blood. Blood brothers." He struggled to find the right words in Elvish. "Family," he said at last.

Giele was stunned. He was a man without name or family, and this young Hork had just made him his brother in a spur-of-the-moment decision, without a second thought. Giele belonged somewhere once again. It felt amazing and powerful, greater than any honor ever bestowed upon him by the Army or King Teirol himself. "I am honored, Wioo."

Wioo released Giele's hand and took a rag from his satchel. They each wrapped their hands. Giele's palm stung, but he was happy; this pain was a reminder of something benevolent.

He wondered if this changed anything about losing the challenge, and asked Wioo about it.

His thick brow furrowed as he considered how to answer. "Wioo not know law so good. Have to ask elders. Maybe they let you return if Wioo speak for you."

Giele nodded, hoping more than anything to be accepted back into the fold of Wioo's village, regardless of the challenge loss.

"Tomorrow we meet other travelers." Wioo unrolled his blanket. "Maybe catch you Greatdeer."

The following morning they awakened early and crossed the plains toward the strangers. Wioo counted six of them, each with a Greatdeer mount.

Two of the strangers rode out to greet them. Spirals decorated their Greatdeer's bodies, like those of the village, but woven garlands of red and yellow prairie flowers festooned their antlers.

The strangers—both males—wore their hair in red-streaked narrow strips that ran from their foreheads to the napes of necks. As they approached, Wioo took one of his spears, stuck it into the ground beside him, and then stepped away from it. He kept his other spears in the bundle strapped to his back. Giele understood it was a symbolic disarmament and slipped his bow over his shoulder.

The newcomers slid off their Greatdeer. One jammed a spear into the ground beside him and stepped forward. The other had a Dwarven rifle slung over his shoulder. Giele was surprised to see it; it was the first example of modern technology he'd seen among any of the Horks. The stranger wore it like he was used to it.

Wioo and one of the strangers clasped hands in greeting. They spoke to each other at length. Their speech was so rapid that Giele could barely pick out one word in ten. Wioo gestured to him several times, displayed the cut on his hand, and asked Giele to do the same. The other motioned to the camp and to the herd of Greatdeer in the distance.

The stranger clasped Wioo's hand once more, and then they climbed back onto their Greatdeer and rode back toward their camp.

"What's going on?" asked Giele.

"He Akak. They traders, not Seekers," said Wioo. "Travel south to trade with pale folk. Elves and Dwarves. They cure Greatdeer meat and hides, trade for guns, silk. They invite us to eat at their fire, and then take our pick of Greatdeer for you."

"That's very hospitable of them." Giele wasn't sure why, but the idea of Horks slaughtering the Greatdeer creatures they bonded with, just to trade for weapons felt wrong. It was like they were trading away their own children.

"I speak small Elf tongue. For trade." Akak pronounced the words with care. "Do you have anything to trade?" The question startled Giele; Akak spoke it with no trace of an accent. Giele suspected the Hork had learned the exact phrase and rehearsed it many times.

"No, not at the moment," said Giele. "Perhaps Wioo can translate for us."

Wioo looked at Giele like the Elf had gone crazy. Giele shrugged. Wioo understood a wider range of Elven than these Horks seemed to, and at least Giele had a working grasp on the Horkish dialect spoken in Wioo's village.

They entered the camp. The traders had familiar dome-style tents, although Giele noticed there was no sense of permanence like there had been in Valley Village. Everything not needed right away was packed onto a travois, ready to connect to a Greatdeer's harness. Drying skins hung from sticks poked in the ground. Two of the Horks rubbed salt and preservatives into strips of meat before setting them on flat rocks surrounded by hot coals while another polished antlers to a high sheen.

Wioo translated as best he could. The new Horks had names full of hard, clicking consonants like *Akak* and *Kekl* as opposed to the soft, flowing sounds of Wioo's tribe. Giele asked what the new tribesmen called themselves but all Wioo said was they were *The People of Six Streams.*

The Six Streams Horks were friendly and open, and they shared food and conversation. The food was strips of meat and vegetables, cooked on an iron grill in the coals of the fire, then wrapped in a seed-filled flatbread. They passed around a bottle of a sauce that made Giele's nostrils flare. After one tentative taste curled his ears, he determined to treat the spicy hot mixture with respect. Akak and the others laughed as the Elf poured most of a canteen of water down his throat, trying to quell the fire that burned there.

Akak seemed to be quite curious about Giele and asked Wioo many questions about the Elf who was blood brother to a Hork. Wioo relayed the questions to Giele, who did his best to answer them. Akak seemed to be interested in any trade opportunities in Aelfland. Giele told him Aelfland might be open to trade with the Horks, but it was the King's decision to make. He smiled and grunted "*Faw.*" He wanted to know about the frontier town Giele came from.

"Goose Creek Crossing." He pointed in the direction it was. "Five, maybe six days' ride."

"Good place to trade?" Akak asked in Elven.

"There's a woman named Cianid who runs a large store. That's a kind of trading post. I'm sure she'd be willing to work something out with you."

Akak snorted. "Woman run trading post?" He switched to Horkish and said something to Wioo.

"He say only Elf women he see work in . . . in what?" Wioo turned back to Akak.

"*Taverna.*" Akak made an exaggerated drinking motion. "They trade too. Bodies for Elf money."

Giele's eyes opened wide. "You haven't . . ."

The Six Streams Horks laughed. "No, no." Akak grinned. "No spend hard-earned money on ugly Elf women when plenty beautiful Hork women give bodies away for free."

The conversation became raucous for a few minutes as the Six Streamers joked about their prowess and lovers—at least, what little of their jabbering slang Giele understood. Wioo blushed under his dark skin, but the bawdy talk didn't bother Giele, who'd heard plenty of obscenity during his time in the Army.

After a spell, the discussion wound down and Akak asked something else.

"He ask what happen to your face," said Wioo.

"Tell him it's a wound I received in battle." The Six Streams Horks didn't need to know that Giele was a pariah. It occurred to him that he hadn't yet told Wioo the truth about the wound. Now that they'd performed a ritual to become blood brothers, he knew he should, and resolved to as soon as they had some time.

"Akak say there is large buck in herd," translated Wioo. "He think even large enough for you to ride. Buck has broken antler. Easy to see."

"Then perhaps tomorrow we should go for that one."

"Wioo think so."

"What is our plan?" Now that they were about to take on the Greatdeer, Giele realized he had no idea how to proceed. Would they have to wrestle it into submission and then drag it all the way back to Valley Village? He didn't relish the idea of having to lug an angry animal on a sledge for dozens of miles.

"You no worry, Elf. Wioo have good magic. Sleep tonight. Tomorrow catch Greatdeer for you. Three, four days you bond to it."

Wioo curled up in his bedroll. Despite misgivings about tomorrow's hunt, Giele did the same.

CHAPTER TWENTY-THREE

The Six Streams Horks fed Wioo and Giele once more with a breakfast of boiled grains, fruit, and salted Greatdeer meat.

"We travel south," Akak said. "We will visit Goose Creek Crossing and trade with Elf woman Cianid."

"She may not want to trade," said Giele. "She doesn't like Horks very much."

Akak grinned. "Then I make her a good deal. Greatdeer leather in much demand among Elves."

"Best of luck, my friend." Wioo and Giele clasped hands with Akak and his partners, then they bid the hunters farewell and broke their camp to continue their southward journey toward the colonies.

Wioo and Giele circled the Greatdeer herd to remain downwind of them. An hour later when they were in position, Wioo pulled a tied bundle out of his satchel that contained some iron spearheads. A pinkish-white symbol was inscribed on each one. He set about changing the heads on his spears to these new ones.

"What are these?" asked Giele.

"Magic."

"I don't understand."

"Blood magic," he elaborated. He pointed to the symbol. "This made from Greatdeer blood. Blood calls to blood."

Giele's eyes widened as he realized what it meant. Wioo had a weapon that would target through magic.

Such a thing would be almost infallible. Giele couldn't imagine a military commander in the world that wouldn't kill to possess such a tool. Elven magic could be targeted, but only by mages. This would allow any soldier, or an entire regiment of them, to target with the accuracy of magic. "What is the symbol, then?"

"This one mean *Greatdeer*." Wioo showed Giele the glyph. Then he flipped over the spearhead and Giele saw another, different symbol in dark red drawn on the other side. "This one mean . . . Wioo not know word. It mean animal is calm, can be tied, will follow."

"Docile?"

"*Faw*. Stupid Elf word as good as any."

"So when you strike a Greatdeer with this spear, it becomes docile and you can capture and lead it?"

"Yes."

"How does the weapon target an individual animal? There must be two dozen in that herd."

Wioo grinned. "That where skill of hunter come in. Spear will strike closest beast unless blood that make symbol come from that beast."

"And how do you keep from killing the target animal?"

"Wioo is careful. Small wound. Cut away spear haft. Leave head inside. Magic keep working."

"*Faw*." Giele wondered if the magic could translate to other mediums like arrows or even bullets."

"Choose your beast." Wioo made an expansive gesture at the herd.

Giele examined the herd in detail. The young grazed near the middle. The does formed a protective circle about them, facing outward, and the bucks circled about them. One would graze while the others scanned the surrounding land. One buck had an antler broken halfway down. Akak had mentioned him and the trader was correct in his assessment of the buck's size. The herd might have exiled a lesser animal for such a feature, but this fellow was strong and rippled with muscle, a head taller than any of the others were. His muzzle showed the white of age, but this grizzled veteran didn't seem to have lost any status to the younger bucks.

Giele felt a kinship toward the Greatdeer and his damaged antler. "That's the one."

"Then Wioo will get him."

"What should I do?"

"Split up. Wioo hide here. You circle herd, startle them, drive them toward Wioo."

Giele's eyes widened. "That's the best plan you've got?"

"You got better plan? How else you get close enough to broken-horned Greatdeer?" He thrust his spear at the air for emphasis. "Wild Greatdeer drive off pumas. Wioo see many dead coyotes over years, trampled and gored."

"What about when they are sleeping?"

He pointed. "Look."

Amid those grazing, Giele saw a group huddled together with their heads down. They weren't eating; they slept standing like horses.

"Always some Greatdeer awake, always some asleep. Never catch them that way." Wioo clapped his hand on Giele's side. "You trust Wioo. Is good plan."

"What if they stampede in the wrong direction?"

"Then we hunt them many more days, then try again." He winked. "Good hunter get herd to run right direction."

Giele's ears burned at his subtle dig. "I'll get them to run right past you. What startles them best?"

He shrugged. "Sudden moves, noises."

That gave Giele an idea. He scrounged a few lumps of wood and asked to borrow Wioo's knife. The Hork huddled down to watch as Giele hollowed out each piece and then carved an angled notch into the side of each one. "What you make?" He fingered one of them with curiosity.

Giele took one and blew into the end. It gave off a slight whistle. He smiled. Elves had used arrow-mounted signaling whistles for hundreds of years. Forges mass-produced the modern variety, but these primitive specimens would work just as well. Wioo's eyes widened as Giele tied the whistles onto three different arrows.

"With luck, I can use these to encourage the herd to move in the right direction."

"*Faw.*"

Giele began his trek around the herd, keeping well out of sight of the watchful bucks while Wioo waited to make his move.

An hour passed before Giele had moved into position. He was sweating and his leg ached as he crept through the weeds and grasses, using every bit of stealthy woodcraft he had picked up over his Army career to get to within a few yards of the nearest buck. Once Giele rustled the tall grass a little too much and the buck's head snapped around. The others caught the quick reaction and the Elf froze, not even daring to breathe. He cursed himself for a fool as the buck sniffed at the air, his eyes rolling in alarm. Giele became aware of every acute physical discomfort, from the way his leg threatened to cramp to the itching of bug bites on his arms. The worst was a blade of grass which had worked its way into the end of his nose and made him want to sneeze. His eyes watered and he bit his tongue to keep from moving.

Just when Giele thought he couldn't stand it any longer, the buck lowered his head to graze and Giele knew the time had come. He clutched his bow, flexed his legs, and sprang straight up from his hiding position, yelling and whooping at the herd.

The buck's tail flared bright white like a muzzle flash and he bolted. The rest of the herd followed a moment later with perfectly-timed precision. Moving almost like a single creature, the entire herd ran away from him at blinding speed, angling left of Wioo's position.

As Giele ran after them, he grabbed his bow and nocked an arrow. He drew it to full between two steps— a difficult move while sprinting at top speed, but one he'd practiced in the Army. Not having to strike a particular target with his whistling arrows meant an easier shot. He released the arrow between the next two steps. The whistler sped to the left of the herd with an unearthly wail like some tortured bird of prey. The herd's response was predictable and they shied to the right just enough to send them right to Wioo.

Giele raced after them, worried for Wioo's safety. The young Hork was in real danger of being trampled. The stampeding herd kicked up a huge cloud of dust in the Elf's face and all he saw was a confusion of flashing tails and hooves and antlers. Then, in the middle of it all, Wioo rose up from his hiding spot, his spear already raised to strike.

The broken-antlered buck reared up in front of Wioo. The young Hork ducked underneath the slashing hooves and drove his magic spear into the beast's muscular chest. He rolled away as the buck's forelegs came back down. The rest of the herd bolted to the south.

Giele ran, worried because he couldn't see Wioo amid all the dust kicked up by the fleeing Greatdeer. As the dust cloud settled, he found the buck standing still, even though the spearhead had barely penetrated his skin. Wioo stood beside the beast, beaming, dust and sweat staining his face.

A gleeful Wioo flapped his arms beside the huge buck. He slapped the animal's neck and the beast quivered but remained still. "*Faw*! Perfect!"

Giele skidded to a stop beside the buck. The wild animal's eyes rolled in his head and his sides heaved.

"Unbelievable," Giele panted. The buck stared at him in confusion, as if he couldn't understand why he wasn't pelting away. Giele reached out a cautious hand to touch the beast's side and felt his blood pounding beneath the velvety fur.

Wioo babbled in rapid-fire Horkish. Giele couldn't make out a clear word of it, but his body language exemplified joy and triumph. He ducked down and cut the cord securing the iron head to the haft of the spear. The Greatdeer didn't move a muscle.

As Giele watched, the animal's flight reflex slowed and his breathing became slow and peaceful.

"How deep did you sink the spear?" Giele peeked between the deer's forelegs at the wound.

"Not deep. Two, three fingers thick. He still run fine." Wioo dug into his satchel and withdrew a small leather pouch tied with a drawstring. He opened it. Within was a creamy salve, which he spread upon the wound.

The buck's ears flickered at the touch but remained still.

Wioo spread a sticky glue around the edges of a woven bandage and then pressed it against the wound to keep the spearhead from working its way out. He withdrew a simple leather harness from his satchel. Giele wondered what else Wioo kept in it, but since he'd tracked down wild Greatdeer before, he must have supplies for most contingencies. They slipped the harness over the Greatdeer's forelegs and neck, and he walked with them without complaint.

"What you name him?"

"Name?" Elves had never used the tradition of naming their mounts. With the exception of the heavy cavalry troops, soldiers never knew if they would be riding the same horse from one day to the next.

"This to be your bond-beast. He needs name so he come when you call, listen to your commands, and so you think of him as more than just legs and a strong back."

A name. Giele looked at the hearty buck with a new perspective. That broken antler was by far the most distinguishing characteristic.

"Brokorn," said Giele.

"Brokorn? What that mean?"

"It's just a combination of *broken* and *horn*."

"*Faw.* Elves make stupid names."

Giele shrugged. "He's the first animal I've ever named." He turned to the majestic creature. "Brokorn. Your name is Brokorn."

The buck regarded him with his soft, liquid eyes and Giele wondered if even magic could ever tame such a noble creature.

In the Army, they hobbled the horses to keep them from wandering during the night, but Wioo would hear of no such thing. "Greatdeer stay with us so long as spearhead inside him."

Giele was skeptical, but this was still Wioo's area of expertise, and the Elf bowed to his knowledge. Brokorn stood to one side of the camp and grazed while they ate.

"What will happen when we return to Valley Village?"

Wioo spat out a lump of gristle. "Grandam Ullu bond Brokorn to you with magic. Then you leave."

"I hope not forever."

Wioo looked into Giele's eyes. "Wioo apologize for challenge. You should stay. If law allows, Wioo speak on your behalf." The Hork bowed his head. "You are good friend to Wioo."

"It's been my pleasure to travel and hunt with you."

He traced an idle spiral in the dirt. "Good turns to yours and Wioo's spirals. Good fortune for us both."

"We could both certainly use it. I know I've seen enough bad fortune to last a lifetime and then some."

CHAPTER TWENTY-FOUR

Two days later, Giele and Wioo saw vultures wheeling for a few hours and diverted their course out of curiosity. They cleared a hill crest and found the scene of a slaughter laid out before them. Someone had gunned down the Six Streams Horks along with their mounts. Vultures squabbled over the bodies or at a pair of coyotes who were trying to drag away a Greatdeer carcass. "*Recha*," cried Wioo, and flung stones at the vultures until they returned to circling overhead, squawking dreadful insults. The fur on Brokorn's back stood up in sharp spikes at the smell of death. Even with the magical spear point still embedded in his flesh, he wouldn't get any closer to the carnage. Wioo hunched over, miserable, and vomited into a bush.

Giele felt sick as well, but if they both fell into the depths of grief and misery, they might miss something important.

"Stay here," Giele tried to be as kind as possible. "I'll take a look."

"No." Wioo wiped his mouth. "Wioo will look too."

Giele tried to keep dispassionate like the career military man he was as he examined the bodies. All six Horks had suffered close range rifle or pistol wounds, as had their Greatdeer. He saw no signs of a pursuit, so their attackers had taken them by surprise. The victims lay where they had fallen, tools or trade goods near their hands. Numerous tracks marred the ground, but

Wioo pointed out the unusual U-shaped marks of shod hooves. It all suggested an attack by colonials.

"Elves do this. Slay these men. Like Wioo's father." He turned to Giele, tears of fury in his eyes. "You come here, destroy the land, destroy the people. Why? What Horks ever do to you?" He leaped to his feet, fists clenched.

"Wioo," said Giele, keeping his voice calm. "Not all Elves are like this."

"Wioo hate you!" He ran away, dreadlocks flying.

Giele let him go. Wioo needed time to grieve. Going after him would give the Hork a reason to attack Giele, and both of them would regret such an action. Giele returned to the investigation, sick at the deaths of men with whom he'd shared meals only two days ago.

Most of the Six Stream Horks had been shot multiple times, but one—Akak, who'd first greeted them three days ago—had been shot once, in the forehead.

An execution.

The Six Streams Horks had fought back. Giele found one spear smeared with Elvish blood. Something glinted in the dust next to one of the victims. He picked it up. It was a knife like the one he'd lost when Rarik and his men rolled him, without question an Elvish blade. The handle had been crushed under a horse's hoof.

Giele had seen many slaughters in his life, but this one bothered him more than any other. These were not random bodies on a battlefield. They had welcomed Wioo and Giele without question, shared their food and camp, and been nothing but friendly and open. Giele wondered if they'd approached the colonials who'd done this with the same naiveté. No, it couldn't be that. Why should they fear Elves? They sought trade, to the benefit of both races. They'd been armed, even with a Dwarven rifle, but that didn't make them warriors. The Six Streams Horks had been murdered like animals. The killers had also pillaged the group's equipment and trade goods; all that remained was bait for scavengers. The single shot to Akak's head worried Giele. It implied he'd been the last one killed and questioned beforehand. Either his answers had been unsatisfactory or his tormentors had gotten what they needed and put him down like a rabid dog.

Giele heard a sniffle behind him and whirled, ready to defend himself, but it was only Wioo. He stood with his head bowed and tears running unchecked down his face. For weeks, he'd looked like an angry young man in Giele's eyes, but now he looked more like the child he still was, haunted by the violent deaths of the Six Streamers.

"Wioo," said Giele, not knowing what else to tell him.

"Wioo sorry. He not hate you. You good man. You blood brother. Wioo know not all Elves like this."

"It's all right, Wioo. Bad men did this. If we can find them, we'll cut short their spirals."

"*Faw.*" He dashed his arm across his eyes, wiping them dry.

"Should we do anything for the bodies? To honor the dead?"

"Their spirals already end. Nothing left of them. They part of the land now."

"So you just leave them?"

He nodded, swallowing as if he had a lump in his throat. "The dead feed the plants and animals. They grow. One death adds turns to many spirals. At home, we float them down river." He made a brave smile. "Remember them as they lived, not as they died."

It was difficult for Giele to leave behind the bodies without consecration or memorial, but he acceded to Wioo's directive and they continued southward. More than once Giele caught Wioo looking back toward the dead.

"What Elves do with dead?"

"We bury them under the ground and erect a marker of stone. Sometimes, if it's someone really important, we put them in a special building."

Wioo stopped walking and turned to look back once more. Giele put a hand on his shoulder.

"That good idea. Mark spot with stone forever."

"Do you want to go back?" Giele hoped he would say yes.

"No. Not now. Better we hunt Elves who killed them." He gave the Elf a solemn look. "If Wioo die before you, bury him and mark spot with stone. Wioo want you remember him that way."

"I ask the same of you, but don't you worry. Neither of us is going to die anytime soon," said Giele in a grim tone. "I swear that to you."

They forged ahead.

When evening came, they stopped to camp in a gully sheltered from the prairie wind and found that someone had been in the same spot before them. A fire ring contained charcoal that was cool to the touch. They found horse manure in several spots among the grass cropped by grazing.

"Only one day old." Wioo sniffed at the dung. "You think these Elves who killed Six Stream Horks?"

"Yes."

Wioo stood up and turned to look back in the direction from which they'd come, and then turned a hundred eighty degrees. Giele realized he was marking a line on the imaginary map in his mind, and it ended at one destination.

Valley Village.

Dread settled across Giele like flies upon carrion. He and Wioo exchanged horrified glances as they realized the truth. They threw their supplies back into their satchels. Giele took hold of Brokorn's lead and then they set out for Wioo's home village at a brisk jog, quick enough to cover some distance, but not so fast they couldn't maintain the pace. They carried on through the night, pausing for thirty-minute rests when their stumbling grew too labored. By the time the sun peeked over the eastern horizon, Giele estimated they were five miles from the village, and both of the hunters were dead on their feet. They staggered on, uncaring where they put their feet down so long as they kept them moving in the right direction.

As they approached the valley, Giele smelled the stink of smoke on the breeze—not from cooking or the forge, but the sharp tang of burned leather and the underlying sweetness of charred flesh. He didn't want to press onward, but Wioo kept pushing ahead. The Hork's head was bowed, dreadlocks hanging in his eyes, and his shoulders slumped in misery. As they entered the last mile, Giele's chest grew tighter. An entire night of running on no rest had taken its toll; the grief of seeing his friends slaughtered might very well kill him.

Wioo had been muttering to himself for hours. As they started up the final hill, he raced to the top ahead of Giele with a final reserve of strength. He reached the crest of the hill overlooking the village and stopped in his tracks. His spears and satchel fell to the ground and he screamed in wordless agony. In spite of his exhaustion, Giele hurried up the hill to join his blood brother. The Elf's legs were heavy and he felt like he might never draw sufficient breath again. He didn't want to see, but stumbled to Wioo's side and looked down upon the ruin which had been a haven to him.

Valley Village lay in ashes.

Horks lay dead, cut down while trying to flee. Bonded Greatdeer stood helpless by their bond-mates, unable to help their downed riders. Possessions that hadn't been burned were scattered and trampled into the dirt— clothing, shattered pottery, children's toys. Across the river, the corral was in shambles and many Greatdeer lay dead or dying in the sun. The forge still stood, but its roof was a burnt ruin and smoke billowed out from within.

On its wall, someone had painted a giant crescent moon in dark Horkish blood. Flies swirled around the drying gore. Underneath it a word was had been scrawled in Elvish.

Pariah.

Giele's world spun around and for a moment he couldn't see, for he knew who'd destroyed this village and slain the Six Streams Horks, all because of him.

Rarik.

"Come on, we must see if anyone still lives." Giele put a hand on Wioo's shaking shoulder.

They descended into the valley. A pall of smoke hung in the air, as if even the wind was too horrified to blow. Giele saw body after body of Horks he'd known, talked with, dined with. Men, women, and children all gunned down without mercy. Everywhere he looked, he found nothing but dead friends and smoking ashes. Tents lay in smoldering piles. They looked to where Ullu's tent had been struck, and it was gone. Wioo put his head in his hands and sobbed.

Then Giele stopped cold. At his feet lay the body of Yerri. Dried blood matted his short hair. Beside him lay proud little Aral, who had died with her bow in hand and her arrows scattered around her. Giele had made it for her and she'd carried it like a warrior. Her unseeing eyes stared up into the sky, her baby face composed with such serenity she could have been imagining shapes in the clouds. Giele couldn't look away from her face or the bullet wound in her chest. Flies buzzed around it, oblivious to their desecration.

She'd died facing the enemy. Giele had commanded soldiers who hadn't been as brave.

Tears streamed down both his and Wioo's faces. Giele was too shocked to be ill, too exhausted to scream.

"Blood-brother," hissed Wioo. He stood by the forge and looked at the message left by the attackers. "What mean these marks?"

Giele didn't move from beside Aral's body. Wioo deserved to know the truth, even if it would end their friendship forever. "It means the men who did this were looking for me." His voice sounded unnatural and hollow in his ears. "They knew I hadn't died before when Ullu rescued me. They wanted to finish the job. When they found I wasn't here, they killed the villagers out of spite."

Giele saw the struggle on Wioo's horsey face as he tried to decipher all that Giele had explained. "This happen . . . because of you? All this?"

The Elf nodded. In that moment, he hated himself.

For a moment, Giele thought Wioo might kill him with his bare hands. God's Blood, he would have welcomed it. The Elf could never atone for these deaths. So many dead.

Giele dropped to his knees, his spirit crushed into the dust. If he'd plunged a knife into his own heart, it would burst from the painful pressure within like a child's balloon.

"Blood-brother," said Wioo again. Giele looked up. Wioo held out his scarred hand to him.

Giele looked at his own hand, with the angular cut across it. It meant something he hadn't been able to lay claim to since being exiled by the King: honor. Giele raised his eyes up to look into Wioo's. A terrible mask of grief covered his face, but despite the sadness, Giele found a resolute maturity there that he could cling to. Wioo waved his fingers a little, encouraging the Elf to take his hand.

Giele clasped his sturdy brown fingers in his slender, pale hand. With strength belied by his size, he pulled Giele to his feet. The Elf towered over Wioo, decades older, and yet Giele still felt like a child compared to the Hork's calm. "This not your fault, this fault of bad Elves. They kill Horks for pleasure. For sport. Like animals." He spat on the dirt. "Horks not animals. Not even animals should die like this. Wrongs must be made right."

Wioo was right. Rarik and his men needed to pay for this travesty, in the currency of blood. There would be time enough to mourn the dead later, after Giele watched the last bit of undeserving life leak from Rarik.

Wherever he fell, Giele would leave him unburied.

He gripped Wioo's hand. "I was a soldier for twenty years. If there is one thing I know, it's war." Giele looked down at his Horkish blood brother. "We'll find those murderers, and when we're done, by God's Blood, they will know they've been in a war."

Wioo's eyes burned with grim passion. "*Faw!*"

Giele slipped back into military mode, quashing all his emotions except the flame of fury burning deep in his belly, which he stoked and fanned with his grief. "See if you can salvage any supplies, Wioo. Does your own bonded Greatdeer still live?"

Wioo looked around, muscles twitching in his jawline as he clenched his teeth. Giele hoped the young Hork could handle the pressure; he was still far more a boy than a man. Then he pursed his lips and let loose a piercing whistle, far louder than Giele would have thought possible from someone so small. Those Greatdeer in the area that still lived perked up their ears and looked in his direction. "*Efraya!*"

A Greatdeer on the far side of the river flashed into motion. He leaped high and landed with a great splash midstream. He heaved his way through the shallow river to race to Wioo's side. The Greatdeer bowed his head to Wioo, who touched the animal's nose with his own and whispered to him.

"Good. This gives us greater mobility already. Do you know how to perform the bonding magic Ullu would have used on Brokorn and me?"

"Wioo not sure exact steps."

"Then as far as I'm concerned, you're the expert. Maybe the attackers left something we can use."

"But Grandam's tent gone."

"Could she have moved her tent?"

"In all Wioo's years, Grandam Ullu never once move her tent."

"Maybe she did now. Let's go look."

They reached the spot where Ullu's tent once stood. The spot was bare. Curious, Giele reached out a hand to touch the dirt where it had been, and his fingers mashed against something unseen.

"Wioo!" he cried in surprise. "Something's here, something invisible."

"What?" Wioo reached out and yelped in surprise as he too felt what must have been the tent.

"It's here. Ullu's magic must have hidden it."

They found the flap by feel. It had been sealed tight and they couldn't pull it open.

"Grandam! Grandam Ullu!" cried Wioo. He beat upon the invisible flap with both fists.

"Wait, we don't even know she's in there. She might be . . ."

"No, quiet. Wioo must think. Grandam told Wioo of sealing magic. To break it . . . to break it . . . blood!"

He whipped out his bone knife and slashed his hand again. His dark blood flowed from the wound. He squeezed his hand into a fist to coat his entire palm with it, and then slapped it upon the hidden tent.

With a flash and a smell of sulfur, Ullu's tent reappeared. Wioo flung open the flap to reveal Ullu huddled with a dozen wide-eyed Horks, all holding one another in terror . . .

. . . but *alive*.

CHAPTER TWENTY-FIVE

Wioo rushed into the crowded tent and flung his arms about his grandam. Giele's knees shivered with the exhaustion of the race he'd run only to lose to Rarik in the end. Seeing Ullu gave him a new jolt of strength and a stab of joy amid the despair of all the dead.

The other survivors stumbled out of Ullu's tent, their faces numb with shock as they witnessed the aftermath of destruction. Elder Leyolo collapsed in the dust, unable to bear the sight. A keening wail rose from the Horks' throats as if the very world itself despaired with them. Giele closed his eyes, helpless as the survivors ran about and cried out in agony when they discovered their fallen loved ones.

Fresh tears cut clean tracks down the Elf's dusty cheeks. On one side, they puddled atop the scar tissue, a gentle reminder that this had happened because of Ullu's compassion. He turned back to where Wioo clung to Ullu. "How many were there?"

"Ullu saw seven Elves and one Dwarf. They called for you." She shuddered. "Leyolo say you not here. Then one Elf tell others, *leave nothing for him to return to.* Ullu pull all who she could into tent. Sealed and hid it with magic." She bowed her head. "Not good enough for rest of village."

Giele touched her shoulder. "You did all you could, Ullu. You saved lives."

She didn't reply.

"I'm sorry. I never meant for this to happen."

"Meant?" She rounded on Giele, as if chastising a rowdy child. "Of course you not meant!"

"If I'd been here—"

"You would be one more dead. Good that you were not. Your spiral has not yet reached its end, Elf."

"I'm going to avenge these deaths, Ullu. God's Breath and Bones, these men will pay for their crimes. Will you assist me with your magic?"

She sighed. "Of course Ullu help. What you need?"

"Wioo and I were successful in our quest to capture a Greatdeer. We brought it—*him*—back."

"Good work. Yes, Ullu can bond him to you."

"There's something else." Giele took a deep breath and plunged ahead. "Will you teach me the magic you use for targeting? For hitting a specific animal?"

"You want to use it on those who attack us." She made it a statement instead of a question.

"*Faw*," said Giele.

She frowned. "Not simple magic, that. Need special ink. Need blood. Need perfect symbol. And . . ." She looked at him with a canny gaze. "Need to know names. You not know for sure who attack village. You not want to kill wrong person."

"I know one name. If he didn't actually participate, he certainly ordered the attack."

"You know this for sure?"

"Well . . . no."

Ullu folded her arms. "Death magic not to take lightly. Kill wrong person. Bad for your spiral to end someone else's before its time."

Giele didn't care what Ullu thought was right. He needed her blood magic. What would convince her to give it to him? Horks might not believe in revenge as a rule, but he was an Elf, and thousands of years' of vengeance ran through his veins. Breath and Bones, he would make Rarik pay for this crime.

"Ullu, what if you give me the ink and show me how to make the symbol? Then it falls to me to use it properly if needed."

She gathered up some of her bowls and dumped them into a large mixing bowl. "All right. Ullu trust you to do the right thing." She looked over her shoulder as she stirred. "Wioo will go with you, yes?"

"Yes." Giele clapped his hand on Wioo's shoulder. "I promised him that much."

"*Faw*. He is young. Full of fire. Ullu glad. It important blood brothers stay together in dangerous times." She turned her attention back to her mixture. Ingredients flew into it from around her tent. "Ullu pleased you form blood-bond with him."

Giele hadn't said anything about Wioo and he becoming blood brothers, and yet she spoke of it with complete certainty. Her insight and wisdom impressed him even more. He watched her work in silence. Wioo went to stand guard outside, his spear held tight, ever vigilant for the return of danger. The poor boy had to be dead on his feet after their rush across the nighttime plains. Giele left the comfort of the tent to join Wioo where he stood, staring out at the dead, but no longer seeing them. One man turned a broken clay mug around and around in his hands, as if he could somehow make it whole. A woman sobbed over the bodies of her husband and son. Two sisters with haunted eyes collected the dead, wrapping them in the shredded remains of tents.

"What we do?" cried one of them.

"Take them into the forge," said Giele. "Too many dead here will attract predators and disease."

"What you do?" asked the other sister.

"We have to burn them."

The young woman's mouth dropped open in complete shock.

Wioo interrupted her before she could dispute Giele's order. "Giele right. Too many dead. Stone forge not burn. It become marker for memories." He looked at the Elf, questioning his interpretation.

"Yes, it will be a lasting marker for their memories. A tomb of stone."

Wioo swayed on his feet, eyelids fluttering.

"Wioo," said Giele. "Get some sleep. I'll watch while you do."

He shook his head. "You tired as Wioo. And older."

"I'm not that old."

"Almost have one foot at end of spiral. *Faw*." Wioo put on a brave little smile. Giele realized he was trying to make a joke, to defuse the horror of death's shadow over the village.

"Don't worry, Wioo. I'm not so far gone I can't stand a full-shift watch on no sleep and short rations."

He grinned for a moment before his expression sobered. "All right. Wioo sleep now. You wake if new trouble comes."

"I promise." They clasped hands.

Wioo wasn't willing to leave his post, though. He curled up on the blackened rug outside Ullu's tent like a dog and fell asleep, his spear poking up like a yucca stalk.

Ullu stepped out of the tent. "Ullu made tea for others. Help them to rest, help them to mourn without so much pain." She offered him a cup. "You want? Help you sleep."

"Not yet. I promised Wioo I'd stand watch."

"Stupid Elf, you need sleep."

"What I need is to get after these men who killed your village," Giele snapped.

Ullu said nothing.

A flush of embarrassment crept across Giele's skin. "I'm sorry, Ullu. I'm not angry at you. I'm angry on your behalf."

She nodded. "Ullu angry too, but no time to yell now. Ullu yell later, when others are safe."

"Where will you go?"

"Nearest tribe is Six Streams. Six days north and west. They will take in Ullu's people."

"We met some of them on the trail. Good people. I liked them. The men who attacked your village killed them after they left us. We found them yesterday."

"This what Elves bring to our land? Death, fire, and noise? Horks lived in peace before now." Her voice was bitter.

"And the Horks will live in peace again." Giele promised himself he would see that happen.

A bowl filled with an aromatic paste floated out of the tent. Ullu pulled out her bone knife. "Where your Greatdeer? Ullu bond you to him now."

Giele looked around until he spotted the patient Brokorn, standing where Giele left him. The Elf went to retrieve him. Brokorn balked at coming into the village and Giele had to fight him all the way over to Ullu's tent. She handed him the knife.

"Need some of his blood, some of yours. Fill smaller bowl with his, larger with yours." Two small bowls appeared beside Giele. The amount of blood she needed from the Greatdeer would be trivial for such a large beast, but it seemed like she required an awful lot of Giele's.

"Why so much?"

"Ullu use rest of your blood for making ink."

"Wait, why do you need my blood for that? Doesn't the magic target whatever's blood was used?"

Ullu smiled. "Ullu not have blood of target Elf. You only Elf around here. Must use your blood to target Elf. Don't shoot yourself in foot, all will be fine."

"Don't shoot myself. Good advice."

"*Faw.*"

Giele cut into Brokorn's hide and caught the blood that dribbled out. It took a minute or two to fill the bowl. Then he cut the back of his hand enough to open the vein there. The stinging pain helped bring the world of smoke and death around him into clarity. He centered himself on that pain like an archer aiming at a distant target. He understood pain, and the familiarity of it helped him to get past the slaughter of the village. By the time he filled the bowl, he was a little light-headed. He handed it to Ullu. She mixed his blood and the Greatdeer's into a paste of mysterious ingredients.

As Giele drifted, he felt he was not alone. While the rest of the world swelled and receded like waves on the shore, Brokorn remained in sharp focus. Giele sensed a connection forming between the animal and him, like a bridge between shores. Her voice distant, Ullu spoke beside him. "You must cut out spearhead. Release Greatdeer spirit. If bond took, he stay without magic."

"Cut it out?" Giele's tongue felt like a giant, dead slug in his mouth, and he feared he might choke on it at any second. "I can barely see."

A thousand miles away, at the end of his arm, Ullu closed his fingers around the handle of her bone knife. "You must. Nobody else can do it for you."

Giele felt Brokorn's velvety fur under his fingertips. His blood pulsed hot beneath his skin. The Elf sensed Brokorn's fear singing below their delicate connection like the air before a thunderstorm. "He's afraid."

"Then calm him, stupid Elf."

Giele didn't use words, but instead sent waves of soothing calm to the Greatdeer, and felt Brokorn's fear lessen. Giele experienced a twinge of discomfort as he cut the embedded spearhead free. It wasn't so much pain as it was deep sympathy.

The moment the spearhead came free, the world returned to normal focus. Giele stood before Brokorn. The Greatdeer raised his head as if to gore Giele, but then bowed it forward and pushed at the Elf's hand with his nose, like a dog seeking ear scratches. Giele looked at Ullu, who beamed back.

"Now you Greatdeer rider."

CHAPTER TWENTY-SIX

Wioo took up the watch so Giele could rest for a few hours. When he awakened, the Horks had salvaged what they could from their burned village. They bundled their meager supplies into travois and harnessed them to Greatdeer. Ullu supervised the packing and loading of all her various ingredients. When she saw the Elf had awakened, she came over to him.

"*Faw.* Ullu wonder if you sleep away whole day."

Giele yawned. "Looks like you're all about ready to go." For a moment, it felt as if the village's destruction had all been a dream, but the pall of death still hung in the air.

"Yes."

He marveled at Ullu's strength. She looked resolute instead of miserable. "There's something we need to do first. Can you call the others to the forge? And have them each bring some wood."

Ullu nodded. She and Leyolo called the other ten survivors to meet Wioo and Giele at the stone building. Of the bustling Valley Village, only a dozen Horks still lived. The rest lay within the forge, wrapped in shrouds of rags. Giele had wrapped a dry stick in rags and soaked it with pitch from Ullu's tent. It burned with fragrant smoke. "Ullu, will you translate for me?"

"Ullu try."

The Elf looked at the faces of the villagers, drawn with stress and exhaustion. "I know you believe a body is an empty shell, one whose spiral has ended. These bodies, your friends and family, died at the hands of Elves who came looking for me, and they left the dead where they lay as a message for me. I want to leave a message here as well. A village was here yesterday, full of people living and laughing and loving, and by God's Blood, it will be remembered." Giele raised his hand to show them the mark of his blood-bond with Wioo. "You are my people now, my family, and this crime will not go unpunished. To honor those who perished, let us consign their bodies to the winds, that their memories will carry the breadth of the world."

Ullu chose her words with care, doing her best to find the right Horkish words to convey his thoughts.

When she finished, Giele raised the torch. "Do you accept this?"

"*Faw*," the survivors shouted. They held their own sticks to Giele's until they all held blazing torches. One at a time, they tossed them into the forge. Sharp-smelling smoke began to pour forth as the bodies caught.

"Go on God's Breath," Giele murmured as the flames rose higher.

"Come," said Elder Leyolo. "We must leave here forever. Too many dead." Giele bowed his head, saddened that with what little Horkish he spoke, he'd understood Leyolo.

All the survivors mounted their Greatdeer, except for Ullu. She squeezed Giele's hand. "You do good."

The others rode out, dragging their travois behind. Ullu knelt down by her packed supplies and rummaged through them while Giele looked on. Wioo sat astride his Greatdeer, Efraya, and watched as the remaining villagers left their valley behind forever. Fresh ink decorated his buck's flanks. His spears were bound together and his satchel slung low by his hip. He looked ready for anything.

"How will I find you later?" asked Giele.

"Ullu make you seekstone." She handed him a small clay bowl with an inverted lip and a leather pouch. He opened it and found inside a small, highly-polished round stone inscribed with an intricate glyph. She took the stone and set it in the bottom of the bowl. Instead of staying put, it strained against the side closest to her. "Watch." She walked in a circle around him. As she moved, the stone circled the bowl, always pointing at her. Giele realized it was a magical version of the Dwarven magnetic compasses used on sailing ships. Except where the compasses were tricky to use without making mistakes and notorious for being easy to break, this was stable and simple.

"This is useful magic." He packed away the bowl and pouch. "Elves use something like it, but it only points in one direction."

Ullu snorted. "Stupid Elves. What good that?"

"Well, when used with a map or star chart, you can always tell what direction you're going."

"With seekstone, you always know where is destination. Ullu think that more important."

Giele shrugged; he couldn't disagree with her logic.

She handed him a narrow, flat pouch and a tiny carved stone bottle sealed with tar. "Quills and ink. Enough for two, maybe three marks. Don't waste." She passed him a tiny leather scroll. He unrolled it to see a complex glyph inked on the four-inch square piece of leather. "This symbol mean *Elf*. Practice until you draw it perfect. It target Elf like spearhead target Greatdeer or sling stone target puma."

Giele laughed. "Is that how you drove away that puma when you found me? All this time I've thought you were an amazing shot with a sling."

"Ullu terrible with sling. Use magic to cheat."

"You ready?" Wioo asked.

"In a minute." Giele turned to Ullu. "Do you have any ink or dye for Greatdeer fur? I need to mark Brokorn."

"Ullu thought you might. Left colors unpacked for you."

With a soft leather paddle, Giele traced and colored in a single crescent moon in red on each of the animal's haunches.

"That all?" asked Wioo.

"It's all I need," said Giele. Rarik wanted to torment him for my brand, but he'd come to fear the crescent moon before Giele killed him

Giele swung up for the first time onto Brokorn's back. For a moment he worried whether he'd be able to ride the Greatdeer without a saddle, but the buck was narrower than a horse, and Giele found that he could stay comfortable by gripping Brokorn's sides with his knees.

"You get in trouble, grab antlers," said Wioo.

The Elf hung his satchel across his back, over his quiver. He was down to seven arrows, but knew in a pinch that he could make more.

Wioo and Giele were outnumbered. Taking on Rarik and his men without help would at best be an effective way to die as martyrs. Giele would need to draw on his best military training and experience to run this campaign to victory. He had a couple days to consider his options on the way to Goose Creek.

"Be safe," Giele told Ullu. "Don't trust any Elves or groups of Elves you run into."

"Ullu run into you, stupid Elf. You turn out all right."

"You know what I mean, Ullu. Just be careful. Most of my people are not evil in their souls, but I'm worried of you running across one of those who is."

"Ullu not young *Faw*n. Know people well enough. Trust instinct." She reached a hand up to him. Giele clasped it. "Come back alive. Both of you."

"We will," said Giele. "Wioo, let's ride."

The Greatdeer flew across the plains. Their natural gait was faster and lighter than a horse's, and though Brokorn was weighed down with a heavy rider, he was quite a bit larger than Efraya, and kept pace with the smaller animal. The wind whipped through Wioo's dreadlocks and made them wave like willow fronds.

Over the next several hours, Giele learned far more about Greatdeer than he'd ever thought possible. They could gallop for a much longer span of time than a horse, but needed longer resting periods between sprints. When Brokorn grew weary, he became stubborn and wouldn't budge for Giele until the Elf slipped off his back to walk beside him.

"You letting Greatdeer tell you what to do. Should be other way around."

Wioo was right. Brokorn was far more stubborn than Giele, and the animal knew it. At times it was all the Elf could do to keep from being bounced right off his back, but he wasn't about to admit his inability to command his bonded mount. "I'm working on it."

Wioo laughed as Brokorn slowed and dropped his head to the grass for yet another snack. "Work harder."

That night they made camp with just the faint light of the crescent moon overhead. Giele felt they were too close to Goose Creek to risk a fire. He couldn't see the lights of the town from the campsite, but there might be late-night hunters out further. Giele recalled the farms were all on the south side of town, opposite from where they approached, so at least they weren't likely to run across any nervous landowners. As Wioo and Giele pulled out their scant rations, Brokorn wandered off to graze further away from us. Giele hissed after him, and in the faint moonlight, he shot a withering glance back at the Elf before continuing onward.

"That one much trouble. Too strong-willed. You never control him completely."

"That doesn't bother me so much, as long as I can count on him in a pinch."

"You can." He scarfed down a slab of flatbread, then wiped his mouth with the back of his hand. "What our plan for tomorrow? You know where to find bad Elves?"

"No." The hard knot of righteous anger in Giele's stomach had killed his appetite, so his own bread sat untouched. He'd been considering options all afternoon. The worst thing any military commander could do would be to rush to a course of action before gathering sufficient information. Since he didn't have the luxury of a unit of scouts at his disposal, he'd try the next best thing—the gossip wagon. "We'll go meet a man tomorrow whom I trust. He's a Padre—that's a holy man—who traveled with me from my homeland." Giele slipped a couple pieces of dried fruit into his mouth and chewed without tasting them.

"Holy man? Full of holes?" In the near darkness, Wioo canted his head to the side as he tried to make sense of Giele's words.

"No, not that kind of holy. He's, well . . ." Giele stopped, out of his element when it came to explaining the Elven religion to Wioo. "He tells people about his beliefs. If they like his words and ideas, they follow them."

"He draw new spirals?" Wioo rubbed his forehead as he tried to understand the complicated concept.

"No. Spirals are a Horkish belief. Elves believe that God guides our lives."

"God, who has Blood and Breath and Bones?"

"Yes, that's right." Giele thought perhaps he should swear a bit less around the Horks.

"God is an Elf? Or a Dwarf?"

"No. God is everything and nothing. Everywhere and nowhere." Giele quoted a half-remembered phrase from his youthful catechism.

Wioo snorted. "What good that? God nowhere and everywhere. You make Wioo's head hurt. Elves stupid. Spirals make better sense."

Giele smiled. "I like your notion of spirals better than my God. Padre Tarvy preaches that God loves us, but a loving God wouldn't allow a massacre of innocents to take place like in your village."

"Elf God cruel then. Bad idea. Wioo talk to your holy man. Maybe he decide spirals better idea instead."

That would be an entertaining conversation to listen to. "You'll like Tarvy. He's a good man, very cheerful and anxious to help."

"That sound better."

"We'll sneak around the outside of town tomorrow before dawn. We'll catch Tarvy before he holds any morning services and talk to him. I hope that he can get us any information about Rarik."

"And then we kill him."

"Something like that." Tarvy wouldn't approve, and Giele worried that he'd feel obligated to warn Rarik. He didn't know who else to go to. He had to trust somebody to be on his side. His gut said it was the Padre. He'd never once avoided Giele's gaze, looked away from the brand on his cheek, or talked down to him.

And what about Piprel? Could Giele count on the mage for help? His exceptional power could do much to tilt the upcoming battle in Giele's favor. With him on their side, Giele and Wioo might have a fighting chance to escape with their lives. That is, if Piprel felt any obligation to aid.

If not, well, Giele had been on suicide missions many times before in his life. So far, he'd always returned.

He intended to do so once again.

CHAPTER TWENTY-SEVEN

The parsonage door handle emitted a slight creak as Giele turned it. Tumblers clicked into place as the latch withdrew. He glanced at Wioo, who waited at the corner of the small building. He huddled next to the mostly-empty rain barrel and kept watch, his eyes bright in the dim pre-dawn light. They'd left their Greatdeer well outside of town and walked in to minimize detection.

Giele pushed the door open, pausing after every creak of the hinges. Inside the small one-room building, he heard Tarvy's slow, even snores. Keeping low to the ground, Giele slipped inside, relieved to discover Tarvy was alone. He shut the door, leaving a crack. It would give them privacy but still let Giele hear if anyone approached from outside.

He moved beside Tarvy's cot and put one hand over his mouth.

The Padre jerked awake. His eyes bulged out of his skull in terrified orbs, and his hands grabbed at Giele's arm. Giele put a finger in front of his lips and made a shushing sound. Tarvy relaxed as he recognized the mark on Giele's face. Giele took his hand away from Tarvy's mouth.

"Giele, what are you—"

"Quietly," Giele whispered.

He lowered his voice. "Sorry. What are you doing here? God's Blood, you smell like a Hork." He paused and looked Giele up and down. "Look a bit like one too."

Giele considered how different he must look to the Padre in Horkish clothing. When he'd left Goose Creek, he'd worn typical Elven attire: high riding boots, dungarees, cotton work shirt. Now he wore soft moccasins, a loincloth with leather chaps, and a woven vest with spiral patterns sewn into it to keep his quiver strap from chafing. Only his wide-brimmed hat, the second one he'd borrowed from Tarvy all those weeks ago, remained from his original outfit. Poor dead Yerri had given Giele a band of colorful beads to wear around it instead of the ratty sweatband.

"I thought you were most likely dead. I'm glad to see that's not the case. I expect coming in here looking like that, you have some interesting stories to tell. I'll make a pot of coffee." He rolled off his cot and stood up, stretching and rubbing his eyes.

"Who said I was dead?" Giele already knew the answer, but asked anyway.

"Rarik. He rode into town weeks ago crowing that he'd killed you. I found it hard to believe." With a match, Tarvy lit some kindling and pushed it into his small stove. "The next day he was in a foul mood and I overheard him say you must have escaped somehow." He looked Giele up and down. "From the look of you, I'd guess you fell in with the natives."

"Yes, exactly. Tarvy, the Horks . . . they're nothing like people say. They're not savages or barbarians. They're a highly-cultured, civilized race. You wouldn't believe the things I've learned about them in the past few weeks. I have pages and pages of notes."

"It sounds interesting. I'd love to read through them. Are you aware you're slipping words into your conversation I don't recognize?"

"I'm what?"

"It sounds like you've picked up quite a bit of the Horkish language and you're mixing it up with Elvish." Tarvy whistled a cheerful tune as he set a pot of water to boil on the stove.

"I didn't notice. I've studied a lot of their language and I've been communicating in a kind of pidgin mixture of both tongues."

Having finished coffee preparations, Tarvy sat back down on his cot to face Giele. "Now, Giele, why have you come sneaking in here like a burglar?"

Giele paused before answering. "I don't want anyone to see me here talking to you."

"I'm not ashamed to call you friend."

"It's not that, Tarvy. I'm worried about your safety. Rarik kept looking for me once he realized I'd escaped. He must have learned the Horks rescued me. Three days ago he found the village where I'd been staying." The words hung in the air without response, like an accusation.

Wood popped in the stove. The first ray of sunlight came through the window on the east wall to highlight Tarvy's cheekbones. His quiet attentiveness turned to dismay. He looked like he was going to be sick.

Giele couldn't keep the pain from his voice as he told the Padre what happened. "He and his men massacred the residents and burned the village to the ground." Breath and Bones, those very words pained him to speak. "A hundred men, women, and children dead with nobody but me to speak for them."

Tarvy's face had gone an ugly pale color. "How . . . how do you know it was Rarik?"

"On the wall of the forge, the attackers painted a crescent moon, with the word *pariah* beneath it in Elvish. Who else would have reason to commit such an act just to hurt me?"

"You weren't there?" The water began to boil, but Tarvy made no move to get up.

"No, Wioo and I were off to capture a Greatdeer. But that's another story."

"Who's Wioo?"

Giele went back to the door and hissed for Wioo. A moment later, the young Hork slipped inside the parsonage. Tarvy's eyes widened at the boy's wiry, nearly nude body topped by the horsey face and mane of dreadlocks. Wioo looked at the padre with a mixture of curiosity and wariness.

"Padre Tarvy, this is Wioo, my blood brother. Wioo, this is Padre Tarvy. He is the holy man I told you about. He can be trusted."

"*Faw*." Wioo stared around the parsonage with interest. The only permanent building he'd ever been in before was the forge.

"Rarik staked me out and left me to be eaten by scavengers. Wioo's grandmother rescued me."

Tarvy stood up, poured some coffee grounds into the pan on the stove, and dropped in an eggshell to cut the coffee's bitterness. The Padre didn't speak, but Giele saw his hands shaking. He must have tested Tarvy's kind nature with his tale of woe.

Wioo's nose wrinkled at the smell of the coffee as it permeated the air. "What he make?"

"Coffee. It's like tea." It felt as if drool was about to run from Giele's mouth in anticipation of his first taste of the dark drink in a month.

"Rarik came through town just yesterday. He made his rounds of the taverns and whorehouses, raising his usual ruckus. I went to the general store, just in case he thought to come in and hassle Cianid. Fortunately he found his entertainment elsewhere."

The mention of Cianid made Giele's heart jump a little. He hadn't so much missed being around Elves during his time with the Horks, but her face was one that had permeated his thoughts with increasing frequency. He tried to sound nonchalant. "Has he bothered her much?"

"No, he hasn't been around much. If what you say is true, he's been out in the wilds looking for you instead." Tarvy poured a cup of cold water from a large pail into the pan and took it from the stove. With a ladle, he doled out three cups and offered one of them to Wioo, who took it with a bemused expression on his face.

Giele blew on the hot liquid and took a grateful sip. "Thank you, Padre."

Wioo parroted Giele's actions and took a sip of his own. His eyes grew wide and he struggled with the mouthful before he managed to swallow it down. Tarvy laughed, and Giele found himself smiling as he reached out to pat the coughing Wioo's back.

"Wioo like it," he said, but Giele noticed how he avoided taking another drink for a long time.

"You've come right back into the teeth of the beast, returning to Goose Creek like this," Tarvy said. "Why risk it?"

Giele's hands tightened around the cup until his knuckles were white. A weaker vessel would have shattered in his grip. "Rarik will pay for the slaughter of Wioo's village. I need your help, Padre."

"You want my help to get revenge?" Tarvy sipped at his own coffee. From the grimace of his face, his was more bitter than Giele's.

"Not directly, Padre, but I need someone I can trust. I also need to talk to Piprel, but I can't easily go back to the railroad when I owe them the maps Rarik took from me and presumably destroyed. Blackpool will think I stole his money and left."

"I see. And with Rarik's family so powerful throughout town, the word will inevitably get back to him if you are seen walking the streets. And your young friend is small, but hardly inconspicuous."

Giele finished the coffee and set the cup down beside him. "Tarvy, you're my friend. One of the only ones I have. Will you help me or not?"

Tarvy stood and went to his shelf. He traced a finger along the tubes of scrolls there, until he found the one he sought. He pulled it out of its case and unrolled the parchment. "*God gave to Aelfkind feet with which to march; hands with which to draw bowstring; a mind with which to seek the truth; and a heart with which to understand it,*" he read. Giele had heard the scripture before at some time in his life, for he recognized the words. For the first time, he understood the real meaning behind them. Beside him, Wioo listened with his mouth hanging open, holding his breath in case he missed something important. "*War without cause is murder, and should be avoided at all costs. If it be that a cause is just, a soldier may fight a war with God's blessing. His feet will carry him; his hands will draw bowstrings; his mind will seek the truth; and his heart will understand whether or not the cause is just. He may fight without fear of jeopardizing his soul.*" Tarvy rolled the scroll back up and turned to face Giele. "I believe your cause is just, Giele. I will aid you."

Relief washed over Giele like cooling rain on a hot day. "Thank you, Padre."

Tarvy shook his head. "I'm not doing this as a Padre, Giele." He held out an open hand. "I'm doing it as a friend. I'm doing it for your young friend here. I'm doing it because it's the right thing to do."

Giele clasped the Padre's hand.

Tarvy squeezed it, his powerful grip lent Giele strength for the battle to come. "And I'm doing it because Rarik is one rotten son of a whore who surely needs killing."

"*Faw,*" whispered Wioo.

CHAPTER TWENTY-EIGHT

After sharing breakfast with Wioo and Giele, Tarvy suggested they rest in the parsonage while he headed into town to see if Rarik was around, and then over to the railroad to find Piprel. At Giele's request, he brought a sheaf of blank paper and pencils from his office in the church. Giele clasped hands with him before he left. Tarvy noticed the healed wound on Giele's palm but said nothing about it.

"You trust him?" Wioo asked as he watched the Padre stroll off, a heavy walking stick in one hand and a cheerful whistle on his lips.

Giele knew Tarvy wouldn't bring harm upon them. He feared the Padre might say the wrong thing to the wrong person and word would get back to Rarik, but Giele had to give him the benefit of the doubt. "I trust the Padre as much as I trust you." He didn't tell Wioo that he was finding it harder and harder to trust any Elves at all.

"If you say so, Wioo say so. What you do now?"

Giele spread out the first sheet of paper on Tarvy's small table, and then unrolled the small square of leather Ullu had given him. Wioo crowded in to watch as Giele started copying the symbol until he was sure he had it right. Wioo watched for awhile, and pointed out the ones where Giele had come close or where he'd failed. By the time he filled the first sheet of paper on both sides, Wioo agreed that Giele was hitting it far more than he was missing. To inscribe the symbol on a bullet or arrowhead would be far more difficult. Giele started practicing on a second sheet of paper, working to trace the glyph much smaller with the same accuracy.

Wioo grew bored with that and started to poke around the small parsonage. He pulled a scroll off Tarvy's shelf and carefully opened it as he'd seen Tarvy do. "What this?"

Giele looked up. "It's a book. A scroll. Words collected and written on paper. You've seen me write notes and such before. That's why I kept using up all of Ullu's ink." Giele smiled at the memory of her gentle chastising.

"Words . . . on paper?" Wioo's face wrinkled up in confusion. He pointed at the page. "These words?"

"Yes."

"Wioo not understand. Words come from mouth."

"Elves and Dwarves write words down so others can read them later."

"Why not just tell them? People listen to voice. Not listen to paper."

Giele smiled. "Wioo, it's complicated. Elves and Dwarves can't always talk to everyone. We're a lot more spread out than Horks. I might take all the notes I wrote down about Horks and compile them all into a book."

"Put your words into a book for other people to read?"

"Exactly."

"Words not change once on paper?"

"No."

"*Faw*. Wioo understand. Good idea. Wioo should put words on paper too, have lots to say." He looked at the print inside the book. "You teach?"

"Yes, I promise. Once this is over . . ." Giele stopped, feeling a chill run down his spine. He hoped he would survive this approaching storm, as he'd survived the one over the Aeresic in the *Allusi*. This was no time to have doubts. "Once this is over, I will have plenty of time to teach you everything I know."

"*Faw.*"

Tarvy returned around midday with a bundle under his arm. He unrolled some cloth and braided cord to reveal a hunk of cheese and some fresh bread. "Light eating, I know, but I think better when I'm a little hungry. How are you with a needle and thread, Giele?"

Giele shrugged. "Ex-military. I've had to repair pretty much every piece of clothing imaginable and made my fair share of them too."

"Good. I have cutting shears in that drawer beside the stove. We need to cut this cloth to make hooded robes for you and the Hork."

"Hork has name. Wioo." Wioo thumped his chest for emphasis.

Tarvy blushed. "I apologize, my friend. I had forgotten."

"Hooded robes?" asked Giele. "What for?"

"I'm going to turn you into Penitents." Tarvy looked pleased with himself.

Penitents were a monastic order of the Church, known for taking unusual vows like silence or vegetarianism in order to become closer to God. Most often, they seemed to be the butt of jokes among the working class people, but Penitents had unlocked many secrets of the world through their focus.

"Penitents," Giele repeated. "I'm not sure that will work."

Tarvy grinned with pride. "Keep your face hidden under the hood and nobody will know it's you. You'll be able to move through town without drawing more than idle attention. Since I couldn't get in to speak with Piprel, this is the best solution I could think of."

"Why couldn't you get in?" asked Giele, alarmed that he'd raised suspicions somewhere.

"He was working and the shift boss wouldn't let him come see me. As Penitents, you should be able to enter the dormitory and speak to him. All you have to do is say it is required of you. People don't generally question a

Penitent's motives." He rummaged through a drawer and withdrew a cooking knife.

"What about Wioo?"

"So long as he keeps hooded as well, people will either think him a short Dwarf or a child." Tarvy broke apart the bread into three equal sections and passed one to Giele and one to Wioo.

"I've never seen a Penitent child."

He sliced and distributed the cheese. "That doesn't mean they don't exist, does it?"

Wioo crammed the bread into his mouth and chewed. He sniffed in curiosity at the cheese, and then nibbled cautiously at a corner. His eyes widened and he gobbled down the rest of his piece. "What this?"

"Cheese," said Tarvy. "Would you like some more?"

"Yes." Wioo thrust out his hand toward Tarvy, palm up, the healed scar on it dark against his brown skin. "Wioo like cheese. Better than coffee."

"What are those scars on your hands?" Tarvy asked.

"We are blood brothers. It is an honor for both of us."

"You really are serious about your interest in the Horks, aren't you? That makes me happy. Nothing helps to heal a wounded spirit like a purpose."

Giele made a noncommittal noise.

Tarvy clapped a hand on his shoulder. "You're strong, Giele, more so than anyone I've ever met before. I have faith you will come through this a better man. Although . . ." He removed his hand. "I pray you will be unscathed."

Giele raised an eyebrow. "You don't sound very convinced, my friend."

"I'm not. Rarik is a dangerous opponent. Couldn't you have offended someone weak and pathetic instead?"

"I'll try harder next time."

They spent the afternoon cutting and sewing two disguise outfits for Wioo and Giele. Wioo wriggled inside his after trying it on. "It make Wioo itch all over."

"That can't be helped, I'm afraid," said Tarvy. "This was the best material to match true Penitent robes. You won't have to wear them long, and only out of doors."

The brown robes hung all the way to the ground, and the ends of the sleeves passed their hands so they could disappear within if needed. The large hoods covered their heads and left them bathed in shadow. A braided cord went around each of their waists, from which they hung small bags that would normally carry the Penitents' medicines or money.

Giele showed Wioo how to walk with his head bent forward so nobody would be able to see his horse-like countenance, which they couldn't cover without it protruding too far from the hood. Giele tied a loose bit of cloth around his mouth so only his eyes were visible within the deep folds of his own hood.

"What about Wioo's spears?" asked the Hork.

Tarvy shook his head. "Penitents do not travel armed. You'll have to leave your spears behind. Your bow as well, Giele."

"Wioo not like being unarmed here."

"I'm afraid I agree with him, Padre. Too many people would like to see me dead given the chance."

They settled on disguising two of Wioo's spears by wrapping the heads in spare cloth and using some of the cord to hang holy symbols from them. As walking sticks, they'd be useful enough if Giele needed to smash anyone over the head, and it would only take a few seconds to uncover the sharp heads. He was no good with a spear, but it would have to make do in a pinch. He felt naked without a bow, but there was no way to disguise one.

"You don't have a pistol, do you, Padre?"

Tarvy shook his head. "The worst weapon I possess is my own walking stick, which is mainly to fend off exuberant dogs or any number of women who throw themselves at me."

They left the safe haven of the parsonage and made for the railroad grounds. The low afternoon sun gave the false Penitent robes a red tint. They walked with slow, measured paces. Tarvy stayed beside Giele and Wioo with his characteristic smile and cheerful whistle to deflect curious questions about the Penitents.

One young woman with a basket full of eggs flipped her hair back and greeted Tarvy with sultry sweetness. "Good afternoon, Padre. Who are your friends?"

"Penitents from the coast, Maddil. They're following a vow."

"Oh, how exciting. I do hope they've brought good medicines to town. I'm feeling quite flushed right now, Padre." She winked at Tarvy.

Tarvy turned bright red and mumbled something incoherent and apologetic.

Giele heard a quiet snort of amusement from Wioo as they walked away from the young woman. "She's lovely, Padre," said Giele, "but we have far more important things to do at the moment."

"I know, I'm sorry. I can't help it if they all seem to find me irresistible."

"When we're done, you'll be an irresistible hero."

Wioo touched Giele's leg and raised one hand to point toward a nearby hill.

Brokorn stood atop it, silhouetted by the low sun.

"Oh no," Giele whispered. "He's supposed to have stayed where we left him. What's he doing there?"

"He have strong spirit," said Wioo.

Giele tried to use the connection to Brokorn to tell him to get lost and stay hidden. He didn't know how successful he was; Brokorn sent back an image of Giele eating soiled grass, which Giele supposed was Brokorn's way of telling him to rut off.

"Damned beast will get himself shot for food, or worse, give us away. I should have left his flanks bare instead of painting that symbol upon them."

"That Greatdeer is yours?" Tarvy whistled, awestruck.

"In a manner of speaking. He's awfully willful. I think he just tolerates me."

Giele tried to will Brokorn to leave the area, but the Greatdeer put his head down to graze instead, showing how well he could ignore Giele when he so chose. "God's Blood," muttered Giele. "If he gets us caught, I swear I'll cook and eat the beast myself."

"Easy, Giele. Don't draw attention to yourself," said Tarvy softly.

They hurried through Goose Creek. Wioo and Giele kept their heads down as much as possible and let Tarvy take the lead. A few people murmured to each other about their unexpected appearance; Penitents were uncommon in the Verigan colonies, but important enough to Elven culture that they were left alone. Tarvy's purposeful strides helped dissuade anyone from asking questions. He gave the appearance of a man with a mission to fulfill, and nobody wanted to interrupt that.

After a few minutes that felt like an eternity, they came upon the gate to the railroad's compound. "Here we are," said Tarvy. "Good luck to us all."

CHAPTER TWENTY-NINE

Giele was amazed at how the Penitent robes seemed to open doors and melt away resistance. All he had to do was mumble about seeking a certain mage and people would point in the correct direction. From the viewpoint of a military man, he was appalled at such freedom. He realized Penitents would make good assassins and spies, and decided that vows or not, they would always bear close watching.

Piprel lived in a long bunkhouse with other boiler mages. Conversations died down as Wioo, Giele, and Tarvy walked down the central aisle between the cots. They found Piprel stretched out on his, reading a book. He was clean, his hair cut, and his workman-style clothing neat and without rumples. A peacefulness resided upon his face that Giele hadn't seen before. When he looked up at Tarvy and smiled, though, Giele still saw shadows under his eyes as if he wasn't sleeping well. His smile turned to a look of confusion when he saw Wioo and Giele. "Penitents?" he murmured aloud.

"We wish to speak to you, mage." Giele reached up and pulled down the cloth covering his lower face for a moment.

Piprel's eyes widened as he recognized the brand on Giele's cheek. "Of course, Brethren." He pulled on his shoes and followed them out of the bunkhouse.

"What are you doing?" he asked once they were outside. "Why the ruse?"

"It's better nobody sees my face right now." Giele went on and explained what had happened over the past month, ending with the massacre at Valley Village.

Piprel shook his head in disbelief. "The evil that men will do . . . It makes me sick. But why come to me with this?"

"Rarik must pay for his despicable acts. I'm going to take him down. I need your help."

"I can't." Piprel wouldn't look at Giele. "I've finally found something to do besides drink. I have you to thank for that, Giele. But I'm no warrior or hero. I'm just a boiler mage."

"Breath and Bones, man, you were a court mage once!" Giele wanted to take hold of him and shake him until his teeth rattled. "You'd rather waste yourself here instead of doing something honorable for a change?"

"I'm not wasting myself, I'm providing a useful skill. I'm earning a living. I'm standing here on my own two feet instead of lying passed out on a tavern floor. I swore to myself I would never use my magic to kill. Not after what happened. Not ever, Giele."

"Piprel, we need your help." said Tarvy. "A good heart beats within you. Put aside your fear. We're not asking you to kill anyone."

Piprel folded his arms and stood tall. "I'm proud of what I've become now. Don't ask me to change." He still wouldn't meet Giele's gaze, though, and he shuffled his feet.

Giele wondered if he could goad Piprel into action as he had before first leaving Goose Creek. And if he did, could he forgive himself if he set Piprel anew upon the path of self-destruction? Giele was proud of the mage for pulling himself out of the gutter by his own bootstraps. But then he recalled little Aral's empty eyes staring into the sky. God's Blood, he'd made Piprel act once before, and he could do it again. "I wish I could believe that. You're appalled at what Rarik did. You just don't have the nerve to admit it. You're as much a coward now as you were before, except now you're not hiding inside a bottle."

"This is not my fight," he said at last, seeming to fold in upon himself.

"No, it's not," said Giele. "And I'm the fool here for thinking you'd stand by me after I did the same for you."

Piprel's face turned a dangerous red and Giele knew he'd hit the mage where it hurt. He hated himself for stooping to such base tactics, but this call for justice was larger than any one of them. Before Piprel could gather his wits to reply, a Dwarf poked his head around the side of the building. "Hey, Pip, shift's starting."

Piprel's rising temper subsided with the opportunity for a graceful exit. Now instead of furious, he just looked sick. "I have to go. There's work to be done here." He turned and walked to the corner of the bunkhouse. "Good luck, Giele. I'm sorry." He hurried away as if he might hear something to change his mind.

"Maybe I can stay and talk to him," said Tarvy.

Giele took a deep breath and forced away his anger. Ullu would have called him a *Stupid Elf* for being stubborn and unwilling to see the truth about Piprel. He had added a new turn to his spiral, and Giele had to respect that. "No. We tried, but this isn't his fight any more than it's yours, Tarvy. I'll resolve this without him."

They hurried back to the parsonage, their robes flapping in time to their quick pace. Once there, Giele and Wioo shed their robes and gathered up their fighting equipment. Giele strung his bow while Wioo unwrapped his spears.

"You're not going to do this, just the two of you?" Tarvy's strong arms hung helpless at his sides as if he couldn't believe it.

"Look around you, Padre. I don't have an entire regiment at my disposal. The longer I delay, the more likely Rarik is to get wind I'm here and come after me and anyone else who's been in contact with me." Giele looked up at the Padre as he dropped his remaining arrows into his quiver. "He'll come after you, Tarvy. I don't want the death of another friend on my conscience."

Tarvy nodded and took hold of his heavy walking stick. "Then I had better go with you."

Giele stopped what he was doing. "Excuse me?"

"You can't go after Rarik with one eye always pointed back this way. At least if I'm by your side, you'll be able to keep an eye on me. I said I'd aid you."

"And you have helped, but I can't ask you to fight alongside me. Breath and Bones, Tarvy, you're a man of God!"

Tarvy spun his walking stick around in his fingers and made it whistle. Giele raised an eyebrow. In that simple display of skill, he knew in a straight-on fight, Tarvy would best him. "There are times even the most faithful must take up arms in God's name."

Having his prodigious strength on Giele's side would be a huge asset. He felt relieved that his forces had just grown again by half. He nodded. "Fair enough. But be careful, Tarvy."

"You have a visitor." Tarvy pointed toward the door. Giele turned to look and saw Brokorn peeking his head in through the open doorway.

"God's Blood, will you never do as you're told?"

Brokorn shook his head in a very Elven gesture, rattling his antler against the door frame.

"It would appear he will not." Tarvy laughed. "You're not used to your orders being disobeyed, are you?"

"No." Giele pushed past Brokorn to look at the sky. The sun rode low on the horizon now. Most Goose Creek residents would be sitting down to their suppers. The time was right to make his last stop. He went back into the parsonage again. "Tarvy, I need you to find out if Rarik is in town somewhere and if so, where. Meet us at Cianid's. I'm going to see if she'll loan me a pistol."

Tarvy tossed Giele his purse. "Here. If she won't, buy one with this."

Giele shook his head and held it back out to the Padre. "I don't want to be in your debt, Padre."

"Then call it a gift."

He was smiling, but his mouth was tight and set. Giele knew Tarvy wouldn't take the money back, no matter what Giele did. He'd have to find a way to repay the Padre. If they lived through this, he'd not only sit in on one of Tarvy's sermons, he'd give the church the biggest tithe it had ever seen.

Giele slung the purse onto his belt. "Thanks, Tarvy."

He clapped Giele on the shoulder, and their eyes met. His face was grave, but behind his glasses, there was a fierce light in his eyes. Giele knew the look. He'd had a few soldiers in his command like Tarvy. Men of justice, of honor, like Kiler. Giele knew then that he could trust Tarvy forever, to the end of the world.

Giele clasped Tarvy's hand.

"Good luck," said the Padre.

"You too." Giele turned to Wioo. "Are you ready?"

"*Faw*. Time to shorten some spirals."

"Then let's ride." Giele felt the thrill of incipient action in his limbs, making his fingers tingle. They might die today, he and Wioo.

But perhaps they might not.

They mounted their Greatdeer. Brokorn and Efraya reared back, slashing the air with their hooves and snorting like they were issuing challenges of their own. Tarvy nodded at Giele and Giele saluted back. "Yah!" he shouted, and Brokorn leaped forward at a full gallop. Wioo urged Efraya ahead and they raced away from the parsonage, leaving behind a cloud of dust.

A few citizens saw them and ducked out of the way as the Greatdeer thundered past them. People gasped in shock when they saw Giele the pariah, riding alongside a Hork upon Greatdeer. They reached the general store and slipped off their mounts. No horses stood outside so perhaps the store was empty of customers. "Once inside, watch the door," said Giele.

"*Faw.*"

He put an arrow to string and pushed open the door with his foot, then he and Wioo hurried inside.

"Rarik, if that's you I'm going to put your rutting eyes out," called Cianid from the cash register. She turned around, saw Giele, and raised a shotgun to her cheek that she must have had behind the counter. Her black hair had been pulled into a bun, but several strands hung unfettered to curl across her cheek in a strange parody of the crescent on Giele's cheek.

Without realizing he had drawn to full pull, the arrow fletching tickled Giele's cheek and his fingers strained at the string. The mouth of the shotgun looked cavernous and he saw her finger quivering against the trigger.

"I'm not Rarik," said Giele.

"I see that. What are you doing here, marked man? I thought the Sheriff ran you out of town."

"I'm here for Rarik."

"To talk to him?"

"To kill him."

Cianid noticed Wioo and gasped in surprise. "Breath and Bones, is that a rutting *Hork* in my store?"

"He's with me." She looked more incredulous than dangerous, so Giele took a chance and lowered his arrow.

The barrel of the shotgun didn't waver an inch. "And that's supposed to make everything all right?"

Breath and Bones, she was a stubborn woman. "Cianid, I need a pistol and some bullets, and then we'll be on our way."

Her eyes narrowed as she considered what he'd said. "You came into my store with a rutting Hork, pointed an arrow at me, and have the nerve to ask me for a pistol? God's Blood!"

"You've still got a shotgun on me. If you don't want to lower it, I'll leave. I thought if anyone in this rutting town wouldn't mind seeing Rarik measured for a pine box, it would be you."

Giele tucked the arrow back into his quiver, keeping his movements slow and careful. She lowered the shotgun. "You're serious about this, aren't you? Look, I know Rarik's a bastard and all and I wouldn't shed tears on his grave, but what's got your fire up?"

"Rarik. He's a big talker. What has he been saying the past couple of days? I have to know."

She shrugged. "Rarik came back here after being gone a few days. He was drunk and talking nonsense like he always does. He said he'd burned down a village of Horks, but that was ridiculous because everybody knows Horks don't live in villages."

"He's wrong. They do, and Rarik and his men slaughtered the men, women, and children who lived in Wioo's village." As Giele told her about the massacre, his voice grew hoarse with emotion.

She chewed on her knuckles as she listened. She looked over at Wioo with a mixture of contempt and compassion. She was hard to read, and Giele wished he knew what she was thinking.

Wioo seemed unaware of her scrutiny. He stayed at his post like a good soldier, watching the door for anyone approaching. Giele felt such pride and love for his blood brother. Breath and Bones, Giele would avenge the Horks' loss even if it cost him his own life. Rarik would pay for his heinous acts.

Giele put his hands on the counter and gazed into Cianid's eyes, letting her see the fire of vengeance burning in his. "Now will you sell me a pistol and bullets?"

She slapped a brand new piece on the counter with a box of bullets beside it. "God's Blood, you can have it. Nobody should get away with that kind of murder." Giele's heart skipped a beat as he saw the fierceness in her face. She had the soul of a warrior. Even though she'd lost her husband to a Hork, she was willing to help avenge their deaths.

It made him see her in a new light; here was a woman that over time he could learn to understand, and might understand him.

He loaded five bullets into the cylinder, dumped all but one of the rest into his pouch, and set the last one on the counter along with one of his arrows. He pulled out Ullu's ink and broke the seal. He repeated the glyph he'd practiced over and over onto the surface of the arrowhead, then blew upon it to make it dry.

Cianid bent down to watch. "What's that? What are you doing?"

"Marking these." Giele forced his hand to remain slow and steady as he traced the glyph onto the bullet. "This is Horkish magic. I shoot one of these at Rarik, it will hit him and kill him." He loaded the bullet into the last chamber and spun it so the bullet would be the last one to fire from the gun.

He hoped he'd been successful at tracing the glyphs. Either they would work or they wouldn't. If they didn't, Giele would need more than just magic; he'd need some luck too.

Wioo hissed at him. "Padre coming."

Giele gathered up the gun and strapped the holster around his waist. The arrow went into his quiver point up so he'd know which one it was without looking.

Tarvy slipped into the store, casting nervous looks behind him. "Rarik's here. Just up the street, and I think he knows you're here."

A jolt of excitement shot through Giele, but he forced himself to stay calm. Every commander dreaded the last sane moments before the insanity of combat began. He needed to face this with a clear head. "All right then."

Behind him, Cianid cocked her shotgun with a distinctive double-click. Giele looked back to see her coming around the counter, a look of grim resolution on her face. "What are you doing?" asked Giele.

"Helping you."

"No. Absolutely not."

"Why?" She raised her chin in pride. "Because I'm a woman? Frail and helpless and weak? There are three kinds of women in Goose Creek, and I'm neither whore nor housewife."

"Which leaves what?"

"Me. You can't stop me. You may as well let me help."

Giele looked at Tarvy, who nodded.

"*Faw*," said Wioo.

Still, Giele hesitated. Cianid stood straight and proud, the shotgun clutched against her slender form. Her strong features were set in grim determination. "Tell me no, Pariah. Go on, if you've got the guts."

God's Blood, she reminded him of Ullu. He expected her to call him a *Stupid Elf.* She was real, and honest, and although he saw the fear in her eyes, her resolve was stronger. He admired that. That's when he realized that the last of his feelings for Terika were dead at last.

If the princess had just one ounce of Ullu's honesty, or was as brave as Cianid, then none of this—Giele's exile, the Hork massacre—would have happened. He'd learned more about love and honor and nobility out here in a month in the wild north than he had in four decades in Aelfland.

He was silent too long. Cianid tossed her hair in impatience. "Well?"

"Fine. Let's go say hello."

Chapter Thirty

The four would-be warriors moved with caution out into the street. Wioo had his spear clutched tight in both hands. Tarvy held his cudgel in similar fashion. Cianid carried her shotgun in front of her, ready to snap it up at a moment's notice. Giele kept an arrow nocked.

"Well, look what we got here," called a familiar voice. "Looks like a bunch of Hork lovers." Rarik stepped out of a nearby saloon along with seven of his men. They had pistols and rifles and spread out across the road. The few civilians on the street realized they were in the line of a potential firefight and ran for cover. "You're supposed to be dead, marked man."

"I am. I came back just for you."

The men's laughter was raucous. "You're a little short, from what I see." Rarik's broken nose had healed badly and looked like a squashed tuber. "Not as short as your ugly little friend, but still . . . two guns against eight, and one's held by a woman and where's yours? Oh yes, I'm holding it. That pistol's still in its holster. You got some kind of death wish, Pariah?"

Giele didn't want to die, but knew at this point it was inevitable. The best he hoped was to take Rarik with him. He couldn't use the magic arrow unless Rarik was alone. Otherwise, it would target the nearest Elf, and Giele didn't want to risk missing Rarik.

Giele glanced over at his three companions, all of whom had joined this crusade of his because it was the right thing to do. They held their heads high and stood proud, willing to die beside him for what they believed. Giele wished he could protect them from sharing his fate, but knew they'd never permit him to stand alone. He gave a small nod to them. Tarvy nodded back and smiled. Cianid's lips twitched. Wioo tossed his dreadlocks. There was nothing childlike about him now. He was a warrior, Giele's lieutenant, his blood brother.

Giele took a deep breath, ready to sound the charge.

Lightning flashed out of the clear blue sky and a blast of wind ruffled all their clothes. Heat flared across Giele's skin and the blast of thunder shattered windows up and down the street. It happened so fast nobody had time to dive for cover or shield their ears. When the peal of thunder died away, Piprel stood beside them. He gave Giele a little embarrassed shrug and a weak smile. "Didn't like that job so much, I guess." Tarvy slapped him on the back and Giele felt a fierce stab of joy. *Now* he had an army.

Rarik whispered something to his one-eyed Dwarf friend Vilnius. Giele narrowed his eyes. They were plotting something. The Dwarf nodded and ran back up the street along with two of his companions. "At least now we're even, five on five," called Rarik. "But even with that drunkard mage, you're out-gunned."

Giele tightened the pull on his string. "And you're a coward, Rarik. It takes a real big man to attack a bunch of unarmed natives, kill them all, and burn their homes to the ground."

"They ain't no better than stinking animals. I gunned them down where they stood." He laughed. "Even a rutting cow's got more sense than that."

Rarik's men put their hands to their holsters like they were about to draw.

Giele felt Wioo take a step forward and knew the young Hork must be blinded by his rage. "Easy, brother," said Giele in Horkish. "Our moment will come." His blood pounded in his ears and he knew the time for battle was upon them.

"You're wrong, Rarik," said Tarvy. "The Horks are a civilized people. More so than some of the Elves on this street. You're a murderer."

Rarik held up his hand to stay his men. "Padre, I ain't got no quarrel with you. You can go. You too, Cianid. We'll settle this later, you and I. This is just between me and the marked man."

"We'll stay," called Cianid. "I'd rather stand with this Pariah than roll over and rut with the likes of you."

Rarik's face grew uglier, if such a thing was even possible, and he stepped back. The tension in the air grew palpable as the other men raised their guns. Giele's gut tightened along with his bowstring. Flames appeared at the ends of Piprel's hands. Wioo crouched down in preparation for a leap to action. Giele aimed the tip of the arrow for a spot just below Rarik's throat.

Rarik's face twisted with contempt. "Arrows and spears, sticks and magic. Don't you rutting drippers know this is the Age of the Gun?" He raised the pistol and fired it up into the air.

A steam whistle rent the air and a clanking monstrosity roared around a corner up the street. It looked like a carriage but without any horses or oxen pulling it. It belched black smoke from its boiler as it charged across the dust. One of Rarik's men sat on the driver's box and worked levers, while another managed the boiler and fed it chunks of black rock. Vilnius crouched down behind a heavy wooden shield in the front, a maniacal grin on his ugly face.

A multi-barreled rifle protruded from the vehicle's nose, and the barrels began to spin. The gun thundered and spat flame. The stink of gunpowder and ash mixed with the soot from the boiler to create a gut-twisting miasma. Giele tasted the dust kicked up from the vehicle's wheels.

Rarik dove out of the way as the horseless carriage hurtled past.

Bullets tore past Giele as he loosed his arrow, only to see it shatter against the wooden shield. Cianid fired her shotgun at Vilnius but the pellets struck the wooden shield before him. Tarvy ducked out of the line of fire and dodged into a doorway. Flame jetted from Piprel's hands, incinerated the man running the boiler, and set the rear half of the vehicle on fire. The mage's face was white with terror, but he clenched his fist with success. Then a bullet struck him in the side and he fell.

"Piprel!" Giele shouted.

Cianid was closest. "I've got him. Go!" She grabbed the mage's collar and dragged him from the line of fire.

Giele and Wioo both turned and pelted for safety, weaving as they sprinted down the street. The one-eyed Dwarf swept his gun barrels back and forth, trying to mow them down, blanketing the street in a hail of lead. Giele knew they weren't going to make it and that any moment he'd feel bullets tearing through him.

Suddenly, hope! Brokorn and Efraya hurled into the street from between Skria Woodyard's Bowyer and Fletcher and the *Goose Creek Gazette*. For once, Giele was grateful the stubborn beast had disobeyed his orders. Without missing a stride, Giele and Wioo grabbed onto their antlers and swung up onto their backs.

The Greatdeer raced up the boulevard, the steam-powered monstrosity behind them belching and churning in relentless pursuit. Giele leaned down over Brokorn's neck and urged more speed out of the giant buck. "Split up! I'll draw his fire!" Giele shouted at Wioo. The Hork hunched down and leaned over. Efraya angled hard to the left. Vilnius tracked his gunfire toward Giele, and Wioo saw his opportunity. He wheeled around on Efraya, balanced for a moment on the Greatdeer's back, and then sprang high into the air with his spear over his head.

The driver never had a chance.

Wioo came down on the driver's box. His spear punched through the driver's chest and out his back, streaked with blood and entrails. Wioo gave an ululating hoot to celebrate his success and dove off the burning vehicle.

A bullet smacked into Brokorn's haunch and his leg collapsed, spilling Giele into the dust. The carriage bore down on them. Brokorn scrambled to one side, limping from his wounded leg while Giele hurried into the stable where he'd bought his horse all those weeks ago. "Watch out!" Giele cried to the Dwarven stable girl just as the vehicle crashed into the door and blocked it with a heap of smoldering wreckage. The young Dwarf lass screamed and ran as fast as her stubby little legs would carry her. She disappeared out the rear entrance. Giele dove for cover as a bullet whistled past his head.

Nearby timbers ignited as the boiler fire spread. Giele whipped an arrow from his quiver and ducked behind a pillar. His bow appeared undamaged despite him rolling across it. He hoped it would hold together.

Vilnius leaped clear of the burning wreck, his pistol out, and ducked behind a feeding trough. The horses in the stable reared and screamed in fear of the sudden collision and flames. Behind Giele, a wide-eyed stallion began kicking at the door to his enclosure.

Giele couldn't see through the rising smoke, couldn't think with the noise of the horses. His heart pounded in his chest. Where was Vilnius? Then he saw motion and caught a glimpse of the Dwarf as he peeked out to one side of the feeding trough. Giele loosed his arrow at Vilnius. It stuck into the trough an inch from the Dwarf's face. He fired two shots at the Elf. Giele leaped across the aisle and pressed himself into a dark alcove, feeling for another arrow. His heart gave a sick lurch as he realized he had three left in his quiver—he must have lost the rest when he fell from Brokorn. Did he still have the one marked for Rarik? Relief washed over him as he felt it, still upside-down in his quiver.

The horses screamed in terror and kicked at the walls. Wood splintered somewhere behind Giele as a mare forced her way through a partition. The Dwarf glanced in her direction. In Vilnius' moment of distraction, Giele scrambled up and over a stall divider to get a little closer to him.

"Give it up, marked man." Vilnius fired two more shots. The loose horse thundered up the aisle toward Giele. She screamed and reared as a flaming crossbeam fell down by the doorway. Vilnius cursed and flung himself away from the trough as it caught fire. He fired once and the horse fell, a hole beneath one ear where the bullet struck her.

In that moment, Giele had him dead to rights, and he was going to put a shaft right through the Dwarf's eye patch. He drew the arrow back and the bow that had served him so well over the past month shattered in his hands. The string lashed across his face and splinters sliced into his hands and cheeks like razors.

"Ha!" The Dwarf leveled his pistol at Giele. "You cling to the old ways like an old fool, Pariah. Only a half-wit brings a bow to a gunfight."

Giele's eyes watered from the sting of the bowstring and the smoke in the air. He shook his head to clear his vision.

The Dwarf's cruel laughter grated in Giele's ears. "I'm going to enjoy this."

Something like a sharp tree branch crashed through the wall behind him, and two points burst out of his chest.

One was broken.

Giele dropped to the floor as Vilnius' final bullet whizzed over his head. The Dwarf's feet left the ground as his life gurgled out. Giele saw the glare in Brokorn's eyes as he snapped his head aside and flung Vilnius' corpse with contempt. The small body landed atop the flaming crossbeam and didn't move.

Giele ran over to Brokorn. Blood ran from a wound between his antlers, making his face a gory mask. He must have charged at the wall with all the speed of a buck in rutting season. The Dwarf's blood streaked his antlers and his own blood ran down his leg from where he'd been shot.

Giele slapped the side of his neck. "Well done, my friend." Brokorn snorted in satisfaction. His fierce pride flowed through their shared bond.

"Giele!" Wioo came in the far side of the stable. His voice was tinged with panic and his eyes bulged as he searched for his blood brother through the smoke and flames.

"I'm here, Wioo. I'm fine. Help me get the horses out of here. Be careful, they're scared."

They hurried down the aisle, opening latches and throwing aside doors. The horses bucked and kicked but ran for the far stable exit away from the flames.

It was getting difficult to breathe in the thick, smoky air as fire engulfed one wall. Wioo had to shout over the roar of the fire. "You hurt?"

"No, are you?"

"Arm broken."

They both scrambled out of the stable so Giele could check Wioo's left arm, which hung at an awkward angle. His face was calm and betrayed no pain, but there was no way he could continue to fight. "Leave Rarik to me," said Giele.

Wioo didn't want to back out of the fight. Giele saw it in his face, but his Horkish practicality made him nod in agreement. "Wioo cannot fight now. Good luck, Brother."

Giele drew his pistol. "Time to end this. Once more, my friend," he told Brokorn. The Greatdeer bowed his head and let the Elf swing up onto his back. Over the crackle of flames, Giele heard the jangle of the approaching fire wagon and the shouts of those running to assist. "Get back to the parsonage," Giele said to Wioo. "It's the safest place for you now. Wait for me there."

"*Faw.*" The young Hork turned and staggered off through the smoke. Wind whipped through the town, kicking up a great cloud of dust and smoke that swirled around the buildings. The breeze was hot and stuffy and reeked of magic, like hot iron in the rain.

Giele spurred Brokorn forward and together they charged forward like a single being with but one mission. They passed by the fire wagon and several Elves and Dwarves on horseback. Giele recognized Deputy Sheksi, who yelled something after him but Giele couldn't hear over the thundering in his ears.

Cianid and the wounded Piprel were trapped behind a fence across a vacant lot between two buildings. Giele's fury rose. Three men crouched behind a wagon, taking occasional shots to keep Cianid from moving. Piprel lay unmoving on his back, blood staining his boiler coveralls. If he still lived, he needed a doctor right away. If he didn't, it was one more death for which Rarik would have to answer. As Giele approached, one of the men charged while the other two cut loose with a withering burst of covering fire. Cianid raised her gun.

"Cianid, don't! It's a—"

Giele's warning fell upon deaf ears, for she popped up, her face blazing with courage and streaked with smoke, and delivered a shotgun blast to the advancing man's chest. A hail of bullets pounded into the fence and she ducked back.

"God's Blood!" Giele didn't know how she avoided being riddled but she appeared unharmed, to his great relief.

The two other gunmen spotted Giele and turned their pistols in his direction. He slipped backwards off Brokorn's hips and hit the ground in a forward roll as bullets whistled over his head. He turned his momentum from the roll into a dive, extending himself out to become as small a target as possible, and fired his pistol with quick, military precision. Two shots, two kills.

Where was that rutting coward Rarik?

With a crash, Tarvy and another man fell out of a nearby ground-floor window and tumbled across the wooden porch into the street. They wrestled over the man's pistol until Tarvy delivered an impressive uppercut to the man's chin. The pistol went flying to one side as they continued to roll around.

Giele took aim but didn't dare fire with Tarvy so close to the other man. "Don't shoot, Cianid!"

She reloaded her shotgun barrels and nodded.

Tarvy rolled on top of his opponent and cuffed the man across the face. The man's struggles ceased. His sides heaving, blood running from his nose, Tarvy looked down at the man and gave him a grim smile. "I'm already forgiven for this. It will take longer for you to earn God's blessing, I'm certain."

Shots rang out. Two bloody stars appeared on Tarvy's chest. For a moment, Giele didn't understand what had happened. As he toppled, Tarvy gasped, "Rarik."

Giele whirled to see Rarik astride a bay horse, a rifle raised to his cheek, pointed at him. Giele froze, caught off-guard. Cianid screamed at Rarik and fired her shotgun, but he was too far for the pellets to do more than sting. Her action galvanized Giele, and he fired a wild shot at Rarik. His first shot hit the ground near the horse's feet. Giele corrected his aim and shot again, but the animal bucked and his second bullet grazed its flank instead of hitting Rarik in the chest. He fired his rifle back at Giele. Fire burned in Giele's right shoulder, his arm went numb, and his pistol fell to the dust. Rarik wheeled his horse around and sped off to the east.

He was running for home, and reinforcements.

Giele staggered back to his feet and choked out a whistle as he picked up the pistol and shoved it back into its holster. "Breath and Bones," he hissed. "I thought being shot in the leg hurt!" Brokorn hurried up next to him. Giele cried out from the agony as he hauled himself onto Brokorn's back.

"Giele!" called Cianid.

He almost turned back, knowing she needed help. Tarvy and Piprel were wounded, maybe dying, but there was nothing Giele could do for them now, and Rarik was getting away. If he made it to the safety of his family's estate . . .

"Get the doctor!" Giele turned away from her and urged Brokorn on after the fleeing Rarik.

Brokorn was faster but wounded, and Rarik's bay had a head start, so it was a race. Rarik rode hard, his rifle held out in one hand while the other gripped his reins in desperation. His hat bounced off his head, and flapped from its chin string behind him. Brokorn's legs were a blur, despite the bloodstains down one. Giele was coming for Rarik, and nothing would stop him. He heard little Aral's laugh in his ears and spurred Brokorn on even harder. As they sped through hills and small groves of juniper and cedar trees, they drew closer and closer. Rarik's horse started to flag and they moved alongside.

Giele didn't bother trying to get cute with his gun; instead, he tackled Rarik right out of his saddle.

They both hit hard. Giele landed on his wounded shoulder and gasped, stunned. Rarik's rifle skittered away. The villain got the upper hand right away, bludgeoning at Giele's face as they rolled through the dust. Rarik dug his knuckles into Giele's shoulder and Giele howled in agony as the bullet ground deeper into the muscle.

Giele's other hand found a handful of sandy dirt and flung it into Rarik's face. He yelled and rolled away. Giele spun around on the ground, braced himself with his uninjured arm, and kicked his heel downward like an axe onto Rarik's ribs. One broke under his foot with an audible snap. Rarik grunted in pain and stopped moving for a moment. Giele yanked his pistol from its holster.

Before he pulled the trigger, Rarik whipped a fallen tree branch into Giele's wrist and the pistol flew away. It landed a few feet away and fired when it hit. The stray round whizzed past Giele's branded cheek. He leaped after the pistol, focusing on the weapon. It held one last bullet—the marked one. Rarik intercepted Giele, swinging the branch back and forth at him and driving him back. Rarik grinned through a mouth full of blood. "You're pathetic, marked man." He swung again. Giele's foot slipped on a loose stone and he fell onto his back.

He was done for.

"Goose Creek is my town." Rarik brought the branch down. Giele rolled to one side. "Mine!" He tried again and Giele moved the opposite way.

Desperate for an opening, Giele planted his boot into Rarik's belly. He flew backward and his branch slipped out of his grip. Giele got to his feet as Rarik scrabbled away, trying to regain his breath.

Giele saw the marked arrow on the ground just as Rarik did. His heart plummeted. It must have fallen from his quiver at some point during the fight. Even in all the dust they'd raised, Giele saw the ink on its head. Rarik sensed his fear. Their eyes met, flicked to the arrow, judging distances. Giele had to get to it before Rarik did. The glyph on it would slay an Elf.

Any Elf.

If Rarik stabbed Giele with it, Giele would die.

They both dove for it. Rarik's hand closed on the shaft and yanked it away, leaving Giele grabbing empty air. Giele staggered away before Rarik stabbed him with it. The villain lunged and drove Giele back, then he feinted an attack to one side and Giele bit on the fake, dodging too far. Rarik jumped inside Giele's guard and drove him down to the ground, pushing the arrow down toward Giele's throat. Giele got both his hands on Rarik's wrists and pushed back as hard as he could.

Rarik's weight pressed down upon Giele as he struggled against Rarik's downward thrust of the arrow. Giele couldn't feel his right arm at all and his muscles began to quiver, growing weaker by the second. The point of the arrow drew closer and closer. Rarik began to laugh. Foul, bloody spittle dripped onto Giele's face.

"This is how it ends, marked man. I win, you lose."

A gunshot roared in Giele's ears. The grin froze on Rarik's face. Blood ran out of his nose and mouth and Giele felt the shudder of Rarik's life leaving his body. His dead weight pressed the arrow further downward, but Giele pushed it aside and it poked down into the dirt beside him. Rarik settled against Giele, trapping him in a dead man's embrace. Giele struggled to push him off, but had no strength left.

"No, you lose." Wioo stood a few yards away, Giele's pistol clutched in his hand, smoke issuing from its barrel. His broken arm still hung at his side and he looked excited and terrified all at the same time.

"Nice shot," Giele gasped.

"*Faw.*"

"I'm—oof—glad you didn't hit me with it."

"Wioo glad too."

Giele grimaced at the pain in his shoulder and the stinking dead weight of Rarik sprawled atop him. "Well don't just stand there, brother. Get this meat off me."

CHAPTER THIRTY-ONE

Giele and Wioo rode back to town. When they returned, the stable had burned to the ground but the fire hadn't spread to any neighboring buildings. Goose Creek citizens stood around with buckets, watching to make sure the flames were out. They shrank back from the bloodied warriors as their Greatdeer approached. A weary Giele wondered if he'd have to fight some of them next, but then one woman started to applaud. It was Shali, the young woman whose face Rarik had cut. Another woman, dressed in the corset and stockings of an entertainer, also clapped. A man shouted, "You got him? That rutting bastard shot my dog last week for barking."

"He cheated at cards!"

"He punched my pappy!"

Shali yanked her veil away and held it clenched in her fist over her head. "He cut me!" she cried.

It was like they'd opened the floodgates. Giele hadn't realized just how much Rarik was detested by many of the townsfolk, but here they were applauding the Pariah for disposing of him. Giele nodded his head, too exhausted to do more.

Tarvy and Piprel were already in the doctor's office when Giele and Wioo staggered in through the door, supporting each other. The town doctor's shirt was hanging open; he must have been half-dressed when the wounded converged upon his office. Underneath the flapping fabric, Giele saw an ornate tattoo across his chest. He looked Giele up and down. "Army?"

Giele managed a weak salute. "Late of the 136th Forest Regiment."

He saluted back. "Viegel Hillcourt, combat medic. Retired from Old Eighty-Four."

The 84th Forest Regiment troops had an excellent survival rate, Giele recalled. He knew he and his companions would be in good hands.

Cianid sat between Tarvy and Piprel's beds, bathing the Padre's wounds. "Did you kill him?"

Giele nodded and flopped into a chair. Wioo collapsed at his feet, too tired even to speak.

"Good." She gave Giele a tight smile. "You can tell the Sheriff what happened."

Giele looked past her, and noticed a stocky, iron-haired Elf with a tin star on his leather vest. His hands were hooked around his belt buckle, and his face was purple in outrage. "I'm Sheriff Wandiel. Deputy Sheksi has some interesting things to say about you, but I have to ask what in God's Blood did you do to my town?"

"What needed to be done, sir. I'll make a full report . . . but I've got a bullet in me . . . and I'm very tired."

Giele shut his eyes.

A day later Giele awakened to find his shoulder wrapped in linen bandages and throbbing in pain. With his first conscious breath, he asked about Wioo, Tarvy, and Piprel. Doctor Hillcourt explained that while Giele slept, he'd pried the bullet out of his shoulder. "You must have been almost dead on your feet. You didn't move once."

He wasn't sure about Horkish anatomy, but he'd set Wioo's arm with all the care he would have used on an Elf or Dwarf. Giele's young blood brother slept on a rough straw pallet on the office floor. "Your other friends will be fine," said the doctor. "The mage was only grazed—just got a nasty knock on the head—and our Padre is made of sterner stuff than most men. God will see him through."

"You son of a wild boar." Giele looked over to see Cianid sitting in the corner. She looked as if she hadn't slept, although she'd washed her face and changed to clean clothes while Giele had been unconscious. "You went and passed out and left me to explain things to the Sheriff."

"I'm sorry, Cianid. Truly, I am." Despite his apology, Giele couldn't find it in his heart to feel bad. He'd accomplished what he set out to do. The Valley Villagers had been avenged, and he hadn't lost any of his friends in the process. "I'm glad you're alive."

"No thanks to you. Riding off like a rutting wildcat without checking to see if any of that gang was left. One was, you know. Oh, don't worry, I dealt with him. But you owe me, Giele Pariah. You owe me."

"It's one debt I'm happy to have."

"It's one I'm not going to get to collect." She folded her arms tight against her bosom. "The Sheriff wants you out of this town for your own good. Rarik may have been the hothead in his family, but the rest of his family might still come after you if you stay in the area."

"It's all right . . ." Giele felt sleep overtaking him once again and yawned. "I have a place to go."

The next time he awakened, he found the newspaper publisher sitting in the office with him. He raised his hawk-like nose up from the pad in which he scribbled when Giele sighed. "Oh, good, you're awake."

"I am."

He shook Giele's hand, careful not to dislodge the bandage over his shoulder. "Jingot. Jingot Longbranch. I realized after you left I'd never properly introduced myself."

"Nice to meet you, Mr. Longbranch."

"Mr. Longbranch is my father. Call me Jingot."

"What can I do for you, Jingot?"

"The rumors have been flying like crazy around here. You were dead, or living with the Horks. Then you come back, fight the local gang and win. You have a story that needs to be heard, Pariah, I'm ready to tell it to the people."

Giele saw no sign of anything but sincere interest in Jingot's face. His pencil hovered over the pad, poised to begin scribbling. Why not? "All right, this is what happened . . ."

A few days later, Doctor Hillcourt allowed Giele and Wioo to leave. Piprel had been cleared after the first day, but the mage had chosen to stay and help care for Tarvy, whose wounds required regular cleaning.

"You're really leaving?" asked Piprel.

"I have to," said Giele. "The Sheriff can only protect me here for so long. Rarik's family might still come after us, and he doesn't want another shootout tearing up the town."

"I'd like to see them try it." A tiny bolt of lightning shot between Piprel's eyes. "This town doesn't belong to them."

"Nor does it belong to you, my friend." Tarvy sounded weak, but he still managed to keep a twinkle in his eyes. "It does my heart good to see you all in one piece."

"Likewise, I'm glad you're alive." Giele squeezed his hand. "It was never your fight."

Tarvy closed his eyes and smiled. "But it was the right fight."

"Look after him, Piprel."

"I will, Giele." The mage clasped Giele's hand. "And thank you."

"For what?"

He made a small flame appear in the center of one palm for a moment. "For showing me the way out of the darkness."

Giele and Wioo went to the street and called to their Greatdeer. They broke free from a temporary corral set up beside the General Store and milled about by the entrance, lowering their antlers at any other Elves who dared approach them.

Brokorn had allowed Cianid to treat the bullet wound in his haunch. She hadn't dared remove it, but through the bond-connection, Giele could tell it didn't bother the Greatdeer much. Ullu would be able to remove it once they rejoined her. Despite his half-wild, untamed nature, Brokorn was pleased to see his bond-mate and anxious to leave. He allowed Giele to sling some saddlebags over his back and fill them.

Cianid watched as Giele and Wioo made their preparations to leave. "Where will you go?"

"Back to the Horks. Frankly, I've felt much more at home among them recently than I have among my own people."

"We're not all bad," she grumbled as she tidied up the entryway of her store. "A few of us did stand by you, you know. Grudgingly, but still."

Giele smiled. "Thank you, Cianid. I couldn't have done it without you."

"Oh, pshaw." Her cheeks colored a little and she looked pleased with herself.

Giele didn't know how to tell her it made her look beautiful, like a sunrise.

"Will you be back?"

"Yes, I promise. I'll need supplies and I'll have notes to turn in. I'm hoping to write a definitive book about Horkish culture."

She turned away from him and busied herself wiping down a window which was already spotless. "Good," she said in a soft voice.

Giele thought she might have something else to say, but no more words were forthcoming. He closed up his satchel and stepped close to her. She turned and for a moment he saw a flash of something on her face he didn't expect. A little secret smile, perhaps, that spoke of intimacy to come someday. He wanted to do something significant, but it didn't feel like the right time. Instead, he pressed a small bag of coins into her hand to pay for his supplies. Blackpool had paid him for his notes on the terrain, and offered to hire him again.

Giele declined; his spiral was taking a new turn.

Cianid took the money and squeezed his hand. Her skin was warm, soft, and friendly.

"Farewell, Giele Pariah."

"For you, I'd rather just be Giele."

"Giele, then. But nowadays, at least around here, Pariah isn't such a bad word any longer."

Somehow, without meaning to, he'd found a measure of acceptance among some of his own people. It made him feel good. Her eyes met his, and he couldn't mistake what he saw in them for anything but wistfulness.

She didn't want him to leave.

Giele was torn. His heart called out to be with the Horks, but here was a woman who he wanted to know better, one who he knew would never treat him as a pawn or an underling. He raised her hand to his lips, a gallant gesture of days gone by. "I'll return in a month or two."

She reached out to caress the scar on his cheek, not out of curiosity, but with a tenderness he didn't know he could ever experience again. He shivered a little as she turned away again. "I'll wait."

Wioo already sat astride Efraya, his arm in a splint. He looked very tired but cheerful. "About time. Wioo waiting for hours."

"It hasn't been that long." Giele climbed onto Brokorn's back.

Shali ran up to him. She'd replaced her veil, but she moved with a confidence she hadn't shown when Rarik still lived. "Giele? The Sheriff said this was yours." She held up a pearl-handled revolver in a leather holster.

Giele took it from her and slid the weapon clear. On the handle he read *Giele Stillwater, Forest Colonel, 136th Regiment*. The weapon had been cleaned and oiled with thorough care. Whatever taint Rarik had given it had been polished away. Giele smiled back down at her. "Thank you, Shali."

He looked up and saw the town Sheriff standing with his deputies at a distance, his thumbs hooked in his belt and a piece of prairie grass dangling between his teeth. He nodded at Giele, who tipped the brim of his hat at him. Giele snapped the holster to his belt, welcoming its weight. It was his once more; he'd earned it. A new bow rode across his shoulders, a gift from Skria Woodyard, who insisted his lifetime warranty also covered theft. Giele hadn't argued with him, for his recent experience had shown he was at best a barely-adequate bowyer.

Wioo looked toward the store where Cianid watched us from behind the glass. "You going to marry her?"

Giele coughed, caught by surprise. "I have no idea. Haven't thought about it."

"She would make you a good wife." He folded his arms across his chest as if the matter was already decided.

"We'll see." Giele was nowhere near ready to get married, but he knew Cianid would occupy a generous portion of his thoughts over the next couple of months. It felt good, to have a woman to think of again; one who wouldn't use him and throw him away when he became inconvenient to her.

They looked over to the doctor's offices. Tarvy sat in a wheelchair on the porch with Piprel behind him. Giele waved to them, his comrades-in-arms. They'd fought hard for him, and he was proud to call them his friends.

"Good luck, Giele," said Tarvy.

"Come back soon," added Piprel.

"I will. Take care, my friends."

They raised their hands in farewell. So did several other town residents. Giele felt he would be missed, and welcomed when he returned. For the first time since before he'd left Aelfland, he felt alive. Whole.

Unmarked.

And perhaps, someday, if she was of a mind, Cianid might very well indeed make him a good wife.

He looked at Wioo and grinned. "Let's ride on, blood-brother."

Their Greatdeer broke into trots, and then full-on gallops, as if they too were as happy as Giele and Wioo to be heading back home.

ABOUT THE AUTHOR

Ian Thomas Healy dabbles in many different genres. He's a twelve-time participant and winner of National Novel Writing Month and is also the creator of the *Writing Better Action Through Cinematic Techniques* workshop, which helps writers to improve their action scenes.

When not writing, which is rare, he enjoys watching hockey, reading comic books (and serious books, too), and living in the great state of Colorado, which he shares with his wife, children, house-pets, and approximately five million other people.

Visit www.ianthealy.com for more information.

www.ingramcontent.com/pod-product-compliance
Lightning Source LLC
Chambersburg PA
CBHW031558240626
47153CB00002B/559